MEN IN UNIFORM

Courteous, courageous and commanding—
these heroes lay it all on the line for the
people they love in more than fifty stories about
loyalty, bravery and romance.
Don't miss a single one!

ROZ
DENNY FOX

TOO MANY
BROTHERS

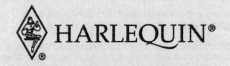

TORONTO • NEW YORK • LONDON
AMSTERDAM • PARIS • SYDNEY • HAMBURG
STOCKHOLM • ATHENS • TOKYO • MILAN • MADRID
PRAGUE • WARSAW • BUDAPEST • AUCKLAND

Recycling programs
for this product may
not exist in your area.

ISBN-13: 978-0-373-36276-9

TOO MANY BROTHERS

Copyright © 2004 by Rosaline Fox

All rights reserved. Except for use in any review, the reproduction or
utilization of this work in whole or in part in any form by any electronic,
mechanical or other means, now known or hereafter invented, including
xerography, photocopying and recording, or in any information storage
or retrieval system, is forbidden without the written permission of the
publisher, Harlequin Enterprises Limited, 225 Duncan Mill Road,
Don Mills, Ontario M3B 3K9, Canada.

This is a work of fiction. Names, characters, places and incidents are
either the product of the author's imagination or are used fictitiously,
and any resemblance to actual persons, living or dead, business
establishments, events or locales is entirely coincidental.

This edition published by arrangement with Harlequin Books S.A.

For questions and comments about the quality of this book
please contact us at Customer_eCare@Harlequin.ca.

® and TM are trademarks of Harlequin Books S.A., used under license.
Trademarks indicated with ® are registered in the United States Patent
and Trademark Office, the Canadian Trade Marks Office and in other
countries.

www.eHarlequin.com

Printed in U.S.A.

ROZ DENNY FOX

A secretary by trade, Roz began her writing career in 1986 with a series of self-help articles. She sold a short story to a magazine in 1987. After much prodding from her then high-school-age daughter, Roz tried her hand at writing a contemporary romance. Roz began writing full-time in 1995.

Roz's second book was a Romance Writers of America RITA® Award finalist in the Traditional category, and she's also been a finalist for the Desert Rose Chapter's Golden Quill Award and the Holt Medallion.

Currently, Roz resides in Tucson with her husband, Denny. They have two married daughters and five grandchildren. Readers can find out more about Roz by visiting her Web site, www.korynna.com.

For Nakita and Savannah.
Dream big. Read much.
Be anything you want to be.

CHAPTER ONE

DAPHNE MALONE put down her phone, threw her hands in the air and danced a zany victory dance around her perpetually unmade bed. She'd just been offered a job. Not the greatest in the world, but a start. In the middle of her jazzy dance to a blaring CD, a strand of curly dark hair caught on one of the four posters, bringing her up short. The jolt sobered her. This was real. A job. In a few hours.

She dashed to her cluttered closet, and because Daphne never did anything slowly, she rummaged around frantically until she uncovered an old beach bag. With her free hand she began pawing through costumes she might use today. She couldn't decide, so she tossed in accessories. The bag was already bulging, and she still hadn't settled on a costume. Maybe she'd phone her mom for advice. Calandra Malone had taught both her daughters how to sew at an early age, which was why Daphne had such a splendid array of clown suits.

She grabbed the phone from her nightstand and hopped around, pulling on a pair of clean white jeans while punching in her parents' number. Daphne juggled the cellular between her cheek and shoulder and braided her long hair into a single, more manageable plait.

"Mom? Guess what?" she said the instant Callie Malone

answered. "I've got a job at a birthday party this afternoon over near Commerce. I am so excited!"

Daphne rolled her eyes. "It's near East L.A., not in East L.A. Yes, Mo…ther, I know Kieran says that part of the city isn't safe for a woman alone. But I'm going to the home of someone who's a friend of a friend of the wife of one of Dane's partners. It's a party for ten seven-year-olds. How safe is that?

"Okay, okay! I'll check in when I get home." Daphne glanced at her watch. "I called to see which outfits you think I should take, but I need to run. Be happy for me, please. It means money, at least, until I get the break I'm really waiting for." Daphne lowered the receiver at the last possible moment, listening to Callie, who continued to spout dire warnings. She ended with one good suggestion. "Take a variety, Daphne, and see which feels right when you get there. Just…be careful, sweetheart."

Daphne added her favorite clown suits to the bag, all the while wishing her parents and her three older brothers would believe she could take care of herself. After all, she was twenty-six. Granted, Kieran subsidized the apartment, but only until she could get herself established. Meanwhile, why couldn't the lot of them stop hovering? Her sister, Becky, was a year younger and they left her alone. Of course, Becky had a solid marriage, a good career, and she was already a mom herself. Daphne's jobs had been a disaster up to now, and her love life—well, that didn't bear mentioning.

Lugging the beach bag down to the vintage chartreuse VW Bug that her brother Perry had lovingly restored, Daphne let a perfect late-summer afternoon rejuvenate her spirits. She was an eternal optimist. She wasn't going to let her mother's undue alarm change that.

Placing the directions to the party on the empty seat, Daphne dropped her sunglasses over her eyes and chugged off along the familiar streets of Culver City—the suburb of L.A. where she'd lived forever.

Like a pro, she cut from the I-10 freeway to the Santa Ana Freeway, eventually exiting on Atlantic Boulevard. A cop's siren screamed over her new Josh Groban CD. Daphne automatically moved to the right and rolled to a stop. Squinting into the sun out her side window, she watched in amazement as five police cars sped past. Daphne couldn't tell if Kieran was driving one. Her brother did sometimes patrol this area. She hadn't spoken with him since the previous Friday because she'd spent the week babysitting her oldest brother's kids. As a rule, she'd know Kieran's schedule. The Malones were a close-knit family in spite of her complaints about their hovering.

Five blocks farther down the road she discovered the police had cordoned off the street she was supposed to turn into. Not familiar with this neighborhood, she wasted time locating an alternate route on a map stored in a side pocket of her car.

The roundabout journey took her down some scuzzy streets. Remembering her mom's lecture, she locked both doors. After making a U-turn, she finally found the street she wanted. The homes here were older, but she was relieved to see they were well maintained. The one she sought was at the bottom of a dead-end street. A partially wooded lot bordered it on the left, intersected by trails. Neighbors probably walked their dogs there or jogged through the trees.

Daphne hefted her beach bag, draping it nonchalantly over one shoulder as she checked the house number. She mounted the steps and knocked.

A harried, very pregnant woman opened the door. She introduced herself as April Ross. After exchanging a few words, April led Daphne into a living room that was a mess of floating balloons. "Forgive me, please. The first helium tank I rented didn't work, so I had to take it back. This is Natalie, the birthday girl. Nat, Daphne Malone, our party clown. Honey, will you take Daphne to the guest bedroom so she can change into her costume?"

April finished tying off a balloon and added, "The guest room has a sliding glass door leading out onto the patio, where I've set up for the party. I know you said you'll probably change costumes during your program. I thought it'd be easiest to run back and forth into the house through the slider."

"Sounds perfect. Thanks, April. I'll scoot off and dress so I can help you greet the kids. Or tie balloon bouquets. Whatever you prefer. In any case, I'd better hurry. I see a couple of moms bringing kids up the walkway now. I'll just go, get out of your hair." Daphne moved toward the hall.

"Thanks for your offer of help. I'm frazzled and I hate being late," April wailed. "Oh, and Daphne, thanks a million times over for bailing me out on such short notice. Nat had her heart set on a clown to do magic tricks. Like I told you, I booked through an agency, but apparently the receptionist flipped two pages at once on her calendar. Another family got first dibs because they'd phoned first."

"No problem." Daphne grinned. "Tell your friends, in fact. I need all the bookings I can get between now and when I find permanent work in my real field."

Daphne chatted with the birthday girl as they walked down the hall. She loved kids, and often babysat her niece and nephew whenever Dane and his wife, Holly, needed her. Natalie Ross was cute and talkative. Before she scampered off, Daphne learned that Nat wanted her to paint the faces of all the kids attending the party.

So, she'd been right to bring all that stuff. Daphne intended to make this the coolest party ever. Humming happily, she dumped her costumes and face paints out across a cheery yellow bedspread. Matching curtains blew gently in the breeze.

She circled the bed and closed the miniblinds. Still feeling exposed, Daphne pulled the lined drape across the glass slider for privacy, leaving the door open for easy access to the patio.

Muted sounds of children's laughter and boisterous shouts drifted through the closed hall door. Daphne kicked off her sandals and skimmed out of her jeans. She had her T-shirt nearly off, when a scraping sound at the slider made her swing around.

It'd be impossible to say who was most shocked, Daphne or a scruffy-looking man who stood poised on the balls of his feet as he stealthily shut and locked the glass door. The drape slipped through his fingers, silently closing them in together.

The T-shirt plopped at Daphne's feet. Her throat tightened and her hammering heart battered her ribs. Feeling the stranger's Delft-blue eyes making a thorough examination of her, she grabbed the first clown suit she could reach and covered herself as best she could with the slithery material. She opened her mouth to scream, but suddenly found her breath driven from her lungs by the agile intruder, who vaulted the bed in a single bound. He covered her mouth with a strong hand. A no-nonsense pistol caressed her ear before she could force air, let alone a scream, past her numb lips.

Her brother Kieran would've said only a fool would fight against those odds, but Daphne wasn't about to die without putting up a fight. She tried jabbing an elbow into her captor's midriff, but hit rock-hard abs. Next she attempted to disable him by stomping on his foot. Except that she was barefoot and he wore boots, as she quickly discovered. And the more she struggled, the more tenuous became her hold on the clown suit.

"Chill out," he growled, jerking her tighter against his own heaving chest. "Who the hell are you?" he demanded in a gruff stage whisper.

"Mmmmf...mmfff," Daphne mumbled against his sweating fingers. He smelled sweaty, anyway, and rough whiskers scraped her neck, although his longish, sun-streaked blond hair was soft where it brushed her cheek. What a funny thing to notice at a time like this.

As her initial shock receded, Daphne tried to store her impressions—for the police—supposing she got out of this alive. He was tall. A rangy build like her brother Perry. She was five foot eight; the man was taller. And stronger by far, she was learning. She couldn't budge him, and twisting only tightened his grip on her.

Her legs felt every quiver of his taut muscles hidden under threadbare blue jeans. A once-black sweat-stained T-shirt hugged a muscled torso. Iron-hard biceps indicated her captor probably kept fit working out or doing manual labor.

For all she knew, he could be April Ross's pool guy.

Although probably not. He seemed inordinately interested in what might be happening on the street in front of the house. Bingo! How close was the Ross home to the area cordoned off by the police? It'd be due east of April's backyard. Quite close. Too close. Daphne began to shake uncontrollably as her mind revolved faster. He could be a hardened criminal. Maybe even a murderer.

That thought came when he forcefully dragged her to the

far side of the front window, where he used the barrel of his gun to tip aside the blind. Apparently he didn't like what he saw. He swore ripely under his breath and flattened them both against the wall, fast.

It wasn't that Daphne hadn't heard such language before. Her older brothers, Dane, Kieran and Perry, were a firefighter, a cop and a long-haul trucker, respectively. Even though she frequently complained about having too many bossy brothers, oh boy, did she wish any one of them would burst through that door right now. If she ever got out of this predicament, she vowed she'd pay strict attention to every one of her mom's lectures, too.

"Where's April?" her captor asked right beside her ear. "Are you keeping her company because Mike deployed again?" Ever so slowly, he slid his fingers off Daphne's mouth. But as she geared up to bellow for help, he waved the mean-looking pistol in her face. The cry froze on her lips.

"Get dressed," he hissed, sounding almost angry. Her fingers felt all thumbs, and there was no way Daphne could comply.

Muttering, he gave her a shake and repeated his demand.

Logan Grant found that he was beginning to be affected by the armful of half-naked woman he'd surprised when he slipped in through April's back door. At first he was too shocked over seeing anyone—let alone a partially clad anyone—in a room he'd counted on being empty. That, coupled with the fact that he was positive his cover had been blown in a big narcotics buy gone sour, meant Logan wasn't having the best day of his life.

Special Agent Grant had spent ten months working his way into a position of power in an organization his agency had been trying to bring down for two years. He'd been minutes from meeting the next big fish in the scummy pond, which would've been another step up the slippery, slimy ladder of crime. Then all hell had broken loose. Cop cars had roared down side streets from all directions. And when push came to shove, Logan had been forced to take sides.

Billy Holt, his superior in the local heroin import ring, had seen him knock out another ring member and steal a pistol from him. Now Holt had more interest in tracking down Logan than in staying to fight local law enforcement, one or more of whom had to be on the take. Only an insider could've made Logan and brought in the cops.

Logan knew too much about the next big shipment due to land on California shores. It made him dangerous to the organization. Dangerous and expendable. Even now, two cars filled with Holt's trusted henchmen were combing the streets, hunting for him.

Under other circumstances, Logan thought he might work up a red-hot interest in this big-eyed, leggy woman—in close proximity to a large, soft bed. Unfortunately, at the moment, saving his skin and hers took precedence over baser instincts.

He'd come here because his sister's home presented his only chance of escape. Though taller than Mike Ross, Logan thought he could borrow Mike's razor and fit into one of his shirts. A change of clothes, use April's cell phone to contact his office, and poof, he'd be scooped up by his associates, leaving Holt to wonder how he'd managed to pull a disappearing act.

Things rarely went according to plan in a special agent's life. This day had gone to hell more rapidly than most, however. Billy's goons cruised the streets, alleys and backyards, leaving Logan—what? With a hysterical, nearly nude female threatening to scream her head off, that's what.

To make matters worse, he'd stayed too long. He'd already put everyone in this house in jeopardy. He let loose another stream of colorful invective. Under current circumstances, it was all he could do.

Daphne's addled brain took in his second barked order—get dressed—and that was what she was trying desperately to do, even though it meant peeling the clown suit away from where she had it plastered to her front. Even though it meant revealing her scanty Victoria's Secret finery to a crazed gunman.

She attempted to shake out the material, bend and slide the colorful, baggy jumpsuit over first one leg, then the other. She nearly tripped and fell flat on her face. It wasn't humiliating enough that the gunman caught her, oh, no. Worse, he zipped the suit up from the vee in her legs all the way to her neck because her fingers were shaking so hard.

"What kind of getup is that?" he asked, eyeing her speculatively.

Fully covered now, Daphne felt a bit steadier. She smoothed back a stubborn curl that had slipped out of her clip and snapped back, "It's a clown suit, you idiot. I'm here to perform at a birthday party. Natalie's. Her name is Natalie. You, uh, called her mother by name. Are you…ah…a fr…riend of April's?"

Hearing herself squeak, Daphne crossed her arms and grabbed her elbows just to have something solid to hang on to. No one, especially her brothers, would ever believe her if she told them she'd stood here trading niceties with a man holding a gun on her.

Logan noticed her wide, tawny cat eyes fixed on the 9mm Luger he'd taken from one of Billy Holt's confederates—a much larger and more lethal weapon than the handgun he usually carried, a snub-nosed Smith & Wesson. All things considered, the party clown was holding up well. He figured that most women in her position would either be dissolved in tears by now, or they'd have fainted long ago.

"So, we're finally making progress," he said. "Dammit, I forgot Nat's birthday. I'll have to make it up to her later. Listen, can I trust you to open the door and call April back here without screaming down the house? I need to talk to her, but I'd rather Natalie didn't see me looking like this."

"I don't think so," Daphne sniffed. "You have one hostage already. I won't be party to helping you get another. Especially not one who's pregnant. What kind of degenerate are you?"

"Hostage?" He grinned then, showing two rows of very white, very even teeth. "I think you've been watching too many cop shows on TV. Just attract April's attention, please. Then sometime, when I'm not so rushed, maybe you and I can sit down over a cold beer and talk about how I'd have done things differently if I really was making you my hostage."

Daphne processed only about half of what he said. His killer smile had, in spite of his stubbly beard, devastated her equilibrium. That smile turned him into the most appealing bad boy she'd ever had the misfortune to meet. Big surprise. She'd always been a sucker for the wrong men.

No wonder her family thought she needed a keeper! She was actually standing in this room contemplating a date with a man who was obviously on the wrong side of the law. Kieran would have a fit, she thought as she let the intruder hustle her toward the door.

"Get April," he said again. "And be quick about it."

Daphne cracked the door open, praying the hall would be empty. No—April Ross was just exiting the adjacent room.

From the way she adjusted her smock, she must have been in the bathroom.

"Psst!" Daphne couldn't think of any other way to get the woman's attention.

April turned, curiosity on her face. Daphne looked quickly at the window, ready to shout a warning, but a ray of sunlight winked through the drapes covering the sliding glass door and glinted off the gun in her captor's hand. That completely stilled her tongue. She merely beckoned frantically, not caring if her hostess thought she was a nutcase.

April walked slowly toward the woman she'd engaged to be her party clown. "Yes? Is there something you need, Daphne? A friend of mine took the children outside to play a game. You'll make your entrance after that winds down, okay? If you don't mind, later on I'll have you help me serve refreshments. Cake and ice cream. I figured the kids would like an opportunity to talk with a real clown."

Still unable to work any comprehensible sound through her lips, Daphne simply reached out, latched onto April's wrist and yanked her inside the room. The door slammed on its own, and Daphne clasped her hands to her breasts. "I'm honestly so sorry to do this to you, April," she croaked.

The woman glanced up at the man who hovered close behind Daphne. Her annoyed expression turned to one of recognition. "Logan! I wasn't expecting you. I thought you were out of town. Nat will be ecstatic."

Daphne gaped from her hostess to the gunman and back again, while he reached around both and locked that door, too.

"April, this isn't a social call. We can't let Nat see me. I'm in trouble. I shouldn't have taken refuge here—I forgot it was her birthday. Suffice it to say, I need a little assistance, and then I'll be off."

Daphne, exhibiting more bravery than she had up to now, insinuated herself between the man and the pregnant woman he appeared to know. "April, don't listen. Even if he's a friend of yours, that's aiding and abetting," she whispered to her hostess. "On the way in, I passed a ton of cops. Something big. Something bad went on. Between us, we can stop him." She waved a hand toward where she'd seen the ruckus.

The man studied her with a half-amused expression. "Aren't you forgetting I have a weapon?"

April snorted inelegantly. "Honestly, Logan. Quit scaring the poor woman to death. Just tell me what's going on. Why do you look like a skid-row bum?"

"Sorry, you know I can't tell you. Just get me a shirt of Mike's and his razor. I've got to alter how I look enough to avoid the men who chased me here."

As if Daphne wasn't attempting to block her, April unlocked the door, opened it and peered down the hall. "The coast is clear. Go into our room. You can take anything in Mike's closet. He's out at sea with his naval unit for two weeks."

Daphne threw her body against the door and slammed it shut. "Friend or not, he's obviously involved in whatever just happened. He's running from the law."

April stared at the woman plastered against her guest room door. "Oh, Daphne, you don't understand. Logan is the law. Logan, this is Daphne Malone. I hired her to perform for Nat's party."

His rough laugh rolled up from his belly. "I love it. I've gotten so jaded, I didn't believe there were still people around who had the guts to stick their necks out for the good guys."

"You're a cop?" Daphne asked, suspicion in every tense

line of her body. "What force? My brother's LAPD. I know cops in a lot of the local precincts. I'm sure I'd remember if we'd ever met."

"Honestly, didn't you tell her you're FBI, Logan? Daphne, meet my crazy brother, Special Agent Logan Grant."

He didn't look altogether happy about the introduction. "April, you can't go blabbing what I do for a living to everyone under the sun. The element of surprise is our best defense. Sometimes our only defense."

Feeling sheepish, Daphne quickly sidled away from the door. "Ohmigosh! Kieran said I was going to screw up big-time one of these days." Her regard changed—became rapt as that of April Ross, who smiled with pride at her brother.

The agent actually got red in the face. "You need to forget my name—Daphne, is it?—and both of you forget I was ever here." He stepped to the window again and made another furtive survey of the street. "Look, here's the deal, April. I've got some real bastards wanting to get their hands on me. Bad enough that they're in no hurry to give up the hunt. They probably have the area blanketed with sharpshooters. I don't think changing into Mike's shirt will make a lot of difference. So I'll wait until the more obvious searchers move up the street. Then I'll slip out through the back and take my chances. At least I can try to lead them away from this house."

"No, Logan!" Worry creased April's forehead. "Nat's party is in full swing in the backyard. Surely you won't risk getting my friends or the kids hurt if those men do spot you."

"You're right. Well, damn! What now?" He paced the length of the room and back.

Daphne had been studying him, trying to figure out how, disguised or not, he'd fooled her so completely. She wasn't easily duped, since disguise was her business. Or rather, it would be her business when some studio hired her. She'd just completed a two-year makeup artistry course at City College. Special-effects makeup was an art. And she was good at it. She'd graduated at the top of her class. In another setting, she could make Logan Grant over. Except she didn't have the proper equipment with her. She'd only tossed in rudimentary face paints for a kids' party. But…

Clearing her throat, Daphne went to the bed where she'd dumped the contents of her beach bag. "May I offer a temporary solution? I wasn't sure what type of clown Natalie liked, so I came prepared with several costumes. I can mix and match false ears, noses, wigs and such. One of them might fit you, Agent Grant."

Logan sputtered, "I've gone out disguised as many things. But never as a woman, and certainly not as a clown. A guy has his limits."

Daphne raked him up and down with disfavor. "Suit yourself. Dying's a whole lot nobler, I'm sure."

April joined Daphne at the bed. She pawed through the costumes. "Logan, stop being such a…such a man. I think Daphne's hit on the perfect solution. The people chasing you have no idea I didn't book two party clowns. Look, she has these big slipper feet in a couple of different styles. I can see this working," she said excitedly. "And…the kids are yelling now to bring on the clowns."

Daphne found herself agreeing less enthusiastically. What had she been thinking? "You'd have to shave. But I have greasepaint in my kit."

"No. Then I'd be back to putting you all in danger. Besides, they'll see through any attempt."

That did it! He'd cast aspersions on her ability. "I promise you, Agent Grant, when I finish with you, not even your own mother will recognize you."

"Quit calling me Agent Grant. That's a dead giveaway," he snarled.

Daphne clapped a hand over her mouth. "Sorry. I'll think of something else to call you. How does Pancake sound? Or Custard?" Her sarcasm was unmistakable.

"I'd rather meet the guys outside with one hand tied behind me," Logan retorted disdainfully.

April, who'd slipped briefly out of the room, returned with a razor and some clean underwear. She passed the items to her brother none too gently.

"I'll need a shirt and pants," he said as he headed for the guest bathroom.

Both April and Daphne shook their heads, but it was April who spoke. "They'd stick out like a sore thumb under this flimsy costume. I'm disposing of those clothes you have on," she said stoutly. "They're disgusting, Logan."

He capitulated, though not gracefully. "Give me the damn clown suit. I doubt it'll fit, but we'll try it your way. If my boss or coworkers ever got a load of me in this, I'd never hear the end of it," he muttered as he tore the clown suit out of Daphne's hand, dived into the bathroom and slammed the door.

The women grinned at each other. In spite of the fact that they'd only just met, it was as if they'd bonded through this mutual accomplishment.

"April, go on out to the party and buy us some time. Tell the kids we'll start the show in fifteen minutes. I'm sure you can come up with another short game."

Nodding, the hostess left, and Daphne spread out her supplies. She set a chair in front of the mirror and began to apply her makeup.

When Logan shuffled out hesitantly in a silly one-piece clown outfit with a wide ruffled collar and baseball-size green puffballs that ran from his neck to his crotch, the outer room was vacant except for his new partner. "When I was a kid," he said, eyeing her, "my dad gave me a talking Bozo the Clown. You look exactly like him."

"I know," she said smugly. "But if I'd known you shared a kinship with Bozo, I might've made myself up to look like his sidekick, Blossom."

He squinted into the bright light she turned on over the mirror. "Wow, I've gotta say I'm impressed. If I hadn't met you without makeup, I wouldn't have a clue what you looked like in real life. Can you really do the same to me?"

"I'm going to try. Sit." She pointed to the chair. "Otherwise I'll trip over my feet."

Logan cast a glance downward at her big, floppy slippers. An automatic laugh bubbled up.

"See, it works every time. The makeup. It's why people see clowns and laugh."

"Not all clowns are funny. Some are downright scary. For instance, our team once arrested a ring of clowns who walked right into houses in broad daylight. They preyed on latchkey kids. Of course, the kids let them in without a peep, and one clown entertained while his pals pulled a disappearing act that entailed backing a moving van up to the house. They burgled freezers, TVs, jewelry. You name it, they heisted it."

Daphne frowned. "That's awful. Especially when you think they might've done worse than clean out a house. They could've murdered the kids."

Logan reared back, appraising her again. "My boss and

I said exactly the same thing. Hmm, there are other kinds of clowns, too. At my buddy's bachelor party, somebody hired one who did a rip-snorting lap dance. I don't suppose you—"

"Absolutely not," she said. But Daphne's fingers, slick with the greasepaint she was applying to Logan's newly shaved face, slipped off just imagining it. After he'd washed and scraped off his beard, Logan Grant looked too darn good. He stirred a heat in her that was better doused. If she had terrible luck with jobs, relationships were even worse. She was hopeless at choosing men—beginning with Kevin McBride, who'd come to pick her up for the prom on his muddy Harley. The jerk had taken a bet cooked up by Daphne's brothers. Those guys always seemed to mess up her love life.

Logan Grant set off all kinds of warning bells in her head. Without whiskers and with his sun-streaked, longish blond hair tied back, there was no doubt he had a rakish kind of sex appeal. Just touching his smooth cheeks, no matter how impersonally, made Daphne's fingers tremble.

It didn't help that his killer blue eyes never left her face. She cringed at the thought of how she must look under his scrutiny. White face. Arched and exaggerated black eyebrows. A wig of red yarn, which was bald on top. Sheesh!

In reality, though, Logan sat there recalling how Daphne Malone had looked before suiting up as Bozo. Once he'd felt halfway safe from Billy Holt's long grasp, Logan had taken time for a cursory once-over of the half-dressed woman he'd grabbed. All her body parts were strung together fine. Very fine, in fact. At first he'd seen her as cute. Later he'd altered that to hot—although she wasn't his type.

After the demise of his short-lived marriage to another agent, a marriage that was probably the biggest mistake of his life, Logan tended to date women who weren't only real lookers but had high-powered careers. Careers well out of his field. And they had to be women whose minds weren't on the M word. One disastrous attempt at domestic bliss had been enough to last Logan a lifetime.

He watched Daphne step back, tilt her head to one side and examine him critically, and he still couldn't shake the other image—the one in which she was barely dressed.

Well, hell! "Are we done?" he muttered.

"Almost." She leaned around him to scoop something off the bed. A bright red felt hat that had bushy white hair attached to all sides. As she straightened, Logan got a whiff of a perfume that nearly had him following her with his tongue hanging out. Damn, but he was a sucker for certain scents. This one did something to his libido. Cranked it up full bore.

Daphne set the silly top hat squarely on Logan's head. She made sure every bit of his own hair was hidden from view. "The flower on your hat has a vial of water attached by this camouflaged button on the brim. You can act like you're tipping your hat to a lady. Instead, you squirt her with a fine spray of water. I don't recommend using it on kids—they often have short fuses and no sense of humor when it comes to practical jokes. But the moms generally laugh."

He stood then, and walked over to the mirror as Daphne pulled on white gloves to cover his big hands. "I can't believe I'm really going out in public looking like this," Logan lamented, lifting first one foot and then the other so she could install his oversize slippers. They felt awkward as hell.

"I can paint on tears so you can be a sad clown," Daphne said tartly, climbing to her feet to peruse him from head to toe. "Otherwise, quit frowning. You'll mess up the paint. The way I see it, I've just saved your scrawny butt."

Logan scowled harder, or tried to. The thick face paint discouraged facial expressions, he discovered.

"Listen up, Special Agent. Here's the plan. I have a few simple tricks I show the kids. I do a few riddles and give little prizes for correct answers. You'll be my assistant. I'll tell everyone you're a clown in training. Natalie asked me to paint everyone's face. If you've had any experience, we can split up the kids. If not, you'll have to hang out and hand me paints and brushes as I need them."

"I think you like humiliating me far too much for someone who doesn't even know me. You say your brother's a cop? Maybe you're getting back at him through me. Or maybe a cop boyfriend dumped you, so making a fool of me gives you a kick."

"I love my brothers. I'm proud of all three. Kieran wears the blue. Dane risks his life fighting fires. Perry transports freight cross-country for a living. And I never dated a cop. I have better sense. I think you're acting pretty ungrateful for a guy in your position. Not to mention that you've endangered lives by coming here."

Logan flinched at Daphne Malone's verbal slap. "You're absolutely right on all counts," he said stiffly. "From here on out, or at least until the party ends, your slightest wish is my command...Bozo," he added under his breath as Daphne thrust a bag in his hands and headed for the door. Logan revised his opinion of her. She wasn't hot. She was a pain in the ass. But he'd associated with worse people to save his hide. So associate with Daphne Malone he would. Temporarily. Logan just hoped this party turned out to be the shortest birthday celebration in history.

He thought that even more as he watched Daphne's sashaying tush disappear out the sliding glass door. Something must be wrong with his love life if he was attracted to a woman dressed like a clown. Her smart mouth alone should deter him. Not only that, Logan was a take-charge kind of guy who didn't particularly like taking orders. Thankfully, his dealings with the dictatorial Daphne Malone would end at the close of this event.

But what if Holt's buddies had already moved on, thinking Logan had given them the slip? Maybe going out there, making a spectacle of himself, would be for nothing. Hanging back, Logan slid across the floor to peer out front again.

He should've known Holt's well-trained goons wouldn't give up so easily. They were out there all right.

CHAPTER TWO

LOGAN STARTED working out a plan to borrow April's car. With a little luck, he'd figured he could sneak past Billy's lookouts. That hope died quickly. A glance through a crack in the blind showed one man from the organization strolling down the street, peering under bushes and over fences into side yards. He stopped to talk to a cop in an LAPD car; Logan wished he could see the cop's face. A second goon followed a trail into the woods adjacent to April's house. Dropping the blind, Logan realized he'd have to play along for a while.

He'd strapped the Luger to his leg with two rubber bands he found in his sister's bathroom cabinet. He'd be walking oddly, anyway, in the big slippered feet. Walking at all was a challenge, he soon discovered, wondering whatever possessed grown-ups to do this for a living.

By placing all his weight on his heels, he managed to make it past the slider onto the patio without falling on his face. Daphne already had the kids sitting in a semicircle, gazing up at her with adoring eyes. A surprising stab of nostalgia rendered him immobile for a heartbeat. An early argument Logan had with his ex had come about because he wanted kids and she flatly refused to discuss it. He envied his sister and her friends, who sat around the pool in deck chairs smiling at their cherubs. Logan again cursed himself for potentially bringing disaster down on them.

Noticing one of Billy Holt's men walking out of the woods on the unfenced side of April's yard, he tensed all over. Logan had gotten into the house undetected by knowing the area. If he ever got out of this, he'd try to convince Mike to move his family to a better location. At the very least, Logan knew he'd come back and help fence their yard.

Feeling protective of everyone here, he waddled up and insinuated his body between Daphne and the deadly onlooker— a man sure to be packing the latest automatic handgun. The availability of high-tech weapons to criminals was something else that made Logan's job more difficult by the day.

Daphne, seemingly oblivious that they were being observed, produced five plastic bowling pins from a flowered bag she'd brought out. She began juggling three pins. Then added two more. When she finally did see the stranger watching from the trees, she faltered and pins flew in five different directions.

Logan scooped them up. Even with gloves covering his hands, he tossed the pins in the air and kept them aloft far longer than Daphne had.

The kids clapped loudly.

"Hey, quit upstaging me," Daphne said, planting her hands on her hips.

The kids and their moms assumed the banter was part of the routine. They all laughed and urged Daphne to take the pins away from her partner.

"That's okay," Daphne told the children. "My magic tricks are way cooler than his."

"What's your name?" called out one boy.

"I'm Bozo. This is Buzzy. He doesn't talk much," Daphne said seriously. "But he'd like another round of applause for how well he juggles. How about if we all show him our appreciation?"

The group of kids and adults clapped harder. Logan knew why Daphne had said he didn't speak. If their intruder stayed at the edge of the party—and he showed no indication of leaving—the guy might well recognize Logan's voice. Logan's estimation of Daphne Malone's ability to think on her feet went up several degrees.

But he thought it was too bad her magic tricks were so pathetic. Bumping her aside, Logan grabbed the coin and deck of cards out of her hands. As a boy, he'd spent hours with a box of magic tricks he'd received for Christmas one year. This was an arena where he felt confident he could hold the kids' interest.

Daphne crossed her arms and tapped one oversize foot, appearing outwardly annoyed at her partner. Truthfully, she was annoyed. What did he think he was doing, horning in on her gig.

Again, everyone present assumed it was part of the act. And Daphne had to admit, albeit grudgingly, that Logan Grant was a whiz at magic. He held the kids enthralled for a good fifteen minutes. Five minutes, tops, was all she'd ever managed. But then again, this clown business was a sideline for her. Her real talent lay in makeup.

At the first sign that the kids were growing bored with Logan's sleight of hand, she clapped sharply and offered a new diversion.

"Time for face painting. Who wants their faces done?"

The kids jumped up and crowded around her. "Me first, me first," all ten shouted as they danced up and down.

"Whoa! The birthday girl is always first. I'll give Natalie a list of faces I came prepared to paint. She'll choose for everyone. It'll be a grand secret until each of you finally gets to look in the mirror." Daphne flipped open a canvas camp stool hauled from the depths of the voluminous beach bag. Next, she produced a tray filled with small jars of paint.

Logan saw that their watcher had left the tree and appeared to be searching the back half of the vacant lot. Logan judged he could safely leave in ten minutes or so. Except that the kids not being painted started milling about. Those with moms on hand whined. The boys roughhoused, and April suddenly wore a panicked expression. She didn't know they were being watched or she would've been downright terrified.

Logan thought he owed it to his sister, to his niece and to Daphne to stay and help out a little longer.

He whistled to regain the children's attention. Elaborately, he pantomimed that they should again gather around. He began slowly pulling out a row of scarves he'd discovered hidden in the false sleeve of his costume. He tied them together and made the lot disappear.

Even Daphne gave him a rolling "Ooooh," followed by applause. Emboldened, Logan marched up to his sister. He made a big show of patting April's burgeoning belly. He pretended to listen to her baby with a fat clown ear, and made cradling motions with his arms. Then, big as you please, Logan leaned down and shot April in the face with the water-filled flower.

She sputtered, wiped her cheeks, and to everyone's glee she swung at his arm.

Daphne tried to keep a straight face, but she had to smother a laugh. Through talking to Natalie, she'd learned that most of the children at the party had attended fairs where they'd had butterflies or lightning bolts painted on their cheeks. No one was prepared for the display Daphne had planned. Natalie had agreed that Daphne would turn each child into a specific animal. Daphne was relieved the girl had liked her idea. Especially since animal props were the only ones she'd brought, and she figured the kids would enjoy taking them home.

First, she covered Nat's face with white paint, then added pink blush to her cheeks. Using a brush, she framed the little girl's face in black, and added a black nose, jet-black arched eyebrows and whiskers. She painted on big ruby-red lips. Rummaging in her bag, she hauled out two red-and-white polka-dot bows. One was attached to round black ears, which she affixed to the back of Nat's head. The second bow she pinned at the girl's throat. "Voilà, meet our pretty house mouse," she announced, presenting the birthday girl to her family and friends. They both curtsied, Nat gracefully, Daphne a bit more awkward given the size of her false feet.

As the children exclaimed over how great Natalie looked, Daphne started on the next child. Whiskers the Cat was followed by a mop-haired boy as El Perro the Dog. He sported a black ring around his left eye when Daphne put on the finishing touch.

Logan was most impressed by the zebra makeup. The boy wore a black-and-white striped T-shirt that made the costume more realistic. The band with pointy ears that Daphne clipped around his head enhanced the total effect of his black-and-white face paint. The kids liked the Bengal tiger best, though.

"Hey, you're really good," Logan muttered when he thought the kids wouldn't be able to hear him talk normally.

Daphne merely smiled in response, but Logan could tell she was pleased. Did she get so few compliments then? He took a minute to really watch her sure and steady strokes.

A boy with a pronounced lisp became another dog. Daphne

quickly cut big paws out of a discarded grocery sack she'd asked Natalie to hand her. Dog-boy ended up with floppy, grocery-bag ears, too.

A two-toothed rabbit caused everyone to laugh uproariously. The girl wasn't shy. She hammed it up, which only increased Daphne's popularity.

Logan watched the moms ooh and aah among themselves. He had little doubt that his partner had just scored more parties for herself. Strangely, he felt a stab of pride at Daphne's accomplishments. It was similar to the way he'd feel about another agent's success.

She finished the final kid, transforming a cherubic girl with naturally apple-red cheeks and a mop of wildly curling black hair rather like Daphne's own, into a hissing, snarling wildcat. Then she screwed a lid on the paint jar and casually nudged Logan. "Don't look now, but our watchdog's back."

At first Logan thought Daphne was referring to one of the kid animals. But with an elaborate roll of her eyes, she turned his attention to the wooded lot.

Sure enough, the worst of Holt's henchmen stood at the edge of April's grass, boldly observing the proceedings.

"Listen up, kids. Buzzy is going to help Mrs. Ross bring out Natalie's cake. While they're gone, I want everyone to practice helping her blow out the candles. I'll dish up ice cream to go with the cake in a minute. Oh—I see an interested neighbor. Maybe he has a child he'd like to book a party for. I'll go tell him how to contact us."

Was she nuts? Logan couldn't believe his eyes. Daphne marched straight up to Billy's right-hand man, a cold-blooded killer if ever there was one. Logan recognized the man nicknamed Razor for the way he carved up his enemies. Jeez. Did Daphne Malone have a death wish? Logan tried to pull loose from April, but his sister had his clown suit in a grip that he feared would tear the material if he resisted too strenuously. Twisting his head to keep an eye on Daphne didn't work, either. April opened the kitchen door and shoved him inside, totally cutting off his view.

AFTER YEARS OF LIVING with an excess of authoritative older brothers, Daphne had learned that the best way to divert a problem was to face it head-on. Even though her knees knocked inside her baggy polka-dot clown suit, she walked right up to a man she knew to be on the wrong side of the law. "Hi, I'm Bozo the Clown," she said. "My partner, Buzzy, and I perform at children's parties all over the valley. I couldn't help noticing the interest you've shown in our act. Unfortunately, I don't have a business card with me." She made a show of holding out her costume so the man could see she had no pockets. "I can give you a phone number, though, if you have a child with a birthday coming up."

"No kid," the man growled. He practically stumbled over his feet in an attempt to back away from Daphne.

"Oh." She actually managed to sound saddened by his revelation. "Well, I'll let you go then. Buzzy and I always help the hostess serve refreshments. This many kids can make a real mess of cake and ice cream. So, if you're just out for your daily walk, Mr...." She let her words trail off.

Daphne knew, of course, that he wouldn't supply a name. As she'd expected, he turned abruptly and all but melted into the woods.

She wanted to grin and pat herself on the back. However, her knees were too spongy. It was all she could do to make it to the patio before collapsing on the camp stool she'd set up to paint faces.

Logan exited the house carrying a sheet cake with seven lit candles.

Daphne saw from the disapproving flash in his blue eyes that she was in for a tongue-lashing. It was only a matter of time. Well, Logan Grant ought to thank her. That was what he ought to do. It was plain to her that the man watching them was suspicious of their act.

When she succeeded in getting her legs under her again, Daphne stood up and flounced into the kitchen.

Logan quickly followed, leaving his sister to oversee blowing out the candles and cutting the cake. "What the hell did you think you were doing out there?" he demanded the minute they were both closed inside.

"He left, didn't he?" Daphne returned flippantly. She pried the lid off a round carton of ice cream and shoved a scoop that lay beside it into Logan's hand. "Make yourself useful," she said haughtily.

He blinked down at the scoop as if to ask how he came to be holding it.

Daphne calmly extended the first bowl. "We'd better hurry. April won't be able to keep the kids from wanting ice cream for long once Natalie blows out her candles."

"You may think this is all a kid's game, like cops and robbers, Ms. Malone. What you did out there was damn stupid. You risked your life and the lives of all those kids and their moms."

Picking up four bowls Logan had filled with ice cream, Daphne bumped her butt against the door to open it. Lowering her lashes demurely, she gave him a sweet smile, which she knew probably looked grotesque with her makeup. "It's a little difficult to take a clown's lecture too seriously."

Practically frothing at the mouth, Logan started after her

to show her how seriously he ought to be taken. But melting ice cream dripped down the handle of the scoop and over his glove. Swearing under his breath, he waddled to the sink and wiped off the sticky stuff. Damn, a man in clown slippers couldn't even stomp out properly.

Logan was two seconds from going into the bedroom to strip out of this ridiculous costume when an out-of-breath April flew down the hall from the direction of the guest room. "I just walked Mariel Weber to her car," she said. "I saw at least three strange men nosing along our street, Logan. Are they the people who want to—well...snuff you?" she asked, lowering her voice to a bare whisper.

Daphne had returned for more bowls. "Hop to it, Grant. The natives are getting restless. Our lives won't be worth a plugged nickel if we don't feed those boys out there chocolate ice cream. I'm not too popular, 'cause I made them wait till all the girls were served."

"You're not too popular with me, either," Logan snapped. "If you hadn't waltzed up and consorted with Razor, he and his pals might've taken a powder by now."

"Razor? No wonder he wasn't eager to share his name." Daphne didn't so much as flinch when Logan swore. She just relieved him of the scoop and quickly filled the next set of bowls. "You cop types all need to clean up your language," she said primly. "You may think swearing is manly, but it doesn't impress the ladies." She hurried back to the patio before Logan self-destructed with apoplexy. Frankly, the only way she could deal with him was to treat him as she'd treat her brothers. Otherwise, if she paused to think about what was really going on, she might fall apart.

At last the party wound down. One mother and daughter had already left, saying they had a family obligation. Daphne knew it wouldn't be long before the others followed. Natalie still had some presents to open, but Daphne knew kids could make short work of ripping through wrapping paper. She'd pack up and leave then. But…what about Logan?

Maybe they could stall through cleaning up the patio, but that was the maximum time she could spend hanging around. Otherwise she'd lose credibility. She sure hoped Agent Grant had more than a few flimsy scarves up his sleeves—although why she cared was beyond her.

Irritated, Daphne pulled empty bowls from children's hands as fast as she could and rushed back to the kitchen. "April, you'd better go on out with your guests. Leave Logan and me to put this stuff away. I think Nat's ready to open her gifts. The kids who already finished eating are poking at her packages."

"I'll go, but will you talk some sense into this brother of mine? He's planning to change into street clothes and take his chances with those thieves and murderers. I think it'd be smarter if you two left together dressed as you are. Those men hanging around out front won't know that you don't usually come and go in costume. Maybe you could swing past Logan's office and dump him out. He'll get your costume back to you somehow. Or else I will. I have your phone number." Bestowing a last unhappy glance on her brother, April disappeared out the kitchen door.

Daphne wasn't at all keen on the idea even though she saw its merit.

"Don't you start giving me lip," Logan told Daphne as she put the lid on the ice-cream carton. Logan, familiar with where to find the freezer, tripped over his feet as he went into the alcove to stow the ice cream. Coming back, he stalked circles around the center island. When Daphne said nothing, he threw up his hands. "If your brother's a cop, you know full well I can't...won't let you help. I'd be in trouble for soliciting help from a civilian, especially a female civilian."

Daphne threw the sponge into the sink after wiping chocolate ice cream off the counter. "I don't know you at all, Logan. I guess your ego's too fragile to ask for help from a mere woman."

"That's not it," he exploded. "It's against rules. Besides, my boss sees me dressed like this and worms the story out of me, I'll be on report from now until I retire."

"Yes," she said sympathetically. "On the other hand, you might actually live to retire." She'd edged over to a window that faced out on the front yard. "I have to agree with April that staying in costume makes the most sense. And believe me, I'm not looking forward to riding in a hot car wearing full greasepaint. It'll run."

"Is runny makeup all you're worried about? If one of those yoyos even suspects I'm his man, your car will end up riddled with bullet holes."

"I drive pretty fast."

"Doesn't any of this faze you? If—and I'm saying if—I go along with this half-baked scheme, I'm driving the getaway vehicle. I've had to dodge tails before, which I doubt you have."

"I've had to shake a persistent friend who thought I was dating her boyfriend. But she didn't have a gun," Daphne said with a grin. "At least I don't think she did."

"It's not the same and you know it."

She sobered instantly. Daphne's tawny eyes revealed that she wasn't nearly as blasé about any of this as she tried to let on. "Let me collect my props and get my check. I owe a lot of people, so if I turn up dead, maybe what I earned today will go toward staving off my creditors."

"Hey," Logan called as Daphne sped around him. "We're splitting today's take fifty-fifty, aren't we?" He winked when she stopped to gawk at him. "Well, I did do half the job," he said, spreading his white-gloved hands. "I thought I was pretty good."

"You did okay for a rookie. But in this line of work it's common for an apprentice to pay a master clown to teach him the trade. If we manage to get out of this in one piece, though, I might buy you dinner one of these days."

"Really? Dinner with a clown? That's an offer a guy doesn't get very often. Okay, Bozo, you're on. Let me go ease April's mind. I'll bring anything you left on the patio to the bedroom. By the way, I'm not driving in these clodhoppers. I'm changing into my boots."

"What kind of special agent are you?" Daphne tossed her head. "Any bad guy worth his salt will spot those run-down boots of yours. That's why I'm driving. I have socks on under my clown shoes. I can slip these off once we're in the car. Your buddies out there will be none the wiser."

"You're a hard woman, Daphne Malone. Okay. You win. Are you sure you're not the cop in the Malone family moonlighting as a clown?"

"Don't ever let my brother Kieran hear you say that. He's convinced it takes a virtual deity to do what he does for a living. A deity with a penis, no less."

"Hmm. Your brother and I would get along fine. Too bad we'll never meet. The agency discourages fraternizing with local law enforcement. In case it's necessary to put us out in the community undercover."

"Yes," she said sweetly. "You're so good at working undercover."

Logan grabbed another sponge off the counter and threw it at her. But she was too quick. It missed by a mile. He found himself grinning in spite of the situation. Daphne Malone was really something. He'd bet she didn't take an ounce of guff from her brother. Brothers, he corrected, recalling that she'd mentioned three. All men in tough-guy fields. No wonder she'd learned to hold her own in a verbal scuffle.

Remembering how she'd looked in skimpy underwear, Logan grinned a moment longer. He pictured scuffling with her across a king-size bed. His smile faded. Ludicrous, he thought, stiff-arming his way out the back door.

April left one of her friends in charge of the children who'd stayed to play after Nat had opened her gifts. She'd received a croquet set and the kids wanted to try it out. One of the other moms promised to help set up while April paid her performers.

"I'm worried, Logan. Phone me as soon as Daphne drops you at your office. It's bad enough that I have to deal with Mike being at sea, without worrying about your safety, too."

"We'll be fine. In fact, I only see one carload of bad guys hanging around," Logan said, brushing a kiss on April's forehead. "Stop worrying. It's not good for the baby. Oh, tell Nat I phoned or something, and that I'm mailing her a gift. What does she want that she didn't get?"

"See if you can find the Barbie with all the camping gear. The stores in this area were all sold out. We're using Mike's leave to go camping before the baby arrives, which is why Nat wants the Barbie that comes with a tent and stuff. She was disappointed, I think, when she found out it wasn't what her dad and I had given her."

"Man, I hate going down Barbie aisles in toy stores. It's more intimidating than Victoria's Secret. Well, almost more intimidating," he said, realizing what he'd admitted not only to his sister, but to Daphne Malone. She'd stowed her check in her bag and waited impatiently at the front door. Logan expected one of the women to ask who he bought skimpy lingerie for. Thankfully, neither remarked on it.

Before either of them could, he relieved Daphne of her bulging beach bag and reached around her to open the door.

"Go on out with Nat and enjoy the rest of her party, sis. I'll call you when I can. Don't worry if you don't hear right away."

April walked onto the front porch. Daphne waved before she and Logan climbed into her Volkswagen.

"You said you had a car," Logan grumbled, trying to fold his long body enough to fit inside the cramped space.

"No disparaging comments, please. I happen to love my little car. She's a classic. And Tootles gets me where I'm going economically. I find parking when bigger cars have to pass up a spot." She patted the dash. "Oops, I see two cars with dark windows. Looks like maybe two occupants in each, and both show an inordinate amount of interest in us. You might want to lean into the back seat so they can't get a good look at you."

"I got a good look at me at April's. I don't think my boss would recognize me."

Still, Daphne noticed he took her suggestion. Agent Grant didn't do anything without bickering, but he listened and eventually took advice—from a woman, no less. Daphne stored that information for tossing up at Kieran one day.

"Hey," she said, flexing her fingers around the wheel. "A dark blue car pulled in directly behind us."

The word that left Logan's mouth wasn't pretty, but Daphne thought it described how she felt at the moment, too.

"See if you can shake him. Keep to the middle lane. At the next intersection, if the light's green, whip into the right lane and make a hard right turn."

Daphne followed his instructions to the letter. But the car tailing them crossed in front of a truck in a real squeaker of a move and ended up behind them again.

"Don't act like you're keeping tabs on him," Logan said. "But glance in your sideview mirror occasionally."

"He's so close on my rear I can almost feel him breathing."

"Yeah, I'm afraid he thinks we deliberately tried to ditch them."

"We did."

"I know, but I'd hoped they wouldn't be expecting it of you. I thought maybe we could zigzag through a few streets and throw them off our scent."

Daphne tried to relax. She leaned back against the seat and loosened her death grip on the wheel. "Where's your office? Can we shake them in five o'clock traffic? The next block will fill up soon with workers leaving a packing plant."

Logan named an address, and Daphne was surprised to learn his office wasn't more than ten blocks from her apartment building. "I didn't know there was a federal building on Jefferson Boulevard."

"There's not." He scrunched down even lower in the seat and rested his hat against the headrest. "Our whole unit is operating on the q.t."

"Phew, that's good. I didn't relish pulling up in front of a federal building to let you out in case I can't lose that blue

Mercedes afterward. But if your whole unit's under wraps, those guys won't know I'm leaving you with feds."

"Don't be too sure." Logan crossed his arms and studied his driver. "They have unheard-of sources. Money talks, and that gang of thugs has gold to burn. Their last heroin shipment brought in half a billion dollars on the street."

"That's disgusting. Think of all those pathetic humans who lie, cheat and steal to pay for their drug habits."

"Unfortunately, in California and elsewhere, plenty of folks with big bucks are dabbling in the hard stuff. They earn their money on Wall Street, or in occupations that are well thought of."

"Like entertainment and sports, you mean?"

"To name two, yes."

Daphne spared him a sidelong glance. "I've lived on the fringes of Hollywood my whole life. I know rich-and-famous kids who spent more than their school lunch money to stay stoned out of their minds."

"Did you know any dealers? Do you now?"

"No. I always figured it was better not to know. I didn't use, or run around with kids who did." She shrugged. "I was never very popular."

"Now that I find hard to believe."

She sent him a dirty look. As dirty, at least, as a clown with a painted-on smile could deliver.

"Are they still on our bumper?" he asked, not wanting to turn around.

"Yes," she said, making a right turn and then a left. "Dang, I thought that maneuver might confuse them. They seem acquainted with all our one-way streets. Shoot, I'm afraid I really tipped them off."

Logan squinted into the sun to read the next street signs.

"Go up Linda Vista and join the Foothill Freeway. From there, see if you can disappear in heavy traffic. Then swerve onto the Glendale Freeway. Follow it all the way down to the Golden State. If they're unaware the feds have a branch office here, it may throw them off the track long enough to let me slip out and double back. I just don't want to leave them following you. By the way, where do you live? And do you live alone or with family—or with a significant other?"

"Alone." She gave him the coordinating cross streets for her apartment. "Why do you need to know where I live?"

"Because I may have to go home with you to make it look convincing to these jokers if they're too persistent."

"What? No way! I just told you I live alone."

"How many people in your building know that?"

"A few. I don't see how that's relevant."

"It is if our tails get nosy and start asking questions around here. If they weren't suspicious of us—of me—I think they'd already be peeling off to look elsewhere. They know where I live. I'm sure someone's watching my condo."

"I suppose you can come up for a little while. How do you plan to leave my apartment, though—and when?"

"I'll think of something. I hate to ask a fellow agent to extract me, but if all else fails, I will. Those jerks behind us don't know your name. You didn't give it to Razor, did you?" Logan leveled a serious look at Daphne.

"I said we booked birthday parties as Bozo and Buzzy. I said I didn't have any business cards with me. Your friend wasn't interested. I pretended I thought he had a child and was checking the party because he might want to book us."

"That was good thinking," he said somewhat unwillingly.

"Thanks." Her response was dry.

"No, I mean it. Have you considered going into police work yourself?"

"Are you kidding? With my work history?" She laughed hilariously as she navigated up the ramp onto the first of the three freeways.

"It couldn't be too bad. You aren't that old."

"Part-time jobs have been my downfall," she muttered with a grimace. "I figured anyone could be a waitress. I've certainly encountered some ditzy ones. But my first day on the job, I dumped Caesar salad in the lap of a really big movie star. I guess you could say I got blackballed from working at any local restaurants where there're decent tips."

"So, your mistake was in assuming that waitressing's easy."

"On my next job, I tried lifeguarding at Santa Monica Beach."

"Can you swim?" Logan asked carefully.

"Yes, don't be an idiot. I swim fine. I just couldn't rescue a two-hundred-and-fifty-pound doofus who almost drowned himself and me. He was drunk out of his gourd, and his buddies thought the way he fought me was really cute."

"Well, jeez, what do you expect if the guy outweighs you? Cripes, you can't weigh more than a hundred and thirty."

"A hundred and twelve to be exact. But the instructor who trained me insists its not a matter of weight but of leverage. So I still got fired."

"That's just two jobs. It's obvious you didn't give up."

"No. I applied for and got a job as a dog walker. I screwed up at that, too." She sighed.

"That job seems like a no-brainer if you don't mind my saying so. What happened?"

"You won't believe it," she responded glumly. "My family

still can't. The agency I signed up with had some high-toned clients. I was assigned to meet dog owners at the valet parking for Rodeo Drive. In a way it was my own fault. My first time out, I was to walk three chows. You've seen chows? They're big and fluffy and red. This particular threesome turned out to be pampered and undisciplined as well. The owner, a star who shall remain nameless, neglected to tell me they had a hankering for a certain French poodle. Her owner operated a ritzy accessory shop on the Drive, where I was told to walk the dogs. I tried my best to hold the chows back when we passed this place. Suffice it to say that before the walk ended, we'd wiped out the awnings of two elite establishments. My dad coughed up for the damages. I won't even tell you what he had to lay out in cold cash. I am going to pay him back, though."

"What made you decide to try being a party clown, of all things? That seems like a job with built-in drawbacks. Kids bite, kick and spit. Mothers never believe their rug rats are at fault."

"Oh, I'm only doing this temporarily while I wait to hear on a job at one of the movie studios. My family talked me into giving college another stab after the last disaster. They weren't overjoyed when I chose to become a makeup artist. But I'm good at it, and I think it'll be exciting and rewarding work. No two movies are ever alike. Plus, I'll meet a lot of interesting people—including single men. But don't you dare ask about my history in that department. I've spilled all of my life story you're going to hear, Agent Grant. It's your turn."

"We'll have to find a different subject, then. Damn, I see we haven't lost our shadow. If I'm not mistaken, the next off-ramp is the one you need to take."

"So it is. Does this mean you're really coming to my apartment?"

"I'm afraid so," Logan said slowly. He checked and re-checked the car following them without giving the appearance that he was doing so.

"Then you can tell me all about Logan Grant. Must be a fascinating life you lead, what with criminals chasing you around, driving you into the back bedrooms of virtual strangers."

"It was my sister's bedroom. She's hardly a stranger. And that doesn't happen often. Agents aren't supposed to talk about their private lives," he muttered. "However, I will tell you that drugs aren't all we suspect these men of trafficking. Don't worry, though, I'm not planning to trouble you for long. Just until I call my office."

Daphne exited the freeway and took the surface streets three blocks west to her apartment. Spotting a sports car pulling out of a parking place, she zipped into it, causing Logan to bump his head against the curve of the windshield when she braked fast.

"Sorry. This parking space is directly in front of my entrance. It means we only have to walk a few steps to get inside. I don't see any other opening. Your friends back there will either have to double-park or wait until someone leaves. This time of the afternoon, when everyone's coming home from work, chances of that are slim to none."

"Good. Hey, I didn't think to ask. Is your main door keyed or do you have a doorman on duty?"

"No doorman. This is a low-budget part of town. Almost anyone who wants to enter the building can get someone to buzz them in. I hate that the people here aren't more careful, but it's mostly college kids and artsy people. Either they have lots of company or they're all in the habit of forgetting their keys."

"It's too late to worry about changing neighborhoods now," he said. "I'll bring your beach bag. You run ahead and unlock the door. Act like we've done this a million times. Pretend this is your Oscar-winning performance."

She stuck out her tongue. "I'm not a struggling actress. Name me one person who's ever won an Oscar for makeup. Well, they do, but no one can name them."

"If we pull off this scam, babe, I'll give you a gold statue myself." Logan scrambled out of the cramped space, retrieved Daphne's bag and actually whistled as he bounded up the steps. When she bent to insert the key, he casually placed a hand on her hip, as if it was habit.

The weight of his palm and the warmth of his long body standing so close sent heat to the pit of Daphne's stomach. She fumbled her key and would've dropped the entire ring had Logan not been agile enough to catch it. Smiling, he kissed her knuckles and left red paint from his mouth smeared across her white glove. Then he opened the door without a hitch.

She refused to meet his eyes, certain she'd encounter a satisfied masculine smirk on his cocky face. Just continue to treat him the way you treat your brothers. She chanted that over and over, even as her brain turned to mush. Damn, she didn't need the complication of a man in her life. But then, she clearly wasn't Logan Grant's type. She knew that instinctively. So at most, she'd have to play hostess for an hour or so. Just until someone from his office figured out how to get here and pick him up.

CHAPTER THREE

THE FRONT DOOR CLANGED shut behind them. Daphne ducked out from beneath Logan's hand without saying a word and raced up the stairs. She'd come inside in stocking feet. Logan was not only grappling with the awkward beach bag, but he still wore the oversize clown slippers.

He stopped on the first landing and pulled off the foam booties that tripped him up on every step. After that he moved better. But the woman leading the charge kept going higher and higher. "Hey," he finally called, wincing as his voice echoed in the stairwell. "Which floor do you live on?"

"Eighth. It's the top floor in this building. I started out on third, but I hated having people tramping around overhead. So the minute an apartment opened up on eight, I switched."

"I can't believe there's no elevator."

"It's an historic building is why. I think the circular stairs are part of the charm."

"Great! Who needs historic?"

Daphne had finally reached the last landing. She turned and headed down the hall, where she stopped outside the last door on her left.

Logan paused to check out possible exits. His hostess appeared to have a corner apartment overlooking the front of the building. The minute she opened the door and he walked in behind her, Logan saw with some pleasure that she also had a big corner window. He made a beeline over there to scan the street below.

Glad he was otherwise occupied, Daphne zigzagged through her living room, picking up items she'd strewn haphazardly about. She wouldn't call herself a slob, exactly, but picking up never seemed a top priority, unless she'd arranged for company. Or if family members phoned to say they'd be dropping by, she made certain the place looked more presentable than it did now.

She hooked an arm around the beach bag Logan had set just inside the door, then threw it and a dirty T-shirt scooped off the couch, plus yesterday's nightgown, into her bedroom. Quickly slamming the door on a rumpled, unmade bed, she hurried out to make a similar survey of the kitchen.

Ugh! Her kitchen was even messier. Daphne enjoyed cooking if she had guests. Otherwise, she'd never been able to work up much enthusiasm for fixing three meals a day. And doing dishes—well, last night's microwave teriyaki rice bowl and her toast plate from breakfast still sat on the counter, along with glasses and an empty orange-juice container. She really ought to develop better habits.

Lord help her if Logan Grant took a notion to open her refrigerator. There was no telling what kind of flora and fauna he might find growing in there. She cast a sidelong glance at him. He was probably hungry, but she needed to shop for groceries because she'd stayed at Dane's house all last week.

"Damn," he muttered. "The car that followed us found a parking place right across the street from your VW. The occupants don't seem in any rush to get out. But it doesn't seem as if they're set to leave anytime soon, either." He sidled away from the window and walked to the front door.

Frowning, he turned. "What did you do with the bag I carried up? I'll think better after I shower and change into my own clothes. Well, not mine but that stuff of Mike's I asked April to pack. Mike's heavier and a few inches shorter than me, but I'm sure his shirt will fit. I'll have to make do with my jeans, though, no matter how grungy they are."

Daphne looked stricken. "When did you ask April to pack some of her husband's clothes? I saw her stuff your old clothes in a department-store bag she sent off with her friend who left the party early. She asked Mariel, I think her name was, to toss the bag in a commercial trash bin. I'll look again, but I'm sure there are no clean clothes of yours in the bag."

She hurried into her bedroom and pawed through the beach bag. She walked back out, shaking her head. "The only things in there are the costumes I took to the party. I'm sorry, Logan."

While Daphne was in her bedroom, he'd removed the hat that had fuzzy white yarn sticking out wildly over each ear. He ran a hand through his own sun-streaked badly matted hair and tugged off the rubber band tying it back. "What was April thinking? I can't go roaming around town wearing this." He gazed helplessly at his wilted costume.

"April thought I was dropping you at your office. Since you're planning on phoning your boss, have him bring some clothes so you can change before you leave."

"Right. Good idea. That wig fit so tight, it must've shrunk my brain."

"Gee, that's reassuring, Special Agent Grant. You're supposed to be our government's finest protector."

Logan delivered a dirty look. "Where's your phone?"

Daphne went into her bedroom and came out carrying a silver cellular.

"I can't use a cell. That group outside has ways of pulling cell waves out of the air. Did you see the array of antennae on the Mercedes? It's set up with every kind of scanner known to man."

"A cell is all I have. I canceled my land line after I lost my last job. I needed to keep monthly costs down."

"So you don't have a computer, either?" He acted as if no one could be that hard up.

"No. If I need one for any reason, I run by my folks' or over to one of my brothers' homes. They have all the latest high-tech toys."

"Which does me no good. Hell, this paint you put on my face is starting to itch like mad. I'll at least go wash it off, if you don't mind."

"There's a half bath off the smaller bedroom down the hall on your right. I, uh, am going to shower in my bathroom. Sorry, but I have a closetful of clothes. None you'd want to share," she said, grinning mischievously.

"Ha, ha. Well, maybe our shadow will give up and leave by the time I get this gunk off. How hard is it to remove? Will I peel off a layer of skin?"

Daphne's smile broadened. "I happen to have this handy-dandy magic cream. Momento! I'll go find you an extra jar."

Logan cooled his heels and inspected her living room as Daphne disappeared again into what he assumed was her bedroom.

He stood in the center of the high-ceilinged space and swiveled in a slow circle. Nothing matched. Not woods, not fabrics, not colors. Oddly enough, the crazy mixture held a homey appeal. The potted plants everywhere added a natural charm.

Personally, Logan didn't own much in the way of furniture or knickknacks. What he and Lizzy had bought during their brief marriage went to her in the divorce.

Or should he call it a bloodbath? By about the third meeting with both of their lawyers, Logan figured he'd be lucky to end up with a shirt. He'd been so naive about what could happen during a divorce. He'd gone into it assuming they'd be fair and split things down the middle because their marriage had been a mutual mistake. But that piranha Liz hired as her attorney had made him out to be the most unfeeling bastard on the planet. Between her and the judge, they'd stripped him of everything except his pride. Even that was rocky for a while.

Logan didn't like remembering how Liz had taken every opportunity to undermine him in the department where they'd both worked in D.C. If it hadn't been for Simon Parrish being transferred to L.A. to head up a team, and the fact that he'd asked Logan to come along, there'd be no telling how his career might have fared.

Daphne popped back into the room. When he glanced in her direction, Logan noticed her face was free of greasepaint. She smiled and passed him an open white jar filled with an opaque cream. "I thought I had a second one of these, but I couldn't lay my hands on it. So I quickly washed my face. You can take this to the bath I pointed out earlier. You'll find washcloths and towels under the sink."

"Thanks. I've gotta say, you've been decent about all this."

"No problem."

"I doubt many women would've faced the situation as calmly as you did."

She uttered a self-conscious laugh. "I didn't feel calm. You had me at a disadvantage from the start. It helped to find out you were on the right side of the law."

Logan remembered how her heart had fluttered when he'd flung his arm around her in order to pull her over to the window. He also had a sudden, distinct memory of exactly how she'd looked standing before him in lacy blue underwear. And how soft and velvety her skin felt under his own rough fingers.

Clearing his throat, which had gone bone dry, Logan nervously juggled the jar of cream. He gave a couple of jerky nods and sped off down the hall to the guest bath.

Daphne noticed the sudden tension in the air as she watched Logan vanish into the back bedroom.

Men could be so touchy at times. Obviously, she'd said something he deemed unacceptable, but she had no idea what. And of course her brothers always claimed she let her mouth run away without ever connecting with her brain. She guessed that was true enough.

Deciding it was just too bad, she ducked back inside her own room, intent on showering. Her hand hovered above the lock for all of ten seconds. Then she curled her fingers into her right palm and went into her bathroom. He was, after all, an FBI special agent. And if he'd had designs on her body, he'd already passed up a chance to ravish her at April's. Of course, his mind had been on other things. Turning back, she engaged the lock. Not that Logan had given the slightest sign he found her even vaguely attractive, or that he'd make a pass if the opportunity presented itself. But better safe than—Daphne frowned. That was exactly what her mother would say.

LOGAN HAD LONG SINCE returned to Daphne's kitchen by the time her door opened and she emerged a different person. She'd put on blue jeans and a shocking-orange T-shirt that read All Men Are Animals, Some Just Make Better Pets.

She missed his fleeting grin because she was busy toweling dry her riotously curly black hair. Logan fought an urge to bury his fingers in the frothy dark ringlets.

"I take it those scumballs haven't gone," she mumbled from under folds of terry cloth.

"No." He eased a bare shoulder away from the wall where he stood to one side of the glass. Long shadows were falling as the day waned, and he hadn't turned on any lights because he didn't want the goons to see him watching them.

As Daphne appeared from beneath the towel, she did a double take at seeing the clown suit hanging loose around Logan's narrow hips. He'd slung a hand towel around his neck, which did nothing to hide whorls of glinting blond hair that fanned across his chest.

He saved her from stepping on her lolling tongue by attempting to explain his unruly state. "That hot-water faucet in your sink needs fixing. I wrenched it too hard and the water shot out, giving me a shower. I hope you aren't squeamish about seeing a half-naked man."

She shrugged to show it was of no consequence. And it shouldn't have been. After all, she'd lived a good part of her life in a one-bathroom house with three growing brothers. Why didn't this feel the same?

Considering the issue settled, Logan turned the conversation back to her earlier question. "Unfortunately, it looks like those dirtbags are determined to stick around. Does this historic building have a back door? And if so, where does it lead?" Logan didn't know when he'd ever been this restless.

His adrenaline still ran high, and suddenly he had to battle masculine urges he didn't need interfering with his good sense at the moment. He began pacing the small kitchen.

"My building has two fire escapes with window exits at the end of every hall." Folding her towel, Daphne fluffed her still-damp hair with her fingers. "The fire escapes actually dump you out on the sidewalk. My brother Dane's always harassing me about this building not meeting new city codes. But I checked, and historic buildings are grandfathered in the city's fire plan. They're considered safe if they provide fire escapes, a monthly check of extinguishers on every floor, and if the building undergoes a yearly wiring inspection. This one does."

"Which one is Dane?"

"My oldest brother. He's a fire captain. And a know-it-all," she said, making a face.

"Look. I'd love to stay and chat, but I need to either go find my boss or get a message to him ASAP."

"There's a phone booth a block down the street on the southeast corner."

"Right! I saunter out partially dressed—like a clown. Guaranteed our surveillance team will see me and gun me down. And say I did, by some miracle, give them the slip. I'd have every beat cop in the area pouncing on me for indecent exposure. Without any ID on me—well, you fill in the blanks."

"You didn't let me finish. I can go make the call for you. Those guys have no way of knowing what I look like dressed normally."

Logan pondered that. "It's too risky," he finally said. "They're not stupid. As well, you're outnumbered. One of them could easily follow the first man or woman leaving the

building who fit our general descriptions. No, I'll just have to
hang out here until after dark."

"And then what?"

"I'll make a run for it. I know this part of town pretty well.
Down a few alleys, over a few back fences, and I've shaken
them."

"Hardly," she said with a sniff. "That costume you're wearing is made of glow-in-the-dark material. The spots that run
down your right side are phosphorescent, as are the white
stripes running down the left."

"That's the dumbest thing I've ever heard of. When would
you play a clown in the dark?"

Daphne treated him to a scowl. "Not all kids' birthday
parties are at two o'clock in the afternoon. Parents who work
nine to five sometimes have after-dinner dos."

"Oh. I never thought of that. I should have, I suppose. My
mom let me have a few campouts in the backyard with pals
on my birthdays. But then, I was probably in fifth or sixth
grade and would've died before I let her book a clown."

"I'm sure," she drawled, raising an eyebrow. "What interests fifth- and sixth-grade boys are fifth- and sixth-grade
girls."

"Wrong," he threw back. "My buddies and I went for older
women. My mom would kill me if she knew Danny Welch and
I smuggled two eighth-grade girls in for one of our campouts."
He shook his head and chuckled at the memory.

Daphne noticed how laughing altered the harsh, hollow
planes of Logan Grant's lived-in face. She'd thought he was
good-looking before, but mainly because of his body and his
incredible blue eyes. Her dad's family had those Delft-blue
eyes. Some of the Malones were even blessed with beautiful Irish-green eyes. Two of her brothers, in fact—Perry and

Kieran. Dane and Becky's were a pretty hazel that changed shades with their moods.

As a kid Daphne used to check in the mirror every morning after saying a novena the night before, praying for her odd gold eyes to magically change color. It so happened that her mom, who was as Greek as someone named Calandra Dimitrious could be, had olive skin, black hair and dark eyes—genes she might have passed straight to her firstborn daughter. But no. If Daphne hadn't resembled her mother's baby pictures, she'd be sure the hospital had switched her at birth. Her eyes were the color of old brass.

Logan continued to prowl the kitchen. By now his over-long hair was practically standing on end.

"I could go down the hall and use Mrs. O'Bannon's phone to call your boss. Her son Shawn insists his mother have a phone, even though she's deaf as a post. I know she wouldn't mind my using it. Shawn's forever calling me to see if she's okay. He phones her, and she doesn't hear the ring."

"Why didn't you say so sooner?" Logan started to pull up the damp clown suit as he headed for the door. "Introduce me as a friend or coworker. I'll phone Simon."

"No. You don't understand." Daphne bit her lip. "Shawn O'Bannon and Dane work together. And his mom, for all that she's half-deaf, is an incurable gossip. That means I'd have to explain to my whole family how I met you, and…well, I'd rather not."

Logan let the costume fall to his hips again, clearly torn between pushing the issue based on his authority as a special agent and complying with Daphne's wishes. "All right," he said reluctantly. "But I'll write down exactly what I need you to tell Simon. It's important you relay the codes exactly as I give them. And keep the call short, Daphne, in case our pals have already tapped the main phone line. Otherwise, Bil—let's just say it could prove dangerous for both of us if you stay on long enough to attract a trace."

Daphne was sure he'd almost revealed the name of an important person in the organization the FBI hoped to infiltrate. Bill something. Obviously Logan didn't trust her, despite everything they'd been through together. And after he said she'd handled herself well, too.

She found that slightly depressing. Her brothers always did that—closed her out, talking over her head as if she didn't have brains enough to know some things were classified information.

Logan apparently had no idea that he'd insulted her. He snatched the paper and pencil she'd rummaged for and found in her desk. He bent over the small secretary with its one wobbly leg, writing in a clear, legible hand. All in capital letters. Facts of that nature interested Daphne. She thought the way someone wrote revealed a lot about his or her personality and she'd read several books about it. For instance, if she remembered correctly, people—usually men—who wrote everything in caps did so to throw up a wall. They'd either been badly hurt or felt betrayed by someone close to them.

She averted her eyes, not wanting to spy. But when she'd completed his call, Daphne intended to look up the specifics in her handwriting dictionary, to make sure she was correct in her analysis.

"All these numbers mean what?" she asked, glancing at the paper he'd thrust into her hand. The bold strokes were mostly gibberish to her. "Does it tell your colleagues you need them to come and pick you up here?"

"The less you reveal at your neighbor's, Daphne, the better. For one, her phone line isn't secure. I haven't seen anyone leave the car, so I don't think they've put a tap on the main phone box. But with those guys, you never know the extent of their resources. They have more devious tricks up their sleeves than the most accomplished of your master clowns. For now, just relay this information to Simon. Let him tell you what I need to do next."

"Oh. Well, fine. Don't worry, though, if I don't rush back. Make yourself at home—help yourself to a beer." Too late, Daphne remembered the state of her fridge. She sucked in her cheeks and crossed her eyes. "Mrs. O'Bannon can talk a visitor's leg off. She doesn't get a captive audience often, so she makes the most of it when she does. Believe me, I know of what I speak. I grocery shop for her. Bless her soul, she lost Mr. O'Bannon early last year. If it wasn't for her dog, Muffy, keeping her from being so lonely, I don't know what the poor woman would do. Her sons have intense jobs and large families of their own. And Mrs. O. flatly refuses to go live with any of them, even though all the boys have tried to talk her into moving in with them." She took a deep breath.

"Has anyone said you do a fair job of talking someone's leg off yourself?" Logan noted dryly, doing his best to shove Daphne out the door. "I'm locking up after you leave. Don't mention me to any neighbor you meet along the way, either. Tap softly three times when you return. I'm serious about this. If anyone hears you banging on the door, they'll come out to investigate. The fewer people who know you're entertaining a strange man in your apartment, the better. I get the feeling it's not the norm for you. And it'd only take one well-placed question for our pals out there to pinpoint my location."

Daphne stopped short of the door, digging in her heels. "You think I'm a blabbermouth and someone incapable of getting a date?" The truth was she didn't date much. Hardly

ever, in fact. But she'd be darned if she'd admit that to a man
who probably had only to crook his little finger to have scores
of dates falling in his lap.

"Go!" Logan opened the door and in spite of Daphne's
resistance, shoved her out. He sighed a huge sigh as he bolted
the door behind her, thinking if he escaped and remained
alive, it'd be a miracle. He was the solitary type, and Daphne
Malone hadn't stopped talking since they crawled into that
joke she called a car.

A beer would hit the spot. He glanced at his watch and was
surprised to see that the afternoon was nearly gone. It was
ten to six. Ordinarily he didn't drink alcohol on the job—
only if an undercover assignment made it necessary to appear
social. But Daphne's offer of a beer bounced around inside
his head.

Logan opened the fridge door and at once recoiled from
the smell. Plugging his nose, he searched for and found one
source of the problem. An open carton of milk that had gone
bad.

No wonder, he mused, pouring the curdled mess down
the drain. According to the carton, the milk was two weeks
beyond its expiration date. After rinsing out the carton and
setting it aside, he returned to the fridge. He had to reach
past a basket of strawberries to get to the six-pack of beer.
Logan noticed a layer of furry mold covering a majority of the
exposed fruit. Extracting the beer can, he let the door swing
closed. Then he opened it again and removed the spoiled
berries. They followed the curdled milk down the garbage
disposal. He ran water from the tap for five minutes before
taking up his former station near the window where he could
spy on Bill Holt's cronies. The men appeared to be settling in
for the night.

Logan savored the brew, realizing he hadn't touched one in weeks. No one in the organization was allowed to imbibe, since Holt believed that booze impaired his people's abilities to do the job. And there were stories about what happened to men who didn't follow his orders to the letter. If Logan had any sense at all, he'd be shaking in his shoes.

Looking down, he smiled as he saw he was still barefoot. Macabre humor played better at times like these than dwelling on what Billy Holt would do if he ever laid hands on him. If the man tortured his hirelings for minor infractions like having a beer, imagine what he'd do to a spy in their midst.

Someone exited the car in question. Logan's heart pounded unexpectedly. He drew back fast, then edged out little by little to see what the guy was up to.

Just stretching. Phew! Logan blotted the sweat that had popped out on his forehead. Where was Daphne? He glanced at his watch again. She'd said it might be a while, but did she think she could take all night? Blasted woman had been down there for a full fifteen minutes.

Goon one was a nasty assassin by the name of Lobo Morales. He sauntered to the end of the block and moseyed back past Daphne's VW. His eyes darted from passersby to people entering the building, to the interior of Daphne's car.

Logan figured people were coming home from work about now and those who were driving slowly by were looking for parking spaces.

Daphne's cell phone rang. Logan nearly jumped out of his skin. Of course his inclination was to answer. He didn't dare. But, he wished whoever the hell it was would give up and stop letting it ring and ring and ring. Her apartment wasn't that large. Was Daphne in the habit of not answering her phone?

Ah! It finally quit. Belatedly, Logan realized he'd lost track of Lobo. "Dammit!" He set his beer on the counter. And because Daphne had turned on a lamp in the living room before she left, he got down on hands and knees and crept up to the window. Once there, he eased his head up by inches, attempting to discover where Morales had gone. It was possible he'd climbed back in his car while Logan was focused on the phone. Long shadows stretched across the street, and he couldn't see anything but the top of the gang's car.

He was preparing to creep back out of sight, when Daphne's lock clicked open, and her door swung inward, causing Logan to whirl in panic—still crouched on all fours. He barely managed to get his feet under him and was ready to spring on his unknown assailant when he recognized her.

Daphne waltzed in as if she hadn't a care in the world. She skidded to a stop, her eyes huge. "What on earth are you doing?" she yelped, slamming the door shut behind her. "Did you drop something? A contact lens?"

His heart thundering a hundred miles a second, Logan sank back on his haunches. Closing his eyes, he draped his wrists over his knees. "I thought I told you to knock," he said through gritted teeth.

"You did." She nodded solemnly. "I forgot I'd left a key with Mrs. O. so she could water my plants when I babysat Dane's kids last week. She still had it. He attended a fire chief's conference up in San Fran, and his wife, Holly, had corporate meetings in Salt Lake City. I have all these potted plants that get thirsty." She waved a hand, taking in the plants Logan had noticed earlier. They added to the homey look, and he'd made a mental note to buy himself a few to spruce up his apartment.

"Never mind telling me the whole story. What did Simon say? When's he sending someone after me?"

"He's not." Daphne calmly crossed to where Logan still hunkered. She placed the sack she'd brought on the kitchen table.

"What? He's not sending anyone? Or weren't you able to get through?" Logan seemed truly baffled.

"I got through on the first try. Simon's a really nice man, isn't he? Kind, I'll bet."

"No, he's not." Logan fell back against the wall and grasped his aching head between his hands. "Simon's a coldhearted bastard who has ice water in his veins, which is why he was picked to head this particular operation. Just tell me in as few words as possible what he said, Daphne." Logan heaved a weary sigh.

"Well, I don't think he has ice water in his veins at all." She made tsking noises. "For starters, he was overjoyed to learn you weren't dead. The reports he'd gotten indicated you'd been captured. I can't imagine why you'd even think he's coldhearted. He's plenty concerned about keeping you safe. He said you're to stay put until he has time to assess the situation. And don't worry, because he has things covered."

"Ah, finally we're getting somewhere. But wait! Stay? Here?" Logan groaned. "For how long? Does Simon know my sister got rid of my clothes and that I'm wearing a clown suit? Or...let me rephrase that. I actually pray to God you didn't mention any of those things to my boss."

"I didn't." She looked guilty as she gazed down to where he sat on the floor. "I tried to stick to what you'd written. But Simon had questions. I'm afraid he never said how long you needed to be here, Logan. He asked if we'd been followed. I said yes, and that two men were parked in front of my building. That's when he said you'd have to stay until he worked out a safe way to extract you."

"You should've told him that's not acceptable."

"Now, wouldn't that have made me sound uncivil and unpatriotic."

Logan cradled his head between his hands.

"Does your head ache? I read somewhere that beer on an empty stomach does that to some people. It's a bit early for dinner, but I doubt you've eaten much today. Why don't I rustle us up something. Although I don't know what I have in the fridge." Pulling her top lip between her teeth, she frowned.

Logan spread his fingers and gazed up from one eye. "Are you kidding? I saw the mold growing in your refrigerator. Personally I think I'd be safer dodging those guys' bullets."

"I've been gone a week, remember? I haven't had time to toss out stuff or go shopping. I came home late last night, and this morning your sister called offering me a job. I may have eggs, oh, and bread. And leftover ham in the freezer. It won't be much, but I can throw together a meal."

"Sure, whatever." Logan got to his feet. "Just tell me again, while it's fresh in your mind, exactly what Simon said. Maybe he gave a clue in code. A time tonight when he'll break me out of here," Logan said hopefully.

She pursed her lips and shook her head. "No. He said nothing else. And you're the one who insisted I keep the call short."

Logan was still muttering under his breath, when someone pounded loudly on Daphne's door. She turned to open it, but Logan's hand shot out and clamped around her arm.

"Do you have a peephole?" he murmured near her ear, bringing back memories of their first encounter.

Unable to speak, partly from fright and partly from the sensation of having Logan's lips brush her ear, Daphne managed a meager nod.

The two of them did a crazy sort of crab-walk across the room. Logan let go of her so she could rise on tiptoe to peer out. He positioned himself squarely behind the door. A second knock nearly made her shriek.

"It's a pizza delivery boy," she whispered to Logan. "He's from the corner pizzeria and he comes here often. You wouldn't think he'd get the wrong apartment."

Logan relaxed. "Simon probably sent him. Open the door just wide enough to take the box. Thank him, but shut the door again fast."

"What about a tip? I always tip him."

"If I know Simon, he'll have been generous up front."

Daphne slid the bolt and opened the door a crack. "Hi, Davey. Is that my usual order?"

"Dunno," the kid said. "Must be. My boss said I should deliver it straightaway."

"I just got home and I have no change. How about if I tip you double next time?" she said apologetically.

"It's okay. Mr. Geller said it's covered." He smiled and passed the box to Daphne, who took it, but hated closing the door so fast.

Logan grabbed the box and opened it before he reached the kitchen. Steam wafted out, along with the aroma of spices that started her stomach growling. "It's like I thought." Logan removed a tiny phone encased in plastic tucked behind the pizza near the back of the box.

"A cell phone?" Daphne eyed the thing skeptically. "I thought you said the guys in the car had scanners."

"This is equipped with a jammer." He took himself off to the side of the kitchen and let her get out plates while he punched in a number.

Daphne heard low arguing. She watched out of the corner

of her eye as Logan raked his hand through his hair and stomped around in circles. It was a wonder the air over his head wasn't turning blue from the language spewing out of his mouth.

He could do what he wanted, but she didn't intend to let a good pizza go cold. She took a satisfying, gooey bite just as he slammed the phone shut and threw it down so it skittered across the counter.

Gazing at her with fire in his eyes, he said, "Simon ordered me not to budge until tomorrow. Actually not even then. He'll reevaluate the situation tomorrow night."

The pizza lodged in Daphne's throat. Her own phone began to bleat, and she answered it still choking. "Oh, hi, Mom." At last the lump went down. "I, ah, am eating pizza. I know, I know. I promised to phone when I got back from the party. Uh...how'd it go?" She gave Logan a sidelong glance. "Actually, the party went really well. I'll probably get several bookings from women whose kids were there."

Logan pulled out a chair across from her and straddled it. He took a swig from what was now warm beer, continuing to glare at her—as if she were to blame for the fix he'd landed in.

"Yes, I'm aware there was a police fracas near my party, Mom. I passed the street they cordoned off. What did it say on the news? You're going to let Kieran tell me? He's swinging by tonight? No...Mother...tell him not to." Daphne's whole body stiffened in protest, as did Logan's. "What?" she yelped. "He's already left? Oh...no, why wouldn't I want him dropping by? It's just that I'm not a baby." She frowned, again at Logan. "Ah...you called ten minutes ago and I didn't answer? Well, I stopped to get my key from Mrs. O'Bannon. Mother! I'm hanging up. For one thing, my pizza's getting cold. For another, I'm going to try and reach Kieran on his cell so he doesn't waste his time coming here after a hard day of his own." She clicked off in the middle of Callie's goodbye.

Logan's arched eyebrow climbed up to meet a lock of sun-streaked hair as he watched Daphne frantically punch in another number—just as another booming knock sounded at her front door.

Closing her eyes, she uttered a word she rarely used. "Too late," she muttered, feigning brightness as she hopped up from the table. "He's here. My brother Kieran. The cop you said you'd like to meet but probably never would. Well, get set to meet him."

Logan lunged for her and missed. "Whatever you do, don't tell him who I really am. Keep with the story that I'm one of your clown friends or something."

"Okay." Flying across the room, Daphne threw open the door. She hadn't given a thought to the fact that her brother's first glimpse would be of a bare-chested man seated at his sister's table.

CHAPTER FOUR

KIERAN MALONE WAS A BIG MAN with eyes as clear and green as the hills of Ireland that his great-grandparents had left behind when they emigrated to the U.S. to build a new life. Dressed in a lieutenant's uniform, he looked as stalwart as a warship and twice as imposing. Past boyfriends of Daphne's had been known to quake in their boots at the sight of him. He, of course, played his part as her protector to the hilt. Yet this evening his entrance had no obvious effect on Logan Grant.

Logan bit casually into his pizza.

Impressed right down to her tingling bare toes, Daphne stepped aside, and motioned Kieran in. "This is my second-oldest brother, Kieran. Uh, Kieran, this is a friend of mine from…uh…school."

Logan acknowledged Daphne's brother with a quick dip of his jaw. "Don't turn on any more lights," he ordered Daphne, who'd reached around the corner to snap on the overhead in the kitchen.

"Okay, sis, what in hell is going on? Who's this bum? And what's with the glow-in-the-dark clown suit he's not quite wearing?" Kieran lumbered across the floor, all the while glaring at Logan's bare torso. Daphne's brother bellied right up to the table and helped himself to a piece of their pizza. "I should learn to listen to Mom when she says she has a strong notion something's not right." Kieran deliberately placed a shiny black boot on the chair where Daphne had been sitting and shifted the pizza to his left hand, letting his right hover inches above his holster. "Okay, joker, bring your pizza along. You can spill your whole sad tale from the back seat of my squad car. My sister might fall for every sob story around, but not me, buddy."

"Kieran, you don't understand. This is—" Daphne abruptly smothered what she'd been about to say, and darted a confused look at Logan. "Please, can I tell Kieran who you are?"

Logan swallowed a wad of crust and cheese, then drew a napkin out of a stack Daphne had dropped on the table and wiped the grease off his fingers. He never lowered his gaze from Kieran's icy eyes. But he gestured with his free hand. "Take a load off your feet, boyo. All afternoon Daphne's bragged on her brothers. It's good to meet you." He stuck out his hand. "Just call me Buzzy the Clown, why don't you."

Veins in Kieran's thick neck bulged. He plopped his pizza on a plate, deliberately ignoring the fingers dangling before him. His fierce scowl, and the fact that he quietly unsnapped his holster, made Daphne's heart sink. She knew that under all his trappings, Kieran was a teddy bear. He'd never remove his weapon unless forced to in a life-or-death situation. But Logan had no way of knowing that.

Unsure what to do, she pulled out a third chair and shoved it toward her brother. "Kieran, sit. You're not going to handcuff him and haul him off to jail. He's done nothing wrong. Are you off duty? If so, why don't I get you a beer."

"I'll take another while you're at it, babe." Logan crushed his empty can, taking care never to let his eyes stray from the opponent who outweighed him by thirty pounds.

Daphne quickly snatched his can. She dumped it into the trash as she hurried to the fridge, wondering what possessed Logan to needle Kieran the way he was doing.

Kieran didn't sit; instead, he loomed closer to Logan, wagging his eyebrows menacingly.

Logan refused to blink, but he did let his outstretched hand drift to the table.

"You're awfully cool for a dude living on borrowed time," Kieran said.

Daphne took two cans from the six-pack and popped them both open. She slammed one down on the table in front of Logan. The second, she shoved hard in the center of Kieran's chest. "Both of you, quit posturing like bull moose. Kieran, I said sit. And for once, stop throwing your weight around. For your information, Logan outranks you. I, uh, think," she added tentatively, all but daring him to deny her statement.

Logan blanched. "Dammit, Daphne. I said—"

"Outranks me? The hell you say?" Letting his burning gaze fly from his sister to the steely-eyed stranger, Lieutenant Malone tensed. "Damn, are you the person of interest we have an unofficial APB on? I should've known. Mom told me three times that Daphne had a job real near today's big mix-up."

Logan's eyes narrowed. Official or unofficial, an APB wasn't good news. He felt exposed and vulnerable dressed as he was—or rather not dressed—to deal with a uniformed cop. Logan had pieced together enough facts in today's surprise raid to conclude that it might have been orchestrated from inside. Billy complained a lot about the possibility of a mole, a spy in the organization, because of the number of times they'd lost shipments. In this case, Logan's boss had purposely elected to skip a crackdown. The FBI wanted the head of the snake. They wanted a Thai leader by the name of

Sarit Ratsami, known to the agents as Rat or Papa Rat. Logan was positive his boss hadn't called for a bust today, but those blaring sirens had given Billy Holt's crew plenty of time to scatter. Only after he'd had a chance to think did it occur to Logan that the whole show had been designed to flush him out. And if he hadn't stopped to save that local cop, Billy still wouldn't have fingered him for the spy.

He'd known that every day he remained undercover the risks of being found out increased. So, who'd tipped Billy off? A rogue agent who'd enlisted a dirty cop? It wasn't hard to buy a hardworking schmuck with the promise of cash. Hardworking cops like Kieran Malone. He seemed to be inordinately interested. What if he really wasn't one of the good guys?

Daphne's head swung first to one deadly quiet man, then to the other. "Good grief. Now that Kieran's here, let's just explain what happened today."

"Don't know what you mean, babe." Logan's eyes remained locked on Malone. "As birthday gigs go, today's was run-of-the-mill. Until one of the munchkins turned a hose on me. Your sister was good enough to invite me up here to dry off. I thanked her with supper, which you're interrupting, by the way." Logan leaned an arm on the table and got right in Kieran's face. "So why don't you trot on home?"

Kieran, clearly close to apoplexy, bellowed, "I don't give a royal pig's eye who bought the pizza. I'm telling you, pal, you pull up that clown suit and come take a walk with me. I don't like your attitude and I'm not leaving you with my little sister."

Daphne didn't trust the sudden quirk of Logan's lips. And she wasn't a bit surprised when he dug in his heels. Still, she could have curled up and died at his next statement.

"No can do, Malone. I'm parked here for the night." Logan

reached across his chair back and picked up the fresh beer. "Right, babe?"

Kieran's mouth opened and closed like a bass trying to spit out a toad. "Daphne's famous for falling into half-baked jobs. But her clown nonsense takes the cake. What kind of job is that for a grown-up? And for a man?"

Logan lowered his beer. "Have you ever actually watched your sister's act? She's a genius with face paints. Today she made a lot of kids laugh." Logan's harsh features softened noticeably as his eyes ran slowly over his hostess.

Kieran Malone plainly didn't care for that. "Flattery might impress Daph, but you don't fool me for a minute. Get this, dude. She's not shacking up with any pansy-assed kiddy clown as long as I'm still vertical."

Daphne doubled her fist and slugged Kieran's shoulder. "Apologize to me and to Logan this minute! I'm not a child. If I choose to have a man sleep over, it's nobody's business but mine. However, for your information, he's been ordered to stay here by his boss at the FBI."

Logan groaned, his expression changing to one of pure dismay.

"So, sue me, Logan," she muttered. "You guys are acting like two-year-olds fighting over the same toy."

"Well, thanks for totally blowing my cover. It didn't enter your head, I suppose, that now I may have to silence you both."

Daphne's golden eyes grew round. She hoped he was kidding. Thought he must be. Frankly, she didn't know if the sparks shooting between the men were indicative of something worse. She had no idea what he'd done with the weapon she'd seen him holding at April's. It'd disappeared before the party. She felt bad for revealing Logan's secret, but it was almost worth provoking him, just to see the wariness steal into her lunkhead brother's eyes.

Kieran turned from apoplectic red to ashen in the blink of an eye. Nearly as fast, he looked chagrined. "Only my sister could go out on a simple part-time job and step in a pile of... you-know-what." The big cop removed his foot from the chair. "I didn't buy for a second that you were a clown. If you are the person of interest I mentioned earlier who bailed out one of our guys, and if you're really a fed, why don't you quit feeding me bullshit and tell me what in hell's going on." Kieran's eyes hardened, indicating that he was finished with dancing around.

Logan rolled the cold beer can between his palms. Malone's right hand still curved around the handle of his revolver. Logan's weapon was rubber-banded to his leg. "Were you at this morning's raid, Malone?"

Kieran admitted he wasn't. "So what?" he added.

"Hmm. If you'd been on hand, you probably would've thought your local team was staging a Hollywood cops-and-robbers film."

"How so?"

"Sirens. All over the place."

"That's true," Daphne concurred. "At least five police cars screamed past me. When I got to the street I needed to turn down, they had it cordoned off. But I could still hear sirens all up and down the avenue."

"No wonder our guys came up empty-handed. Any drug dealers for blocks around would've had enough advance warning. They'd take off."

"Give the man a Kewpie doll."

Kieran's eyebrows dived together over the bridge of his nose. He picked up and folded over a piece of pizza, and munched on it in silence. At last he washed it down with a swig of beer. "It could've been that a rookie got excited and broke the rule of silence. But that would hardly set off the chain reaction you've described. Which only leaves the possibility that someone deliberately hit his siren in hopes of giving the drug dealers time to flee. If the cops in other cars saw them scattering, they'd use their sirens to warn off passing motorists."

"That's what I figure." Logan stiffened his spine, and he stared at Kieran Malone with shielded eyes.

Daphne stopped in the act of tearing off a piece of pizza. "What are you guys saying or rather, not saying? You're implying one of our local cops is in cahoots with the horrid men who want you dead, Logan?"

He linked his arms over the chairback and waited for Kieran's response—a response that didn't please Daphne. "Put a sock in it, kid. Better yet, isn't there some TV show you're dying to watch?"

She shoved a chair aside. "Honestly, Kieran. Anybody who reads the newspapers knows the LAPD has as many internal investigations going on as they have busts going down. Dirty cops isn't exactly news."

Kieran scowled. "Just because that's true doesn't mean you wanna be loose-lipped on the subject around law types you don't know real well. And maybe not even in front of those you think you do know well. Let's just say there are some real nasty characters suddenly operating around town, virtually unchecked. Far as I know, our attempts to quash them have met with no success. Now I'm wondering if someone inside our department is the reason. So, who to trust? I hate this, but it's better not to say anything about police work to anybody."

"Amen to that," Logan put in.

Daphne picked the peppers off her pizza and laid them on a napkin. "Kieran, I wish you'd just go out and arrest those creeps who followed us home. Then I can drive Logan to his office."

"Who followed you home? Why can't you drive Logan anywhere he wants to go?" Kieran nailed the other man with a pointed once-over.

Logan heaved a giant sigh. "Logan Grant, Special Agent, at your service. I'm currently in a deep freeze." He cast a sidelong glance toward Daphne but spoke to Kieran. "Until a few hours ago, I worked undercover. I've got no ID on me and therefore I can't prove anything I say. But I hope you believe me when I tell you it wouldn't be wise to try rounding up the boneheads staking out this building by yourself. Even if you and I team up, there's a fair chance neither one of us would get out alive. And if you called for backup, we'd run the risk of attracting more of their kind or—maybe worse—having the cops who helped them escape show up."

Kieran dragged his chair closer to the table. It wasn't hard to tell that he was playing out a range of possibilities in his mind. "I'm gonna take you at your word. Like I said, only my sister could get mixed up in something so crazy. But may I ask why they're staking out her apartment?"

"I was made by a ranking member of the organization. He saw me take down one of his men who'd drawn a bead on one of yours. The senior man in the ring saw me come to his defense. His semiautomatic jammed, which is the only reason I got away. It was sheer luck the warehouse is two streets away from my sister's house. I went straight there. The senior knew I couldn't have gotten too far on foot, and I think he knew

I could only have taken cover in a home somewhere on that block."

Daphne tore each of them off another slice of pizza. "Logan's lucky I happened to be doing my clown routine at his niece's birthday party. At first he scared the heck out of me, appearing in the room the way he did. But after his sister vouched for him, I volunteered to lend him an extra clown suit I'd thrown into my bag. When the party ended, we drove away still dressed as clowns. So, while the people who chased him are suspicious, they can't know for sure he's the man they're after."

Her brother unbuttoned his uniform jacket and sat back as if he planned to hang around a while. "I recall Daphne mentioning that your boss ordered you to stay put. That means you've been in contact with the agency?"

"She has," Logan reluctantly admitted. "I didn't want to use her unsecured cellular to call out. Daphne borrowed a neighbor's phone to touch base with my office." Logan deferred to her for verification.

"The man I talked to said Logan shouldn't leave here. He sent us the pizza and a safe phone. But you spoke with Mr. Parrish after I did, Logan."

"Yeah," Logan said, sounding glum. "He claims I'm too hot a commodity at the moment to risk rescuing. Cops put out an APB on me. One, at least—probably more—can't afford to let me walk. As well, the organization wants me gone."

"Not an enviable position to be in, man," Kieran said. "Our chief is interested in why you, our person of interest, saved our man. He suspects something's going on in his town and that he's being left out."

"If there's a snitch on your team, that would be why." Logan swung his leg over his chair and stood. "I hate waiting worse than anything. I like involving civilians even less. I'm kicking myself for not making a run for it before I got Daphne sucked in."

Kieran noticed how closely his sister watched Logan rubbing a hand idly back and forth over his flat belly. Brotherly hackles rose immediately. "The least you could do is go get decent," he snapped.

"Aren't I? Decent?" Logan glanced down, and quickly hitched up his sagging clown suit.

"He doesn't have any clothes," Daphne supplied when Kieran continued to glare. "Logan's sister sent the stuff he'd been wearing off to a commercial trash bin with one of her friends. April's husband is a sailor who's currently out on a ship. Apparently, he's shorter than Logan."

"How tall are you?" Kieran asked. "And what size pants and shirt do you wear?" Turning to Daphne, he added, "I'd guess he's nearer Perry's size than mine or Dane's. We're storing some of Perry's gear while he's on the road. I'll check to see what he left behind."

"Hey, that'd be great. Then I could shower and feel halfway human again." Logan scraped his knuckles over his jaw. "I used my brother-in-law's spare razor. It's a good thing. No one in the organization has seen me clean shaven."

"You'll want to stay that way. I'll buy you a pack of disposable razors. Any preference for soap or aftershave?" Kieran picked up the pad and pencil Daphne had left on the table after she'd torn off the message Logan had written for his boss. Shoving it at Logan, he said, "List what you want and I'll deliver it in the morning. I'll load up my gym bag. If those goons watch who comes and goes from this building, they might feel a need to check out shopping bags."

"Since you don't live here, Kieran, won't they be suspicious of you hauling in a gym bag?" Daphne asked.

"Possibly. But I'm here a lot. Anyone they might randomly stop to ask can probably attest to the fact that I come and go frequently. Hopefully they'll choose to steer clear of you if they discover you're the person I visit. The last thing they probably want is to get crosswise of a cop who's not in their pocket."

"I pointed out to Logan that none of them saw me out of clown makeup. And my neighbors know I've been gone all week. So, it'd be perfectly natural for me to run out to the grocery store later."

Logan voiced an immediate objection.

And Kieran promptly agreed. "You've handed out those dumb clown business cards of yours to everybody in the world, sis. What if those thugs are as sharp as Logan thinks and they get it in their heads to ask about your partner? I don't like it." Turning to Logan, Kieran muttered, "Your people won't leave you here long, will they? I mean, by this time tomorrow they'll have you smuggled out, right?"

"I hope so," Logan said, not sounding altogether sure.

"Sheesh! Your boss say something to make you doubt that?"

Logan shrugged. "I couldn't pin him down to a time. I said sooner rather than later. He said safe is as safe does. Whatever the hell that means."

"Sounds to me like he's not going to rush in and rescue your sorry hide."

"Why take chances?" Daphne rose and began clearing the table. She brushed by Logan, hunched over the counter, writing his list. "We faked out those guys. Sure, they may wonder if it was you in the other clown suit, but they can't very well conduct a door-to-door search. If you ask me, the best plan is to let things cool down naturally. Let them think you slipped through their net."

"Nobody asked for your two cents' worth," Kieran snapped.

Daphne smashed the pizza carton, folding it double, then walked over and flung it in the trash, her temper simmering.

Logan felt for her, regretting her brother's careless dismissal. He murmured, "Kieran's just worried, and so am I, that they'll get more aggressive in their search. They have nothing to lose, after all. They have no conscience, either. I can't blame him for wanting me gone. I want it, too."

"No, Logan, that's not it. My brothers all assume I need taking care of. I love them dearly. But I'm tired of their smothering." She faced Kieran. "The fact is, if you hadn't come to check up on me, you wouldn't know Logan was here."

"Blame that on Mom. She's the one who sensed something was wrong. And you can't deny her hunch was right. It's your history, Daph. It speaks for itself."

She said nothing in return, because of course Kieran was correct. Her history of oddball accidents was legend in and around Culver City. Family friends called her Madcap Malone. It was as if she were a magnet for trouble. Had been her whole life, she thought unhappily.

"Look, I don't want to be the cause of a family feud," Logan said. "Kieran, I promise I won't stick around a minute longer than my boss decides is necessary. By this time tomorrow you two will probably be able to talk about me in the past tense. Although I'd rather you didn't mention me at all."

Kieran definitely looked happier about that prospect. Daphne's face revealed nothing. Watching her, Logan experienced a sudden pang in the center of his chest. Which wasn't good. Not good at all. If Kieran Malone could read even a smattering of what was going on in Logan's mind, the big cop would throw him to Billy Holt's wolves without a qualm. Edging away, Logan breathed easier when he was out of range of Daphne's enticing perfume.

"Kieran, does Diana know you're going to be so late getting home?" Daphne bent her wrist toward him and tapped her watch face. "It's almost eight."

"Diana's been in Spain all week. Did I forget to tell you?"

"Kieran's wife is a model," she said for Logan's sake. "You've probably seen her on covers when you've passed magazine racks. I have all her back issues. Remind me later, and I'll show you some. Diana puts the rest of the women in the Malone family to shame. We'd hate her, except she's too darned nice."

Logan swung toward Kieran with renewed interest. "I guess it's every man's fantasy to marry a model."

Kieran flushed in embarrassment, but Daphne gave an ungracious snort. "Everyone thinks modeling is the most glamorous job in the world, and that all women want to be one. Diana says it's plain hard work. To say nothing of how irritating it is fending off drooling mashers like yourself. Ask Kieran how the two of them met."

Logan glanced at the cop, but it was Daphne who told the story. "Diana was being stalked by some sicko who'd developed an obsession with her. The jerk wrote her graphic love letters, and she never knew where they'd turn up. He broke into her apartment when she was on location one weekend. He stole all her underwear and left a letter in the drawer saying she had to quit ignoring him. Because if he couldn't have her, no one else would, either. He left awful pictures of mutilated women."

"I hope she turned the notes and pictures over to the FBI."

Kieran dredged up a grin. "No. She had the good sense to call local law enforcement. Lucky me, I drew the assignment of protecting her." He laid a hand over his heart. "Conscientious public servant that I am, I never let her out of my sight. Well, except when she goes abroad for a shoot."

"I take it you caught the bastard."

"It took six weeks, but yeah, we got him. He was only eighteen, and his folks are loaded. They thought they'd get Junior off with a slap on the wrist and maybe some community service. But, thanks to the way our legislators beefed up California's stalking laws, we were able to try him as an adult. We found Diana's pictures wallpapering his bedroom, complete with some scary captions. To say nothing of nabbing his computer, which was filled with sadistic porn."

"Nice kid. I could say disgusting turkeys like him mean job security for the likes of you and me. But I'd be a happy man if all criminals suddenly went straight and I had to find a new line of work."

"Really?" Daphne asked. "What would you do if you weren't in law enforcement?"

"Fish."

"No kidding?" Kieran, his demeanor instantly softening, reached over and punched Logan on the shoulder. "A man after my own heart. Same goes for my brothers. Dane, Perry and I pooled our money and bought a used Boston trawler last year. We moor her at Marina del Rey." Kieran stretched his long legs in front of him and laced his hands behind his head.

"Oh, boy, you've done it now," Daphne said out of the side of her mouth. "I hope you're not sleepy, Logan. One fishing story leads to another in this family."

Logan straddled his chair again and made himself comfortable. "I probably have a few good fish tales myself. A buddy and I did our fair share of fishing the coast of Maryland. My friend owns a sweet little thirty-foot sloop. We ran up her sails when there was wind. Otherwise she operated on a honey of an inboard-outboard system."

For the next solid hour, the men swapped tall tales—until Daphne's eyes glazed over. Great, all she needed was another fishing superstar hanging around. Like three wasn't enough. Four, counting her father.

She yawned repeatedly, but they didn't take the hint. She leafed through a magazine that had come in the mail. She hated the way men rambled on endlessly about sports or fishing. They could simply close out any woman in the room.

Still, seeing how relaxed and animated Logan Grant had become almost made Daphne wish she didn't get horribly seasick every time she so much as set foot on a boat. He was a man she wouldn't mind being marooned on a desert island with. Idly she flipped the pages of her latest cosmetics-trade magazine, and daydreamed about what it might be like to sail the Pacific with the likes of Agent Logan Grant, all lean, tan muscle. She pictured him dropping anchor in some secluded inlet, the sun beating down on his smooth back. She, of course, would have prepared a picnic lunch designed to show off her culinary skill. Ha, what culinary skill?

Okay, so maybe she'd surprise him by unpacking a few sex toys. Wow, where had those notions come from? Her breath was in danger of steaming the words right off the pages of her magazine.

Oh, right—she'd reached the last two pages, where advertisements abounded for items promising to enlarge breasts, psychic readings that offered guaranteed love spells and a video in which a "high priestess of love" claimed she could restore passion and teach women to satisfy their sexual desires. Oops, make that sensual desires.

Heat had built so high, Daphne's eyes were practically crossed. She closed the magazine and fanned her cheeks with it.

The move attracted Logan's attention. He straightened, and smiled sheepishly. "Gosh, Kieran, I think we're boring Daphne to death." He lazily scratched his chest, never imagining he was making her tongue cleave to the roof of her mouth. "Do you by chance have coffee tucked in one of your cupboards?" he asked, delivering another of his killer smiles. "Not that I couldn't talk fishing all night, mind you, but we should probably act civilized enough to drink a cup of java and include you in our conversation. What's so interesting in that magazine you've been engrossed in?"

"Nothing. It's nothing. Just ads for greasepaint and stuff."

Glad of the opportunity to come back to earth, Daphne hopped up and quickly shoved the magazine in one of her junk drawers. She'd hate for either man to idly thumb through it and maybe realize which section she'd been poring over. "Coffee would hit the spot, all right. I'll fix us a pot. Kieran, how does that sound to you?"

"Good, as long as you don't brew that flavored crap."

"I agree. My wife's favorite was something called raspberries and cream. I'd haul in half-dead after a marathon stakeout, pop a cup of leftover coffee in the microwave, and yuck! Liz actually had the nerve to pitch a fit when I spit the first mouthful all over the kitchen floor. She didn't understand why I couldn't smell it and know it wasn't the regular kind."

Daphne yanked her head out of the cupboard. "Wife? You're m-m-married?"

"Was." Logan grimaced and stretched his arms high over his head. "Didn't last," he said, hoping to end the questions then and there.

Daphne wasn't the only person interested in the particulars of Logan's split with his spouse, though, and Kieran ventured the first question. "Statistics on marriages in our business are really grim. Everybody says so. Not to be nosy, but would you blame your breakup on the job?"

Logan disliked talking about his failures, and he considered his divorce at the top of that category. But Daphne had been decent about dragging him out from under Billy-boy's nose. And her brother had come around; he also had reason to ask. Kieran and his wife were both in fields not conducive to successful relationships. "There's never just one reason, I suppose," Logan eventually mused aloud. "A big problem was that we were both special agents. You might think shared interests would help hold a marriage together. But not, I guess, when one half of the couple is more ambitious than the other." He screwed up his face.

"You?" Daphne asked hesitantly as she shoved the filter into the automatic coffeemaker and turned it on. "You were more ambitious, right?"

Unwilling to dump the blame squarely on Liz's shoulders, though she'd done some unspeakable things to get the promotion they were competing for—including sleep with the department director, who was old enough to be her grandfather—Logan jumped up and mumbled something about needing the facilities. He couldn't meet her eyes.

When he was out of sight, Kieran chided his sister. "I hope you have sense enough to drop the subject of the poor guy's divorce. Logan obviously feels bad about losing his wife. Maybe he was at fault. Maybe this move to California caused the rift. If they send him back East again, who's to say he can't mend fences? If some other woman doesn't try and get under his skin in the meantime, that is."

Daphne knew precisely where her brother was going with that line of talk. Perry, now, would've said flat out to back off and leave the man be. Dane, he'd pull her aside and talk her to death about every failed marriage he'd ever heard of, hoping the examples would warn her off. Kieran made his point by skirting the issue.

"You can relax, Kieran. Logan Grant is merely passing through my life. How many times do I have to tell my family that I have my sights set on a career as a makeup artist? Sheesh!"

"I know that's what you say. I also couldn't miss the way you followed Grant's every move with your eyes. Those aren't the eyes of a disinterested woman, Daph."

"So he's not bad to look at." She hiked a shoulder negligently.

"No, but he's a lonely man working in a tough, lonely job, where the odds of surviving to a ripe old age are slim at best. Sometimes situations like the one he's in now—well, they cause men to grab any slice of normal life they can. You know—live fast, love hard, die young, but create a beautiful memory?"

"If that's his philosophy, shouldn't you be giving Logan this lecture instead of me?"

"What lecture is that?" Logan reentered the room. Brother

and sister were so engrossed in heated dialogue, neither saw nor heard him walk up.

Daphne laughed self-consciously. "The lecture where my brothers threaten to maim you horribly to protect my virtue."

Logan's jaw went slack. He stopped well short of entering the kitchen.

Kieran blew out a harsh breath. "Jeez, Daphne, you're so blunt it's no wonder you scare off the guys we bring around. The ones we consider marriage material."

Logan put the skids to the conversation by holding up both palms. "Stop right there. I'm the last guy in the world who'd be judged marriage material. I screwed up once at that game, and I'm not about to play again. Uh-uh, no way!"

"See, Kieran?" Daphne batted her big eyes at her brother. "You heard it from the horse's mouth. There's no need to worry about leaving us here together."

Kieran studied her morosely. "Considering your track record, that's exactly why I worry."

"My track record? What track record? Like I've been so successful finding and keeping a boyfriend. Shoot, as fast as I lose boyfriends, it's a wonder—"

"I didn't mean your record with losing guys," he broke in. "I'm thinking more about how you seem to collect strays all over the place. Mom and Dad have two dogs and two cats. Dane and Holly have three dogs. Diana and I ended up with a dog and cat, and I've lost count of exactly what all you wheedled Becky and Jerry into taking."

"Well, lost and injured animals, sure. If this apartment house allowed pets, you wouldn't have to worry about that. I'd have a dog or two for protection." The coffeepot gurgled, signaling the last of the water had run through it, and Daphne turned away. She quickly filled three cups, and reached up to dig through a cupboard.

"Drat. I have sugar substitute, but no sugar. No cream, but I think I left a carton of milk in the fridge when I went to Dane's. I know Kieran likes milk in his coffee. What's your pleasure, Logan?"

"I'll take mine black. And if you mean to give Kieran milk from that carton sitting on the counter behind you, think again. It smelled worse than an open sewer, so I dumped it. God only knows what was growing in the carton. Sort of resembled brown cottage cheese."

"Oh, no! I really have to run to the store. I can't eat breakfast without milk."

"No!" Kieran and Logan both yelled at once. "Black coffee will do me tonight," Kieran said quickly, pulling one cup toward him and handing another to Logan. "Hey, it's almost time for the local news," Kieran announced, pausing to blow across the dark liquid in his cup. "I suggest we adjourn to the living room where we can see what the media has to say about today's police screwup. There's always more in-depth coverage when a bust fails. You rarely hear about our successes."

Daphne carried her coffee to the other room. She turned on the set, then sank into one corner of the couch. She didn't know why she was disappointed when Logan grabbed the only other chair in the room, leaving Kieran to sit next to her. Talk fell off as the local news anchor started with the story they wanted to hear.

When that part of the broadcast ended, Logan sat back, obviously more relaxed. "They really have nothing. If they knew my name, they'd give it. I'm betting this will blow over fast."

"You're right. You may just come out of this unscathed,"

Kieran said. "Of course, you won't be any good to the agency. They can't send you back undercover."

"True, but at least I didn't come away empty-handed. And the really good thing is the bastards don't know I overheard them making plans for a huge shipment of opium and other contraband. Stuff equaling a couple of billion dollars."

"Billion? Did you say billion?" Daphne gasped.

Kieran flashed her an irritated glance. "Listen, sis. Since you've finished your coffee, why don't you trot off to bed. Logan and I have some serious business to discuss."

Daphne took a deep breath to tell Kieran where he could put that edict. But she saw something in the set of Logan's shoulders that said he wanted the same thing. And she was exhausted. Playing cops and robbers for real took its toll on a woman. "Sure," she said agreeably. "Maybe when I wake up in the morning I'll discover this day's been nothing but a dream. A bad dream."

CHAPTER FIVE

DAPHNE HAD NO IDEA when or if Kieran left. She was dead to the world less than five seconds after her head hit the pillow. She discovered Kieran had gone and Logan remained her houseguest early the next morning when an insistent knocking on her front door sent both of them flying into the hall where they crashed into each other.

"Sorry." Logan grabbed her arms to steady her. Drawing away, he aimed his Luger at the ceiling and unlocked the release. He was bleary-eyed, tousled and wore nothing but a pair of tighty whities, undoubtedly a pair that belonged to his sister's husband, Mike.

While Daphne stood there, unable to assimilate what was taking place, Logan held the weapon she'd hoped he'd ditched. She was relieved to see his hand was steady.

She scraped her hair out of her eyes and yanked up drooping straps on a sleep-camisole she'd pulled on last night, along with matching bottoms. The straps of this particular camisole perpetually fell askew.

Ever the man with questions, Logan demanded gruffly, "Give me a rundown on who's in the habit of visiting you at 6:00 a.m."

"Six—a.m.?" she parroted. "Not a soul I can think of. It's

pretty well known that I'm one of those folks who think if God had wanted me to see a sunrise, he'd have arranged for it to appear at noon."

Motioning her forward with the Luger, Logan ended up bodily moving her down the hall. "Look out the peephole and see who's there. It could be another delivery from my boss."

"How will I know?" she muttered, balking at how brusquely he hustled her along. Daphne found it hard to collect her thoughts whenever her sleep was interrupted. Like now.

Logan's answer was to press her flat against the door. It certainly didn't help her equilibrium to feel his hot breath on her neck, or the pressure of his broad chest against her back. She wondered if the man had any idea how sexy he looked with so little on and the merest shadow of a beard.

Gathering what wits she could muster, Daphne rose on tiptoe. Another loud whap on the door very near her nose had her leaping back, slamming into Logan. They both stumbled. "Oh, no," she babbled. "It's Dane."

"Dane?" Logan rubbed the center of his breastbone where he'd taken a solid hit from Daphne's hard head.

"You know—my oldest brother. He's a firefighter. We talked about him."

"Oh, yeah. So, ask him in before his hammering has some helpful neighbor calling the cops."

"Are you kidding?" she yelped. "Look at you. You're almost naked," she hissed. "Come to think of it, I'm not dressed to receive guests, either. Dane isn't half as understanding as Kieran. Of all the Malones, he has the hottest temper. Dane knocks heads first and asks questions later."

Logan leaned over Daphne and fit his eye to the round eyepiece. He saw a distinct resemblance between this man and Kieran, especially in size. Dane might even be taller—unless that was a distortion of the peephole magnifier. If not, Dane Malone had four inches on his younger brother. He had a dusting of gray at the temples of his otherwise dark hair, but Logan couldn't detect one soft-looking thing about the man.

Easing back, Logan rubbed his jaw. That was also about the time his sleep-fogged brain made contact with other portions of his anatomy. And Daphne's words started to make sense. Plastered against him as she was, Logan couldn't begin to deny the desirability of her soft, lightly freckled shoulders. Foggy or not, his mind—and other select sites—began getting ideas all their own. Part of him said to hell with the man at the door. Instead of letting him in, Logan could tussle with this woman across the sheets. Unless he was more out of it than he'd realized, her thoughts were starting to match his own.

"I have to let him in," she said, breaking the spell. "Dane isn't one to go quietly away. He'll accomplish his mission if he has to climb the fire escape and break in my window."

"What is his mission?" Logan refastened the gun lock and let his gun hand drop.

She bit her lip. "From the way he's dressed I'd say it's his day off. He and Kieran will have met for coffee this morning at the Starbucks a few blocks from Dane's house. The rest is simple. Dane wouldn't take Kieran's word that you were an okay guy, even if he swore on a stack of Bibles. He's here to check you out for himself."

"Great. Just great. Of all the women in the world I could've walked in on at April's, I get an innocent lamb who just happens to be guarded by a flock of six-foot-tall battering rams. Pun intended."

"I'm hardly an innocent lamb," she stated frostily, continuing to ignore Dane Malone's banging at the door.

Logan's eyes lit. Self-assured women attracted him, both

in and out of the bedroom. And Logan rarely passed up a challenge. "Under other circumstances I'd be all for exploring that statement further. Under these, however, I'm gonna do the smart thing and help preserve your virtue. I'll go put on that dumb clown suit again. Just give me a head start. Then let the gorilla in before he blows a gasket."

Daphne pictured how her brother would react to being called a battering ram or a gorilla, and she had to grin. She watched Logan sprint off. In the time needed for her to undo the three locks her brothers insisted she have on her front door, the flush of lust brought on by Logan's disappearing butt cooled just enough to allow her to greet her brother civilly. "Good morning, Dane. Please...come in."

"What in hell took you so long?" he demanded, shoving past her. He scanned everything that was visible in the room before he remembered to reach behind him and shut the door. "So where's your new roommate? Fat chance he's FBI if he doesn't even roust himself when somebody comes knocking at your door."

Arms crossed, Daphne gave him an irritated glower. "What makes you think Logan doesn't have you covered even as we speak?"

Her brother checked over first one shoulder, then the other. Chuckling, he shrugged out of a weighty backpack Daphne hadn't noticed he wore. "Still amounts to hiding behind your skirts, sis. Call him out here. Kieran sent him some duds, and I was instructed to bring you milk, bread, cheese and eggs."

Daphne accepted the pack he handed over. She removed and set aside the supplies. "I'll go give the rest to Logan. Don't let the door hit you in the butt on the way out, big brother."

Just then, Logan appeared in the archway that led to the bedrooms. The Luger had magically disappeared. True to his word, he again wore the clown suit from yesterday, although he only had it zipped to his navel. And because it was still early morning and not yet fully daylight, the costume's spots and stripes glowed eerily green.

Dane Malone took one gander at him, threw back his head and hooted with laughter.

Daphne bristled on Logan's behalf. He, on the other hand, caught a glimpse of the spectacle he made in a mirror hanging on the back wall of the living room, and joined in laughing at his image. "Well, you did say I'd glow in the dark, Daphne. I'll admit I never guessed I'd rival a hooker straight off the Vegas Strip."

"Hey, you're okay, buddy," Dane said, still holding his sides. "I like a man who can poke fun at himself." Plucking the backpack from Daphne, Dane tossed it to the other man, who adroitly caught it with one hand.

"Good reflexes, too," Dane remarked. "Kieran sent over a change of clothes and a pair of boots. He said all he could find of Perry's stuff was two pairs of sweats. They're clean. Kieran's wife wouldn't let them hang in her guest closet otherwise. But if I were you, I'd be glad of the opportunity to change into anything other than what I had on." His grin expanded to a merry chuckle again.

"Quit ragging on my costumes, you two. I'll have you know it probably saved Logan's life yesterday. By the way," she said, "Logan, this is my brother, Dane Malone. Dane, Logan Grant. Unless he prefers you to call him Special Agent Grant." She batted eyelashes coyly, knowing Logan was steamed at her.

He didn't disappoint. "Hell, woman! Not so loud. Somebody could be listening at the door. Which reminds me. Have you checked to see if our watchdogs are still keeping tabs on us?"

"No. I'll do it now, though." Daphne bent and collected the groceries before starting across the room, angling toward the kitchen.

Dane gave a shrill whistle. "Let me store that stuff in the fridge so you can go put on something that covers more of you than that skimpy whatchamacallit. For Pete's sake, kid, you can't even keep the straps up."

Daphne had forgotten what she was wearing, but it wasn't uncommon for her to wander around in the morning in her nightwear. "I call it a camisole, Dane. And if I'm not mistaken, you and Holly gave me this for my last birthday."

His eyebrows drew down. "What in hell was Holly thinking when she bought you that outfit?"

Daphne deliberately twitched her rear at him before marching into the kitchen. "Your wife thinks I'm a grown woman, not the little girl my brothers keep trying to tell me I am," she said loudly. Although the effect of her statement was somewhat diminished since she had her head in the fridge by then.

Dane didn't strike back, but he sure sent a warning to Logan. Because it would've been flat impossible for anyone sharing the room with him to miss the expression on Logan's face, or the desire that flamed in the depths of appreciative eyes that followed every move of Daphne's shapely body.

"According to Kieran, your boss plans to get you out of here today, Special Agent. Any idea when? In case it's soon, shouldn't you be dressed more appropriately?"

Logan finally shook off the searing awareness of the woman he'd tried hard to forget about. He'd spent a restless night being all too conscious of her sleeping not twenty feet down the hall. It crossed his mind to tell Dane Malone where to stick his suggestion, except, dammit, the advantages of dressing normally again, even in borrowed clothes, won out hands down.

Wheeling on bare feet, Logan slung the backpack over his shoulder and walked off without waiting to hear if Billy Holt's pals were still on their stakeout. He was pretty sure they hadn't budged since he'd last checked at midnight and again at 2:00 a.m.

"It's a different car, parked in a slightly different location," Daphne announced from a position she'd taken up at the kitchen window. "This one's big and white instead of navy blue. But it has even more antennae. I think I see two sets of knees. I hate to say this, but it doesn't seem as if they plan to move anytime soon."

"Grant left to go change clothes." Dane spoke from behind his sister as he leaned over her shoulder to see what she was talking about.

"Oh. Why did he ask me a question then, if he had no intention of waiting until I had an answer?"

"He probably figured he'd look more professional with clothes on," Dane said meaningfully.

Daphne ducked under the big man's arm. "More professional wearing Perry's sweats, when we both know what a slob our dear brother is? Why don't I think you made the point you were hoping to make, Dane?"

"Such as?"

"Such as that I ought to follow suit."

"Capital idea."

"Hmm. I thought I might toss together an omelette and toast for breakfast before I go in to shower. I generally have breakfast before I dress."

"Go now. I'll fix the omelette."

It was so tempting to needle him by refusing, but Daphne

knew Dane was a far better cook than she was. Married or
not, he had to take his turn at the station house like all the
other firemen, many of whom were gourmet cooks.

"Is this one of your days off?" she asked when it finally
dawned on her that he wasn't in any rush to leave. "Why aren't
you home taking care of the kids? Or if Holly has the day off,
too, shouldn't you be spending time with your family?"

"Holly's working, and Mom's taking the kids to the San
Diego Zoo. Dad and Mom both are. In fact, we dropped the
little angels off with them last night. Holly and I had an opportunity to go out to dinner alone. Somewhere other than a
restaurant with a kiddyland attached."

"Ah, so you had an entire night to yourselves. Must've felt
like a second honeymoon."

"Yeah." Dane drawled the word slowly and got a goofy
grin on his face. Just as fast, he scowled and gave Daphne a
little push toward the hall. "Never you mind about that. I'm
serious about starting breakfast while you get decent."

"Decent? What's with you and Kieran? He used the same
word last night when he referred to how Logan looked. You
know what I think? I think you big apes are showing your age.
How long since you've hung out at our local beach? By those
standards I'm way overdressed. I'm talking skimpy bikinis,
Dane," she said, using hand gestures to indicate minuscule
tops and bottoms.

Logan appeared silently, which Daphne concluded was
habit with him. It was downright spooky, and she wished he'd
give some type of warning.

He only grinned at her discomfort, clearly enjoying the
subject brother and sister were arguing about. "If we're talking
bathing-suit size around here, I can see I definitely need to
look into fishing the Pacific. In Maryland, the babe scenery

was mostly nothing to shout about. The wind blew so hard, women walking on shore or riding in boats generally had to cover up from head to toe, except for a couple of months during the hottest part of the summer. And then there were too many boats to relax and enjoy the view."

"You fish?" Dane's interest perked up immediately.

Rolling her eyes, Daphne elbowed her way between them. "Not again! What is there about slimy fish that all but makes men orgasmic?"

Both men's heads snapped toward the retreating woman. "A lot you know about that subject," Dane shouted at the same moment Logan muttered, "There's no comparison between the two."

"Yeah, yeah, yeah." Daphne waved airily. "Logan, I thought you and Kieran discussed every aspect of fishing there could possibly be last night. I wouldn't think there'd be anything left to say on the subject."

The men smiled at each other. It was Dane who said, "Men wonder the same thing about women talking fashion all day long."

Daphne paused at the arch that led down the hallway. "Fashion's a multibillion-dollar business."

"Don't I know it," muttered Dane. "My wife contributes to it big-time. And the worst of it is, she wasn't like that until Kieran married Diana. When Holly and I dated, and after we first got married, she went camping, fishing, hiking and water-skiing with me. Now if I say 'Let's do something on the weekend,' she wants to hit the malls."

Logan had gone to the window to assess the situation below for himself. Turning, he gazed at the other man without much sympathy. "At least you don't have to go shopping by yourself. Yesterday, I promised my sister I'd get my niece a Barbie with camping gear. And my mom's birthday is next month." He groaned.

"Then you're going about it all wrong, my friend. I have single buddies at my station house who meet all kinds of women in stores. They troll for the hottest clerk, make cow eyes and beg her assistance. They get the gift they need and a date for the upcoming weekend. The women even help with wrapping the gift."

"I've got a better way, Logan," Daphne said from where she still lingered near the hall. "Phone your favorite department store, order the Barbie sent to April and put it on your credit card. No hassle, no wrapping—"

"No hot weekend date," Dane remarked from behind Logan.

Logan actually seemed more interested in Daphne's method. "You mean someone at Robinson-May will wrap and ship the Barbie Natalie wants if I call the toy department?"

"If they have the item in stock, sure. If not, we have two toy stores at our local mall that take phone orders, too."

"Do you have a phone book? I should call today and get the gift shipped. I'd hate for the kid to think Uncle Logan forgot her on her birthday."

His thoughtfulness touched Daphne. Her brothers were generous men, but they needed prompting several times to shell out money for birthday presents. And more often than not, they got someone else to buy it for them. In Dane's case, his wife, Holly. "The phone book is in the bottom right-hand drawer of the stand beside the couch," she called. "Help yourself, and to my cell phone as well."

"Thanks, but I'll use the safe phone Simon sent. All I need is for those jerks downstairs to intercept a call sending a gift to the address we were at yesterday, and signed from Uncle Logan."

Dane chewed on his lower lip. "If you were working undercover, they won't know your name, will they?"

"I can't count on that. You'd be surprised at how many sets of ears those organizations can buy. Say someone in my agency tells another agent having a cold one in a local bar that I've gone missing. Say the bartender's taking kickbacks from the organization to listen for tidbits of information. Their leader puts two and two together, and the word is out, that the man they want dead or alive is Logan Grant."

Daphne heard the serious thread running through Logan's tone. Up to now, this had all seemed unreal. Even sort of fun. It wasn't. Logan's life was on the line. And maybe hers as well. She hurried in to shower and change, shuddering as she did so. She hadn't thought she'd lived such a sheltered life. She was still a schoolgirl when Dane joined the fire department, and Kieran the police force. Their dad was a psychiatrist, so Daphne knew evil existed in the world. But it was always in other people's worlds, not her own safe little corner.

She spun the faucets and stepped under a hot, steamy spray, determined to keep a positive perspective on this. Simon Parrish, the man she'd spoken with on the phone yesterday, had a calm, deep voice, one that reminded Daphne of her dad's. Simon had thanked her for helping Logan, and he'd assured her they'd have the situation under control as quickly as possible. She believed him.

Remembering that made her feel a hundred percent better. She dried off and threw on jeans and a T-shirt. Someday she'd remember this incident and laugh. It'd be something to tell her grandchildren. If she ever got lucky enough to have grandchildren. First, she had to find a husband. Considering how her too many overbearing brothers came on like gangbusters, that seemed highly unlikely, she reflected, pausing to clip her unruly hair in a knot at the back of her head.

The tantalizing odor of coffee and bacon wafted under Daphne's door and drove her out to claim her portion of the meal.

Logan met her at the arch. "There you are. Dane sent me to fetch you. I don't know what he's cooking in there, but until I began to smell it, I hadn't even realized how starved I am."

"I was just thinking the same thing." She smiled broadly and slipped past him as he stepped politely aside and motioned her out first.

In the kitchen, he reached around her and pulled out her chair. Daphne had already observed how impeccable Logan's manners were. His rough edges were all in his looks. In everything else, the rough corners appeared to have been sanded smooth. That set her to wondering about his background. "What made you choose the career you did, Logan?"

"Are you kidding, sis?" Dane gave a snort. "Most boys grow up dreaming of being men in black. Spies. G-men. We're tantalized by the hype Hollywood dangles before us."

"I thought all little boys wanted to be cowboys."

"No, Daph. You watch too many old movies. The new breed of cowboy is a cross between Delta Force and an undercover agent. The recruiters say working for the FBI or CIA is the last bastion for a man with machismo." Dane brought plates with individual omelettes and neat sides of toast piled next to them. He set a carafe of coffee on the table, and sat down opposite Daphne.

Logan smothered a laugh. "Our recruiters can sure lay out a line of bull. There's a lot of boring desk work involved. Sifting through stacks of evidence. We also surf the Web for hours, hoping to tap into illegal gambling online, or loan-sharking, or kiddie porn. Then there's an occasional kidnapping to investigate."

"Lovely," Daphne mumbled around a mouth full of egg. "Now I wonder even more why any sane person would choose that as a career. I have to discount Dane's cheerleading, though. I've always known he's iffy when it comes to sanity." She jerked to the side, knowing he'd smack her arm. Dane settled for an evil glare, instead.

"Ignore Daphne. All of us in the protect-and-rescue business—and I include firefighters in that—know how to understate what really goes on in the trenches."

"Why would you?" she interjected. "I asked an honest question. Why not give me an honest answer?" Daphne rose and pulled out napkins, which she handed around before sitting back down. A phone rang, one that sounded close by. She'd seen hers on the coffee table in the living room. It turned out Dane had put Logan's safe phone on the other side of the coffeepot. Daphne retrieved it and handed it to Logan, who'd already set aside his fork and was half out of his chair.

"Hello," he said, lowering his voice. "Simon. Ah, glad it's you. I hope you have good news." Logan listened a moment, his frown growing deeper with each second. "Here, Simon wants you," he said, shoving the phone at Daphne.

"Me?" Her fork fell from her hand and clattered to the table. She took the phone gingerly. "This is Daphne," she said, barely speaking above a whisper. "Uh, yes. No. No, I can't think of a problem. Sure. Always glad to do my part. Do you want to speak with Logan again?" She got his attention by glancing over at him. He sat there stiffly, his frown having expanded to a full-fledged scowl. "No? Then you'll phone when you have something more?"

"When will that be?" Logan spat, grabbing at Daphne's hand to stop her from ending the call without relaying his question.

"Sorry, he hung up," Daphne said. Showing her discomfort, she closed the phone and slid it closer to her surly companion.

"What was that all about?" Dane asked, glancing from Logan to Daphne and then to Logan, who'd shoved back from the table. He stalked to the counter and threw the phone down on the stack of napkins Daphne had left there.

"Logan's boss, ah, asked if it'd be all right if he stays here a while longer."

Dane pushed his empty plate away. He was the only one of the three to have actually finished his meal. "How long is a while, sis?" Dane's unhappy expression matched Logan's.

"You heard me say Simon hung up before I could ask. He mentioned that trying to get Logan out now might jeopardize another agent he's placed with that group of thugs."

The men both swore colorfully, employing different words.

"What's wrong with you two? I don't see any problem. I'd think your boss would get you out if it was possible."

"Meanwhile, I'm on ice, while some other agent ends up cracking the case I've worked on for ten damn months."

"I see." Daphne's eyebrows shot up. "This isn't about saving the life of another agent or about taking these guys off the streets. This is all about numero uno. About who gets credit for doing the deed."

Dane, who hadn't sided with Logan previously, aligned himself squarely behind the other man. "Daph, keep quiet. You have no idea what you're talking about. Logan opened the door and probably fed back crucial information his boss used to plant another informer. We know from listening to Kieran that there're damn few 'attaboys' in the thankless job of law enforcement. All too often the praise handed out doesn't reach the deserving. I see what Logan's saying."

"It's not the credit I'm concerned about." Logan swung around, his hands clenched at his sides. "I came so close to making inroads into an upper layer in that network. For weeks I've known dope isn't all their elaborate preparations are about. It's really a smoke screen for something even more sinister. I bet I know who the other agent is that Simon's embedded. He's really new. Al Jorgeson will never ferret out the information I feel certain I would've learned if I could've stuck it out longer."

"What else are they into?" Dane's whole body came to attention.

Logan shook his head. "I can't tell you."

"No matter how you cut it, Logan, the bottom line is, you blew your chance of sticking it out, and now it's up to someone else," Daphne said pragmatically.

"Thanks for pointing that out." Logan threw himself back in the chair, propped his elbows on his knees and plunged his head into his hands.

"Sis, why don't you just eat and stay out of this." Dane rose and walked to the sink with his plate.

"Look, Dane, I know you and Kieran would love to pretend I'm not involved in this situation. The fact is, I thought up the scheme to smuggle Logan out from under their noses. And it's me his boss asked to keep him safe for a while. Not you. Not Kieran. Not even Logan himself. Me, guys." She thumped her chest with a closed fist.

Neither man looked pleased by the truths she'd just uttered.

Satisfied, Daphne picked up her fork again and began calmly eating her rapidly cooling food.

"Daph." It was Dane who cleared his throat and made an effort to sound reasonable. "Kieran and I can't help seeing this fiasco as another of your lunatic jobs that's gone to hell."

"Not even close. The job went very well, I thought. Tell him, Logan. I was a hit with the kids and with your sister."

"She's right." Logan sat up and scooted his chair closer to the table. But that didn't change how morosely he stared at her—or how his body reacted automatically every time he gazed at her, as he was doing now. Daphne's eyes were bright, and her pretty face, scrubbed clean of artificial enhancements, appealed to a side of Logan's libido he'd neglected ever since his tragic and ruinous divorce from Liz. Tragic because Logan had really been ready to settle down with one woman. And ruinous because it had cost him a promotion and shattered his trust in friends at the agency. To say nothing of cleaning out his savings.

And the more days Logan was forced to share close quarters with a woman as decent and genuine as Daphne Malone, the harder it was going to be for him to remember the consequences of his marriage. She stirred needs in him that ran deep. Needs he'd vowed after his divorce to ignore forever.

"Why are you looking at me like this is all my fault?" Daphne asked, frowning faintly at him. "You just admitted to Dane that your being here is a separate issue from my job. Well, going out as a birthday clown isn't really my job. As I keep explaining, I'm only using it to help pay the bills until my application at one of the major movie studios reaches the right executive's desk."

"Sis, realistically, what are the chances of that? How many people graduated from that program you took? Fifty?

A hundred? They all put in applications at the same studios. And how many of those actually get hired?"

"The best ones do," she said. "May I remind you that my instructors said I have a better than average chance because I was at the top of my class? They all wrote recommendations I copied and attached to my applications. You just have no faith in my abilities, Dane."

"No kidding. Probably because we know your track record."

Logan didn't like hearing the man shred his sister's confidence. "It's like I told Kieran last night. Daphne is talented. You ought to watch her paint kids' faces, Dane. She came up with this clever gimmick, too." He turned to Daphne. "You made those animal ears yourself, right?"

Daphne nodded. She might have elaborated on what Logan had said, except that her phone rang.

Logan stiffened. "Be careful what you say. Wait and make sure you know who it is."

"I have caller ID," she informed him, tossing her napkin aside before she got up and went to find her phone.

She came back holding it. "I don't recognize the number or the name. Jones is the name in the readout. It's a local call."

The phone rang again. "We'll be quiet. You find out what they want. Maybe it's a wrong number. On the other hand, Jones might be an alias used by our friends across the street."

Daphne said hello and listened intently to the speaker. She said nothing for so long that both Logan and her brother began to fidget noticeably. They tried giving her high-signs and hand signals that made no sense.

"Could you hold on a minute? I need to check my calendar." Burying the phone against the side of her jeans, she said in a stage whisper. "It's Lori Jones. Her sister's daughter was at Natalie's party. This woman, Lori, wonders if I can entertain tomorrow afternoon for her little girl's birthday celebration."

"Tell her no." This from both men simultaneously.

She hesitated momentarily, lifted the phone and held it back to her ear. With a cheery lilt in her voice, she said, "You're in luck, Lori. I find I had a cancellation. Just let me grab a pencil so I can jot down the directions. What? My partner? Oh, you mean Buzzy. I…ah…" Daphne struggled as she tried to decide what to say. She sucked in a breath, ready to apologize and say that for this party she'd be a single act.

Logan snatched the pen out of her hand and wrote in block letters on the page TELL HER WE'LL COME AS A TEAM.

Stumbling over the words, Daphne managed to convey the message to her caller.

CHAPTER SIX

"ARE YOU BOTH NUTS?" Dane stomped back and forth, raking his hands through his hair. "Until this mess is settled, you can't be running around in clown getups, inviting death and destruction on the unsuspecting people who attend those parties."

"You're right, Dane. I'll call Lori Jones and cancel."

Logan clamped a hand over hers, quashing her attempt to open the cell case. "Wait. If we go boldly about doing what we hope our relay team below assumes is our normal business, maybe there's a better chance they'll give up and go away."

"That's true," Daphne murmured. She believed Logan ought to know best.

"Which is it, sis? Am I right or is he? You agreed with both of us."

"I know. There's merit to each suggestion. It seems to hinge on what the guys surveilling us decide to do."

"Why take chances, Daph?" Dane said.

"Why not?" Logan asked. "Tell me—if there was a burning building and someone said there might be a person left on the top floor, what would you do?"

"I'd go in, of course. But that's different." Dane watched

the wry quirk of Logan's lips. "All right. You go play clown by yourself. My sister isn't an agent. That's your job, not hers."

Daphne jumped into the fray. "This party is my job, Dane. I'm the person Mrs. Jones called. I trust Logan to see that no harm comes to me or Lori's guests."

Logan's head snapped up. He gaped at her. Daphne's blind faith in his abilities placed a whole new spin on things. "Uh… maybe Dane has a point. For obvious reasons, agents aren't always heroes."

She looked crestfallen. Not liking to think he'd been the cause, Logan brushed a tangle of curls over her ear. Their eyes met and held until Dane cleared his throat.

"You're not a novice, Grant. Can't you see my sister's caught up in the romance of danger? Not separating a man from his job is a common mistake women make. The majority wake up too late to see they've fallen for a regular guy whose underneath is like any other. Except that his job makes him moodier and harder to live with than Joe Blow who pushes a pencil from nine to five."

Daphne exerted an effort to disconnect from Logan. She'd missed everything but the last part of her brother's rambling. "Honestly, Dane, I can't make heads or tails of what you just said. Logan and I will be entertaining a dozen or so kids for an hour. Two, max. You act like we're embarking on a lifetime journey together."

"No. No, Dane's made a valid point. I didn't think this through. It's not a good idea." Logan knew exactly what Dane Malone meant. "We might've fooled them once with clown suits. But if they look closer they'll see my costume's too short. Too small all over. It was never designed for a man."

"If that's your only objection, I still don't see a problem." Daphne stood ready to override him. "Mom gave me yards and yards of a fabric that's perfect clown material. I can zip you up a costume that fits better in no time." She glanced at her watch. "In fact, if you two clear this table while I go find the material and one of my patterns, I'll stitch up a new outfit before suppertime."

Of the two men in the room, Logan alone caught her enthusiasm. For one thing, he was going stir-crazy being cooped up in this apartment. For another, he needed to get out and judge what was happening with Holt's men for himself. Simon hadn't been all that forthcoming. This was, after all, still Logan's case to crack. Not far below his need to examine the lay of the land, another issue loomed. The desire he felt for Daphne. If it wasn't for her ever-vigilant brothers, chances were good that by now he'd have acted on those feelings. And if there was anything Logan was well aware of, a man in the throes of falling for a woman left himself open to all manner of mistakes. Ask him; he was an authority. He'd made them all when he stupidly tumbled head over heels for Liz.

Dane Malone didn't offer to help clear the table. He watched pensively from a distance, plainly wanting to wage more opposition. But he wisely said nothing, and when Logan finished loading the dishwasher, Dane inquired whether Logan played cribbage.

"I don't, but I've always wanted to learn. Since we both have time on our hands," Logan said dryly, "let's leave Daphne to her sewing and you can teach me."

"After you then. She keeps a board in the living-room desk."

The men were hunched over the cribbage board when Daphne reappeared, lugging her portable sewing machine and an armload of orange, red and yellow polka-dot cotton chintz.

Logan sprang from his seat and relieved her of the weight of the machine. "Why do I think I'll like wearing a costume made out of that eye-popping stuff even less than I liked glowing in the dark?"

"This is more traditional clownish fabric. Don't freak until I'm done and you see the full effect. Stay here a minute, please. I need to measure you across the shoulders, around your waist and from shoulder to ankle. I want to make your suit roomy enough," she said, unfurling a tape measure. "I guarantee, in this outfit, and once I paint your face, the men outside won't have a clue as to your real looks."

"Gr...ea...t," Logan groaned. Nevertheless, he stood still while she flitted around him taking measurements. Standing quietly wasn't easy. Especially when she got down on her hands and knees to wrap the tape around his ankles. Her butt wiggled provocatively, and the sweet scent of her perfume or shampoo drifted up to drive him crazy. To say nothing of the feathery play of her fingers over his ticklish parts.

By the time she okayed his leaving, Logan was clenching his back teeth and digging his nails into his palms to keep from yanking her up and kissing her senseless. Which wouldn't have gone over well with her brute of a brother seated in the living room.

And Dane appeared to know exactly what was on Logan's mind. The man punished Logan by whipping his ass mercilessly in ten out of ten cribbage matches. Nor was Malone satisfied with just doing that. When Logan admitted final defeat and set about storing the board and pins, Dane reached for Daphne's phone, casually delivering another low blow. "Hey, Daph. Kieran said Perry's due in tonight. He's dropping off a load of cigarettes he picked up in North Carolina. Then he has a two-week layover here before heading to Frisco to collect a load of school supplies coming in on a boat from Taiwan. He'll be hauling that to a distributor based in St. Louis. Can you believe in less than a month school's starting again?"

"If you're calling Perry to see how far out he is, say hi. I'm sure Mom will have a family get-together during his layover. I'll see him and catch up then."

"You'll see him sooner. He'll be crashing here tonight."

"Why?" Daphne's head came up fast. "Perry always bunks in with Kieran and Diana."

Logan, who'd lost all ten games because his gaze had strayed to Daphne so often, sensed the sudden tension between the siblings.

"Yeah, I know he generally hangs his hat there. But this morning, Kieran told me Diana phoned and left a message on his answering machine last night. She's catching an earlier flight home. Instead of arriving tomorrow night, she'll be in about the time Kieran's shift ends today. Guess I forgot to mention it earlier."

"No kidding. Well, Perry won't want to hang around those lovebirds, for sure. But he can't stay here. Logan's using my only spare bed. What's wrong with your house? You have plenty of room."

"That's why Mom and Dad took Victoria and Tanner to the zoo today. Holly's off this afternoon preparing for Vic's annual slumber party. I can't ask Perry to suffer the giggling of eight girls all night. Not after he's spent weeks on the road. You know he sleeps two days straight when he finally gets the chance."

"Well, he'll have to bite the bullet and move into his old room at home. Let him put up with Mom nagging about how he should find a nice girl and quit being a traveling man. She's always on my case. It'll do my heart good to see Perry taking the heat for a change."

"How long has it been since you've been by the ol' home place?"

"Gosh, three or four weeks, I guess. I do my best to stay away. It's my only defense. When I've got Mom on the phone, I can at least hang up on her as soon as she starts running through a list of losers she and her friends have heard are wife hunting. Or else they've got a list of jerks who are recently divorced. You have no idea how bad it gets, Dane. Mom quit picking on you the first time you brought Holly home from college."

"Maybe you ought to let her fix you up with someone. The new guys they're hiring in my station house are too young for you. Same goes for the new recruits at Kieran's precinct. Face it, in your age range the prospective husband pool's getting shallower with every passing year."

"Stop!" Daphne could feel her ears burning. "You're going to give Logan the impression that there's something wrong with me and I can't find a man."

"So? It's true."

"Is not. Men are everywhere. It's just that I'm choosier."

Making yakking motions with his fingers, Dane punched in a series of numbers on the phone pad. "We got off the subject, Daph. Perry can't sleep at the folks'. Our old rooms aren't our old rooms anymore. They've started remodeling our bedrooms into a home office for Dad, a den and a sunporch, plus a sewing room for Mom."

"When? I know they talked about it over Christmas, but... how can they just wipe out our best memories of growing up in that house?"

"Easy. They hired a wrecking crew. Mom tried to get you

to come and box up your high-school treasures. She said you put it off and put it off. We all did. Tanner finally glommed onto my football trophies, and Holly rescued my yearbooks." He shrugged. "I don't know why they'd want to clutter our house with junk from yesteryear."

Waving her scissors aloft, Daphne began to respond, but Dane shook his head as his phone call was answered.

Logan sensed the news had truly shocked Daphne. Hurt her. He got up to console her, and heard Dane talking with their absent brother.

"Hi, Perry? How are you, buddy?" Kicking back on the sofa, Dane kicked off his boots, then propped both stocking feet on one of Daphne's accent pillows. "Your Kenworth broke down outside of Beaumont, Texas, and you had to be towed to town? Blew the tranny, huh?" Dane jackknifed, coming to his feet to begin pacing the room. "That sets you back, what? Two, three days?"

Dane's disappointment over Perry's news was almost palpable. And amusing to the room's other occupants. Logan and Daphne traded smiles. Not because they had plans to pounce on each other the minute Dane's back was turned, but because his well-laid plans had just evaporated so completely, and he was clearly stymied.

"Are you okay?" Logan asked Daphne. "Your mother wouldn't throw all your keepsakes in the trash, would she?"

"No. Would yours?"

"Probably not. She's a saver. It's embarrassing to see the stuff she hangs on to. Pictures of our house and family I drew in kindergarten. Stick figures I colored with crayons when my dad was still alive. Poems I wrote in second grade."

"You wrote poems?"

"Doesn't everybody?"

"I wouldn't have guessed you'd be the type. Poems are pretty touchy-feely."

"Oh, yeah? I guess that must be why I got into trouble in fifth grade for writing love poems to Marcy Clark and Bridget Taylor." He grinned.

"I think that's sweet. Why would you get in trouble?"

"The girls were rivals. They launched a knock-down, drag-out fight on the playground. I haven't been moved to write a poem since. Nothing happened to the girls, but I lost playground privileges for a month. Worse, neither they nor any of their friends spoke to me for the remainder of the school year."

"Ah. Sounds traumatic. Is that why you sneaked older eighth-grade women into your backyard camp?"

Logan feigned taking a blow by lurching and clasping both hands to his chest. "You have a steel-trap memory, woman. I'll have to be careful what trade secrets I let slip around you."

"I imagine having a good memory is required to work for the FBI."

"Are you thinking of signing on?" Logan's eyebrows lowered.

Daphne removed a row of pins and checked the seam she'd just finished. "No. I told you, I'm hoping to get work at one of the studios. I'd think, though, working undercover like you do, you'd come across documents that might be dangerous for you to copy. Don't you have to store tons of facts in your head?"

"Early guys with the agency did. Those of us who came later owe our thanks to the electronic wizardry we use today. I can't fathom what agents did without them."

"Oh, that reminds me. Dane, are you finished talking to Perry?"

Her brother clicked off, tossed down the phone and came to see what his sister wanted.

"When you leave, stuff that backpack again so the guys in the car won't see any change from when you brought it this morning. Whichever of you visits me next, either you or Kieran, needs to smuggle Logan in a laptop. He should have one, and I always borrow yours."

"If you're going to that party tomorrow, stop by the house and I'll give you a laptop Perry left for Victoria. You can give it back to him when he hits town. He is going to bunk on your sofa."

"If he's broken down in Texas, when does he plan to get to Culver City?"

"With luck he'll make it by tomorrow."

"Then Kieran and Diana will be past their lovey-dovey stage. And Vic's slumber party will be over. So Perry can use one of your spare rooms."

"No, sis. He's staying here. We decided."

"Who did?"

Logan stood quietly listening to the exchange. He leaned against the kitchen table, where Daphne was sewing his costume. His ankles and arms were negligently crossed. His lips quirked as he listened to their byplay. How long, he wondered, until Daphne caught on?

Not long at all, as it turned out.

"I get it. You toads put your pea brains together and came up with this plan so I won't be left here alone with Logan."

When no one disabused her of that theory, she huffed disgustedly. "Dane, you're treating me as if I'm some airhead who can't be trusted to breathe on my own. How many times do I have to point out that I'm not a child?"

"I'm thirty-two," Logan put in. "I suspect that's the bigger worry for your brothers."

"Big damn deal. Men are such imbeciles. All men. Go away and let me get over being mad about this, or I'll open the door and shove you both into the street."

"Jeez." Logan straightened. "What did I do except sympathize? Just say the word, and I'll leave. I've offered to more than once, if I recall. You—well, you and Simon are why I'm still here causing your family heart seizures."

"That's the point, Logan. They shouldn't have heart seizures or any other kind of seizures over me. The only reason they do is because I foolishly elected to remain in the same town where I grew up. What if I'd gone to an East Coast college? What if I'd joined the military or the Peace Corps? Women younger than me are fighting wars halfway around the world. Every time I poke my head out of my shell, I have three brothers pushing me back inside and throwing a lock on the shell door."

"It's not your shell—er, your apartment door," Dane said flatly. "Kieran's footing the rent on this place."

"Is that why you all feel you can butt into my life all the time? Is this about my spotty job record?"

Logan stepped between the battling siblings. "You know, when I'm not on assignment and if I know Mike's out with the fleet, I keep an eye on April and Natalie. My mom doesn't call me or April all that often. Be glad you have a family that cares, Daphne. In my line of work, and I'm sure in Dane's and Kieran's, we see plenty of families who don't. And remember, I'm not in your life to stay. They are."

"Well put." Dane clapped Logan on the back a few times. "It's this new breed of women, Logan. I lay the whole problem on the doorstep of Title Nine."

"What's that?" Logan probably ought to know, and Title Nine sounded familiar, but he couldn't dredge the term out of his memory. Not when his thoughts centered on Daphne Malone—and on how sweet and unguarded she looked.

"Title Nine is the government regulation instituted to ensure girls' athletics get funding that's equal to what's spent on boys'."

Logan bobbed his head. "Sounds reasonable."

"You'd think. Except women took it way beyond its original intent. Now they feel they have to kick men's asses at everything." He ignored Daphne's loud sighs and mutterings. "The NFL, Logan. That's about the only true male bastion left. Pro football. If those guys cave, life as we know it today is over. Kaput."

"How so?"

"Do you play fantasy football?"

"I must lead a sheltered life. Can't say I've ever heard of it."

"Come on, I'll explain. It's got nothing to do with Title Nine—except that there aren't any women in our circle of players. Perry just reminded me that tonight's when all the guys who want to play ante up their three hundred bucks to register. How it works is we divvy up all the pro football players among a dozen guys. We do it like the draft, except by phone or instant messaging, and according to a set of rules. I might end up with a running back from the Broncos and a quarterback from the Dolphins, and so on. As the real games are played, we get whatever points our individual players earn in every game. We keep running tallies with the help of our software. If one of your players gets hurt, you cross him out, or trade him if anyone will trade. The guy with the highest

points each week wins part of the pot, through to the finals.
That's where the winnings really mount up."

"Sounds like fun. Count me in. Uh, provided I can pay once
I'm able to access my funds." Logan followed Dane into the
living room where he snapped on Daphne's TV set.

"What it is," she said loudly to be heard over the sports
channel, "is a monstrous waste of grown men's time. Time
they could spend doing something constructive."

Neither Logan nor Dane acknowledged her. She'd lost them
to a game.

They were still huddled in front of the tube two hours later
when she walked in carrying a one-piece clown suit that was
an assault on the eyes. She'd sewn furry red balls up the front
of a pear-shaped suit. A giant orange bow perched at the neck.
Neither helped tame the gaudy polka dots.

"Oh, man," Dane muttered. "You don't really expect the
poor guy to wear that out in public."

Logan was aware that Dane's comment crushed the antici-
pation in Daphne's expressive eyes. "It's, ah, going to attract
attention," he said lamely.

"Including that of the yo-yos waiting out front for you,"
Dane put in explosively.

"Logan said we should act bold so they'll think we have
nothing to hide." Daphne dropped the costume in Logan's lap.
"Try it on. I only have to sew elastic around the wrists and
ankles and it'll be done. I think I cut the arms and legs long
enough to allow for ruffles that'll cover the top edges of your
clown boots and gloves."

"Ruffles, oh hell." Logan's face took on a sickly hue, while
Dane tried but failed to hide his snickers.

Logan climbed slowly to his feet. "Really, it's fine, Daphne.

It'll get me out from under wraps. If we pull this off, I'll owe you another big one."

"Owe her a big what?" Dane's geniality fled. Before anyone could answer, the cell phone near his hand rang. At first, they all stared at it as if it were a snake come to bite them. Being closest, Dane picked it up and thumbed the case open. He mumbled, "'Lo." Then, "Hey, Holly! What's doin'?" The corners of his mouth turned up, indicating his pleasure. "You want me to go get the food trays already?" Twisting his wrist, he read his watch. "No, it just seems early. Way too early. Loga—uh, Daphne's roommate and I are watching the predictions on which pro teams are trading players. Babe, we're gearing up for this year's round of fantasy football."

His wife obviously didn't care and apparently wasn't willing to budge. Dane cupped a hand around the phone and lowered his voice to a shade above a whisper.

In order to give Dane privacy, Logan flung the costume over his shoulder and sauntered out of the room. "I'll go try this on."

Daphne suspected her brother's concerns weren't related to watching sports at all. She knew he wasn't keen on leaving her and Logan by themselves with so much time on their hands. Some people might think it laughable that his wife had thwarted his plans to stick around, but Daphne didn't find anything remotely amusing about the way her brothers were treating her. It'd serve the lot of them if she locked them out after Dane left and spent however long she and Logan had together making mad, passionate love with the man.

As Dane droned on, Daphne discovered her passing fancy was harder to shake than she would've guessed. Not that she would ever instigate making love. No. Ludicrous. What did she know about seduction? Only what she read in the hot women's magazines she bought every month. Magazines she hid from her family.

Daphne figured she fell somewhere between the not-so-innocent lamb she'd thrown back in Logan's face and the I've-got-my-life-under-control fearless female she tried to convince her brothers she was. A few boyfriends had managed to get past her family's screening process. Well, one had. But that liaison, when it came to the sexual-experimentation part, could not be classed as a rip-roaring success.

However, she continued to believe in possibilities.

Dane signed off and glanced up to find Daphne studying him pensively. "I've gotta go." He picked up the backpack he'd discarded earlier. "Come home with me, sis. Let Logan stay here by himself until his agency works things out."

"You want to subject me to a night you finagled to get Perry out of?" Daphne grabbed the backpack and stuffed a pillow inside to make it look full.

"Holly said you'd throw that in my face. She gave me hell, too. She really did after I admitted Logan seems like a nice guy. Where is he?" Dane slung the newly plump pack over one shoulder.

"He went to try on the clown suit. I'll tell him you said goodbye. Listen, Dane. I hope you'll give Victoria some space as she grows up. You can't protect her—or me—every blessed hour of every day."

Dane walked to the door without saying a word. "You're asking too much, Daphne. I wouldn't be me if I didn't try." He leaned down and kissed her forehead. "Watch your step. I work tomorrow, but if you need anything at all, phone Kieran. One of us will come running to your rescue."

She sighed, closed the door and banged her head briefly on the wood.

"You're asking a jaguar to change his spots," Logan said from across the room. "They love you, you know."

Daphne straightened away from the door before she turned the locks. "I—they...you don't understand. Where's your costume? Didn't it fit?" she asked, concern etched across her face.

"It fit fine. Looked damn dorky. You won't understand, either—but I didn't want Dane busting a gut laughing."

"I do understand that feeling, believe me. But I still need to know where to run the elastic."

"I stuck pins where you need to start and end."

"Hey, fantastic." She took the garment he held out. "How did you know to do that? Not one of my brothers would have had a clue."

"You're not giving them enough credit. The ones who're married, anyway." Logan followed her to the kitchen. He eased up to the window and moved the curtain aside to check the street below. "Tailors pin everywhere when they fit you for a wedding tux."

Shifting her eyes from her sewing machine, Daphne stared at Logan's profile. She imagined him in a tuxedo and her mouth grew dust dry. She had to remove the pins she'd stuck in her mouth to keep from swallowing them.

"How long were you married?" she asked over the hum of the machine.

He let the curtain drop, but didn't fully turn back to face her. "One year from the ceremony to when the final divorce papers arrived. Did I tell you she was a fellow agent?" He gave a negligent shrug. "We probably only lived together a total of five months."

The lines bracketing Logan's lips should have served as a warning to drop the subject then and there. But Daphne had been known to jump in with both feet where angels feared to tread. "That hardly seems time enough to work through the bugs that come with anything new."

"Yeah. In my case it was too bad marriage didn't come with a money-back warranty, like refrigerators or cars." One edge of his lips curled up wryly, and he hooked both thumbs into the pockets of his too-big sweatpants.

"You sound bitter. I don't mean to be nosy, but I like to learn all I can about relationships gone bad so I can avoid the same pitfalls."

"First, don't marry a clown." Logan kept a straight face.

She smiled. "I take it you mean that literally. Although you seem to have the same mental block my family has toward my real occupation. I'm going to be a movie-makeup artist one day."

"What exactly does a movie-makeup artist do? I thought all movie stars have their own plastic surgeons who shoot them full of Botox, and do nips and tucks that make them look half their age. Even if that's not the case, I can't picture Catherine Zeta-Jones wanting to step out as one of the cute characters you turned those kids into at Nat's party."

She laughed outright and the sound caused a ripple of goose bumps to skitter up Logan's spine.

"Actors shooting a film spend a third of their day in the makeup chair. I can do far more to change someone's appearance than a plastic surgeon can. And not everyone comes out looking like cartoon-animal characters. A face is a blank canvas. You think actors don't show up hungover, depressed or ill? They do, and when they step out of the makeup chair, not a soul would know they had a care in the world."

"Sounds hard. Sounds impossible. Do you give demonstrations?"

"I would if anyone asked. Not one person in my family has ever asked to see what I can do." She pulled the fabric from under the feeder foot, and raised her eyes to Logan's. It was probably foolish to bare her hopes and fears to this man who was practically a stranger. But he stood there as if waiting for more. "After we come back from the birthday party tomorrow, I could show you a bit of what I've learned to do. Daylight is a truer light, or I'd offer to show you now." She nervously chewed her lower lip.

The vulnerability in her eyes moved Logan to agree. "Sure. That would be cool." He didn't really have any interest in Hollywood, or in vain people striving for the adoration of millions. And he felt almost like a fraud because those few simple words had brought such happy animation to Daphne's face. Her comment about faces being a blank canvas, though— that didn't apply to Daphne Malone. She revealed her every insecurity in those incredible cat-gold eyes.

"Well, this project is finished," she announced, handing back the costume. "I can't decide if I should give you the same hat and phony hair, or if I ought to change your character. At April's I was forced to rush. If any of those men knew you well, they might have seen through your disguise."

"Nat didn't." He bundled the suit under one arm. Daphne appeared so anxious to do the right thing. So anxious to keep him safe from harm, and also to please him, Logan experienced a sudden, swift urge to kiss her cares away. A physical reaction slammed him hard in the gut.

Daphne read his intentions. She didn't believe what the quiver that ran through her body was telling her, but she waited expectantly nevertheless. Still, she felt shock waves of major proportions when Logan's lips settled on hers. Softly at first, then harder as the costume slipped from his hold and landed in her lap. He used both hands to anchor her lips to his. One hand cupped the back of her head, and the other stroked the side of her neck. The rough pad of his thumb rasped back and forth along her jaw. She was a mass of heat and nerves and unfamiliar wants and desires.

Daphne didn't know what to do. She knew what she wanted to do. Heck, her addled brain said go ahead, girl. Do it! Almost as if directed by someone else, she lifted her arms and wrapped them around Logan's neck. He raised her up out of the chair.

Uh-oh. Big mistake. Sweatpants, even oversize ones, hid nothing. She felt Logan's heat, his strength, and the hardness of his erection.

In some part of his brain, Logan was aware that what had started out as a simple kiss of assurance had erupted into more. Far more. Dane and Kieran Malone would call him a bastard for not stopping this now. And the charge fit. He'd started something that generally ended with two people naked and in bed.

But sweet, sweet Daphne deserved the one thing Logan had sworn he'd never risk again. She kissed like a woman with stars in her eyes, too much love in her heart and a white picket fence in her mind.

Although it took every ounce of determination he had, Logan finally wrenched his lips away from hers. He shut his eyes. Even then, behind closed lids, he saw her parted, damp lips, her shuttered gold eyes glittering with desire. Desire that was his for the sampling.

He didn't know how many men who'd gone without a woman for as long as he had would turn and walk away from the gift Daphne Malone was clearly offering. The hell of it was, Logan had to do exactly that. Walk away. Before it was too late for both of them. He could feel his fingers, which had slipped to her shoulders, kneading the soft flesh underneath. As gently as he could, he pressed her back down into the kitchen chair. "I...ah...probably owe you an apology," he finally choked out.

"No. None required," she said in a shaky voice. With fingers that didn't seem to work properly, she hurriedly began setting her sewing machine to rights. She rolled up the cord, stored it in the lid and attempted to drop the lid down over the machine.

"I wanted to thank you for all your hard work. The costume is great. And you've been—" Logan sucked in a deep breath "—you've been such a good sport, when I know you'd like nothing better than to have your life back the way it was."

"No. It's okay. My life wasn't so fantastic, to tell you the truth." She managed to get out of her chair, but failed when she tried to lift the heavy machine.

"Here, let me get that. Tell me where it goes."

Daphne wiped sweaty palms on the back pockets of her jeans. Her brain froze for a moment. "Uh, I keep it in the closet in my bedroom."

Logan swung the portable machine off the table. He'd sprinted four steps into the living room when her full statement hit him. He couldn't walk into her bedroom. Not with her hot on his heels. There were limits to a man's self-control. He knew a woman's bedroom revealed all kinds of secrets about her. Private things, from the pictures on the wall, to the frilliness or nonfrilliness of her bedspread. A woman's closet disclosed how she liked to dress. Stuff lying on nightstands and dressers showed a man what she'd be like without trappings.

And Logan had lain awake much of last night concocting

detailed fantasies about Daphne Malone. He didn't want to go into her room and find out he was wrong. Or right, for that matter. Lord, but he'd never leave if he'd guessed right. Because whether Logan wanted to admit it or not, his dreams had included traits that had been lacking in the woman he'd married. Traits like kindness and loyalty. If Daphne possessed some of them—and he was almost positive she did—he'd be drowning in deep water.

She saw the hesitation in his stride, as if the mere thought of entering her bedroom was like running into a brick wall. While she was admittedly disappointed, she supposed she ought to be grateful. Special Agent Grant had made no secret of the fact that he wasn't a man looking for a committed relationship.

Perhaps she was as gullible as her brothers tried to let on. They'd scoff and call her a moron for thinking that after one kiss, she'd know her heart's desire. But one kiss from Logan had shown her she probably wouldn't survive an affair. Not with him, anyway. No, not with him.

Drawing a huge breath aimed at driving out the taste of him that lingered on her lips, Daphne found her voice. "You don't have to go into my messy room, Logan. Just set the sewing machine outside my door and I'll take it from there."

"Are you sure?" he said, his own voice still wobbly.

"Positive. I'll put it away and then we need to decide what to have for supper."

Relief coursed through Logan when it shouldn't have. Sharing a meal with her he could handle. But sharing anything more…

They'd both end up burned.

CHAPTER SEVEN

DAPHNE STOLE A MOMENT after she put away her sewing machine to return to a more even keel. She was afraid she'd still act gauche and awkward around Logan, even after she went out again.

But he made it easy for her by seeming perfectly natural. "I'm digging through your cupboards," he called from the kitchen. "We have limited supper choices here."

She wracked her brain wondering what they might eat as she made her way through the living room—only to learn when she reached the kitchen that Logan already had a pot of water simmering on the stove.

"From what I see, we can eat spaghetti with pesto sauce, spaghetti with tomato sauce or spaghetti with clam sauce."

"Darn, you've exposed my deepest, darkest secret," she said, trying to sound lighthearted. "I subsist on bread and peanut butter, cheese and crackers, or spaghetti with seven kinds of canned sauces. Don't tell my mother, whatever you do."

He laughed. "Did I sound like I was complaining? Me, who orders in anytime I'm stuck at my place for any meal?"

"Stuck there?" She leaned against the end cabinet and

lazily rubbed one bare foot overtop of the other. "You mean the agency always has you out on assignment?"

"Even when they don't, I generally eat out." Affected by the slow sweep of her polished pink toenails, complete with winking gemstone toe ring, Logan turned his focus to his task, plunging a handful of noodles into the boiling water.

"You can't mean you eat three meals a day in restaurants."

"I feel hemmed in by apartment walls."

"Yeah, I noticed, but I figured you were just restless because of being followed."

He considered her observation. Logan didn't want to tell her that after Liz had pulled up stakes and moved out, his life tanked. If he told her how awful it was sitting around an empty condo, that would make him sound pathetic. It wasn't as if he'd ever really depended on Liz. After all, they were both extremely busy at jobs that weren't regular nine-to-five. Before she moved her stuff in, he was a man who hadn't needed anyone. A loner, everyone said. Now they called him footloose. He didn't know why the two terms felt at odds. They just did. And it was a difference that mattered to Logan.

"Maybe I'm just an action kinda guy," he finally muttered.

"Hmm." Daphne leaned her elbows on the countertop and considered him briefly. The only noise in the kitchen was the ticking wall clock and the bubbling pot of spaghetti. "Odd that you like fishing, then. My brothers can sit like bumps on a log for hours doing nothing but tossing out a line and reeling it in again. And they don't care if it comes back minus bait and without a fish every time."

"I wasn't a solitary fisherman. I fished with a buddy. His engagement fell apart a few months before my marriage caved.

Fishing is only a part of going out on the water. Camaraderie is a larger part. Your brothers don't fish alone, either."

Slowly nodding, Daphne figured his statement revealed more personal information than Logan had been willing to share up to now. It wasn't so much walls that suffocated him but the loneliness of not having anyone to talk to. That, she understood. Although she'd always thought living alone bothered her because she'd grown up in a large, boisterous family. "Did your mutual friends avoid you like so much garbage after you and your wife split?"

Logan stirred the noodles so long after he'd lowered the gas under the burner, Daphne figured the whole subject of his divorce must be taboo.

Eventually, he roused, but he still seemed to address the steam rising from the pot. "I can't remember—did I mention that Liz and I worked together? I may not have said we were both up for the same promotion. I expected the director to choose between us based on past performance and qualifications. Turned out Liz really, really wanted that promotion—any way she could get it. All our friends apparently knew how far she was willing to go. Not me. So, yeah, our coworkers had a tough time facing either one of us after the ripples quieted. In fact, it was damn messy until Simon transferred me here."

"So, you owe him, I guess. That must be why you haven't disobeyed his orders. I've wondered about that. You don't seem the type not to power through on your own terms."

Logan smiled oddly. "Here I thought I was doing such a good job of hiding my irritation."

"Hardly. Those noodles ready? If they are, I'll grab bowls."

"You never said what topping you wanted."

"Surprise me. Since meeting you, I've learned to enjoy living dangerously."

He stared at her slender back. She'd stepped over to the cupboard on the opposite wall and rose on tiptoe to reach the top shelf. "Living dangerously isn't all it's cracked up to be, Daphne. TV and movies dress up what agents do to make it appear exciting. The guys we're after are dirtbags—and too often we have to act like them."

"Oh, I'm not thinking of joining up." Daphne set the two bowls and napkins on the table. "Do many women work for the FBI?"

"Enough." His eyes bored into her back. "You ask a lot of questions about agency work for someone who isn't interested."

"Boy, you're touchy. I'm trying to make conversation, Logan. I don't fish. You aren't big on face paint. What does that leave?"

"Tell me more about your family. Your brother, Perry— what's he like?" Logan set the bowl of spaghetti tossed with creamy pesto sauce between them. Then he pulled a foil-wrapped pack from the oven.

"Mmm. You found enough butter to make garlic toast? Gosh, I could get used to being spoiled like this. But it's not much of a meal to tide over a man, is it? That's one thing I'll tell you about Perry. He's a meat-and-potatoes person."

"A bruiser, huh?"

"Not at all. His metabolism works better than anyone in the family. I hate him."

"Like you have to worry about calories." Logan stopped with a forkful of noodles halfway to his mouth, sending an unmistakably appreciative glance her way.

She blushed and bent over her food with exaggerated

interest. "My mom, Kieran and Becky are the ones who have to watch what they eat."

"Becky? You have a sister? Maybe you told me that, and it went in one ear and out the other."

"Like all you have to worry about is keeping my family straight. Becky's the baby. She married an engineer. They have an eight-month-old daughter who is currently the apple of her grandparents' eyes. Not that the folks don't spoil Dane's kids, as well. They do. There's just something about babies." A smile lit her face, and she sighed softly before stabbing at her noodles again.

"So, Dane's the oldest and you're...somewhere in the middle?"

"Next to the youngest." She crossed her eyes and made a funny face. "Dane's thirty-nine. Kieran's thirty-four. Perry is thirty. I'm twenty-six, with Becky a year younger. I get the bulk of all their matchmaking attempts, because Perry's hardly ever around."

"Mike and April bug me a lot, too. It's gotten worse since my divorce. Why is it married folks share a common goal? If you're single, they mount a crusade to find you a suitable mate."

"If only suitable played a part. With my family, it's more like...you're single, Daphne. This guy I just met—somewhere—is also single, so it's gotta mean a match made in heaven." She propped an elbow on the table and rested her chin in her hand. "Do you ever wish Mr. Right, or in your case, Ms. Right, would simply fall out of the sky? I do. Yeah, I admit it. To shut them up, you know?"

Logan, trained to read nuances and signs, thought he knew what else was going on in her head. Who was she trying to kid? Daphne Malone wanted the same thing for herself that her family wanted for her. A husband, home and babies of her own. It wasn't something Logan felt qualified to comment on. Instead, he veered down another path. Finished with his meal, and feeling exceedingly restless again, he shoved back his chair, rose and carried his bowl to the sink.

Gravitating to the window, he surveyed the landscape below. "Damn, the blue car is back. They're double-teaming us. The boss isn't willing to give up the only lead they've got. Namely, us."

Daphne brushed aside his observations and steered the conversation back to where they'd left off. "I think it's easier to meet someone you can be compatible with at work. That's another reason I'd like a studio to hurry up and hire me."

Logan pushed off from the wall with his shoulder. "I worked with Liz. We weren't compatible."

Undaunted, Daphne waved a forkful of noodles. "How much time did you give yourself to get to know her? Did you meet her family?"

"No."

"Her childhood friends? People who knew her values way back when?"

"Not really. Coworkers pushed us together. They paired me with Liz at parties, other after-hours activities. Agents are a tight-knit group. We progressed from hanging out to sharing an apartment for a month to finding a justice of the peace."

"No church wedding? Wow, getting married is such a special event. I think it deserves more than a ten-minute trip to the courthouse."

"We'd moved in together. I had a mission coming up that was going to take me out of town for several weeks. Liz suggested we make it legal so if anything happened to me—well, you get the drift."

"Sounds pretty cold. But I suppose if you're sure you love each other…"

"Love?" Logan gave an inelegant snort. "I've never met anyone who can really define what love is. I'm not sure the type of romantic love you're talking about even exists."

"If you see it, you know it. My parents are still in love even after forty-two years. Dane is. Kieran, too. And Becky. Are you suggesting your sister doesn't love her husband?"

"Are you kidding? She was sappy over Mike Ross beginning in fourth grade. My mom got upset because April never dated anyone else."

"Between them, our two families sort of prove love exists."

"Okay, some people have the capacity to love and be loved. Not all of us."

Her face fell.

"Look, Daphne, I didn't mean to lump you in with me. I was a lone wolf before I hooked up with Liz. The hell of it is, I was a happy loner. You know what I mean?"

Daphne nodded because he clearly expected her to say yes. But she didn't understand. Frankly, she doubted Logan was aware of how many things he said, how many little signs he projected, indicated the exact opposite of the way he perceived himself. And maybe he didn't know that the majority of wolves preferred traveling in packs. She recalled reading somewhere that wolves mated for life. But she supposed there were renegade wolves….

"Do you mind if I go watch the news?" Logan jerked a thumb toward the TV.

"No, no. Go right ahead. While you're here, *mi casa es su casa.*"

"Thanks," he said, his voice serious. "If you hadn't come to my rescue, it's conceivable I could be dead."

"Don't say that." She shuddered.

"It's true. This organization has too much at stake and zero to lose by putting men on every lead they've got. You have no idea how badly I want to see them toppled."

"I hate to think how much manpower they must have in order to keep rotating men outside our door, Logan."

"And their organization is one of a jillion operating on this coast. There are so many of these gangs, you'd need a calculator to add them up."

"Luckily the world has crimefighters like you and Kieran. Still, you must get discouraged."

"Oh, sure. That's why the small victories are so important, and why it's so damn hard to catch the idiots, only to see them walk five minutes after we haul their butts to jail. I'm really glad no one in your family's a lawyer, Daphne. Creative lawyering is what's killing us in this country."

"Not all lawyers. I have a friend who's a victims' rights advocate. She admits she could make a whole lot more money if she was a criminal lawyer."

"Money. Now, there you have the key. It all boils down to greed. If there wasn't big money to be made running drugs, weapons, smuggling people—you name it—I'd be out of a job."

"Hmm. Like you told Kieran, there's always fishing for profit as well as fun."

Logan threw back his head and laughed.

Laughter changed his somber features, making him even handsomer and more appealing, if that was possible. Standing there, watching him, realizing how much she liked being able to lighten his heavy burden, even momentarily, Daphne knew she was in trouble. She thought she could grow to like doing this way too much, like him way too much. Logan made no secret of the fact that he wasn't looking for another romance, and any woman who'd fool herself into thinking she could soften or change his resolve would end up hurt.

"I'll tidy up in here," Daphne said, waving him away, toward the TV in the living room. She didn't want Logan to see that her heart had begun to pound a bit harder. He'd already shown he wasn't a man to take advantage of a woman's weakness. On the other hand, she couldn't be sure if there were limits to his willingness to walk away. And it'd be twice as hard to resist a happy Logan Grant. In short, Daphne didn't trust herself.

Logan didn't question why she rushed him out of the kitchen so fast. But it was plain to her, from the way Logan made sure he collected the safe phone before he went off, that he hadn't lost hope that his boss would call at any minute with a promise to spring him—saving him from her clutches.

She scrubbed everything in her small kitchen until the counters gleamed and the chrome sparkled. When she finally emerged, Logan was sprawled across the couch, his feet bare. The news was over, and he'd switched to one of the late-night talk shows. He sat up when she walked into the room. "All done, huh? Hey, if you'd prefer the couch, I'll move to a chair."

Daphne shoved back drooping hair that had fallen over her eyes. "Don't give up your spot on my account. I might read for a while. Also, I'll need to get ready for the party tomorrow— make sure I have enough props. In case some of the same kids who were at Natalie's show up at the party tomorrow, I want to make up their faces differently."

"Can you do that?"

She raised a questioning eyebrow.

"I'm not doubting your ability, Daphne. It never dawned on me there'd be as many variations as I saw you pull off at Nat's party. Now you're saying you've got even more."

"Eventually I'll run through my whole repertoire. But that's only a problem if you get repeat kids. Hopefully I'll have a studio job before my stuff gets too stale. With the mobility of today's population, party clowns can only hope to garner enough referrals to keep going if they venture into different parts of town."

"Tomorrow's party takes us back to the same area where we met?"

"Not next door or anything. The kids and parents know one another through the elementary school, I gather. You look troubled. Is that a problem?"

"No. Er…maybe. I guess it's a bit like an arsonist returning to the scene of a fire he set."

"Speaking of returning to the scene… Did you order Natalie's gift?"

"No. I can't imagine what I was thinking when you suggested using my credit card. Those guys can easily check activity on my card. It'll have to wait until Simon gives me the all-clear."

"That's too bad. Is it okay for me to use Simon's phone for a local call? I'll give Dane's wife, Holly, a jingle and ask her to order the gift but have your name signed to the card."

"She'd do that? Those Barbie things aren't cheap. Dane's wife doesn't know me."

"She knows me. And Dane will have told her about you. They don't keep secrets from each other, which is another reason their marriage is so solid. I'd ask my mother to take care of it, but Kieran said—and I agree—it's better Mom doesn't know you're staying with me."

"Ah. Gotcha," Logan said, and indeed a knowing light came into his brilliant blue eyes. "Mama Bear would come to save Baby Bear from the man who's been sleeping in her bed, huh?"

"Something like that. And it's not helpful for you to joke about where you're sleeping. Mom draws strict lines between right and wrong."

"Dane takes after her, then? You said he knocks heads first and asks questions later."

"My folks are really salt of the earth. It's just that we kids go to great lengths to keep Mom in the dark about small transgressions."

Logan passed her the phone without another word. But he patted the cushion next to him as an invitation for her to sit there.

Daphne faltered. However, not wanting to be viewed as schoolgirlish, she plopped down next to Logan and immediately punched in her brother's number.

"Hi, Holly. This is Daphne. Oh, fine. Things are fine here. No, I'm not calling Dane, it's you I need to talk to." She proceeded to lay out Logan's request.

"No, I don't know if his niece wants the version with the pickup and camper, or the one that comes with a boat and tent. Just a minute, I'll ask him." Covering the phone with her hand, she left the decision up to Logan. Then she returned to the phone.

"He says, go for the one with the tent. I think it's a man thing. You know, Holly, that back-to-nature, roughing-it's-fun gene all men seem to share?"

Daphne's low, husky laugh triggered a sexual response in Logan. It should've set off warning bells in his head. He knew he should get up and walk away, leaving Daphne to wind up the call to her sister-in-law. But some demon not only possessed him to stay where he was, but also prompted him to reach out and play with the thick cloud of Daphne's night-black hair.

Her eyes roamed wildly from side to side as she attempted to see what he was doing. "Uh, thanks for the favor, Holly. You've saved a little girl's faith in her uncle. What are we doing?" she squeaked. "No—nothing. Watching TV. Logan is. That's what you hear in the background. I'm headed for bed as soon as I hang up. Oh, will you have Dane contact Perry? I understand he's planning to crash here whenever he hits town. My fridge and cupboards are nearly bare. If it's not too much of an imposition, Perry needs to stock up on staples again before he comes."

She ducked her head and hid her ear against her shoulder, thinking it was the only way to escape whatever Logan was doing with her hair. "Mac and cheese and beer? Good grief, is that still Perry's idea of a good meal? Sure, make a list and have Dane give it to Perry. You'll earn my undying gratitude. Plus, I'll throw in free babysitting for a month." Daphne was still grinning when she clicked off.

"Logan, what are you doing? I was trying to ensure we won't have to eat spaghetti every night this week."

"Oh, like macaroni and cheese is such a big improvement." Logan took back the phone she shoved his way, but he didn't turn loose her hair. In fact, he playfully dusted the tip of her nose with the curl she could never tame to stay behind her ear.

"Are you trying to pick a fight?" Daphne faced him, pulling one foot underneath her. She knew immediately that was a mistake. Since this couch was a castoff from her parents' family room, the cushions sloped to the center, sliding the occupants together.

"Why would I fight you, Daphne?" Logan crushed her shoulder-length hair in both his hands. "I suppose everyone tells you what gorgeous hair you have."

Daphne made a second mistake, looking directly into Logan's eyes. That got her caught in the storm of desire she saw brewing there.

Get up now. Something rose like a burst of lightning inside her brain and zapped that fleeting sane thought. Instead, she let herself tumble headfirst into the eye of the hurricane.

Logan's face loomed ever closer. Straight nose. Firm lips. The chin with a faint cleft she hadn't noticed before. Drawing nearer and nearer, until she could no longer define any single feature. Her lips parted, perhaps in protest. Or perhaps not, because no sound escaped. Not until their mouths touched. Then Daphne felt, more than heard, a moan of exquisite pleasure.

Logan was admittedly surprised to discover that a second kiss between them had turned out to be as cataclysmic as the first.

But they had a long night to kill, and there were certainly worse ways to spend the time than kissing, or even indulging in some heavy petting. After all, they'd called it quits before, and neither of them felt ill will toward the other. At least that was the thought running through Logan's mind as he pulled Daphne astride his lap.

Her jeans caused friction to an area that created a rush of heat so swift, Logan had no defenses to fight it. Not that he really wanted to. It felt good. Great, in fact. As she moved against him, a lethargy stole over Logan. Somewhere in the center of his sluggish brain, he was positive the Malone broth-

ers would do Billy-boy's job for him were they ever to discover
the heat and fire Logan had unleashed in their sister.

They believed she was an innocent. Daphne appeared to
know what she liked from a partner. And damn, he liked that
in a woman.

He also liked the feel of Daphne's skin. So he lost no time
hitching up her T-shirt. She tensed just enough when he released the catch on her bra to drive home the reminder that
she wasn't too experienced at this game. Her hesitation slowed
Logan's headlong rush. He gentled his touch, and endeavored
to break free of her luscious mouth. "Things are moving awfully fast," he murmured, sliding his hands around her rib
cage until his calming strokes up and down her back eased
the frantic beating of her heart.

"You're not stopping again, are you?" she asked, an air of
disbelief evident between the dragged-out breaths.

"Not by choice." He stole another quick kiss because he
couldn't help himself.

"What else is there?"

"Necessity." Logan kept her from raining kisses all over
his face. He made her pay attention.

"Necessity? Like…protection?"

Logan held her still, afraid that if he didn't, there would
be no reason left for discussing anything. It'd been so long
for him. He wasn't going to last if they didn't settle this soon.
"Yeah. Fooling around like this leads to sex, babe."

"Not to worry. When I moved into the apartment on the
third floor, I took over the lease from Perry. He'd bought his
truck and was going on the road full-time. Let's just say he
left a lot of things I threw out—and some I decided to save
for a rainy day."

Logan tried to follow her disjointed explanation. He got the gist of it, anyway. Good old Perry had left rubbers. "I'm not big on chatter at times like this, Daph. And if we don't get this show on the road, my role's going to be a big disappointment to us both, I'm afraid."

She slid off his lap, grabbed his hand and tugged him up from the couch. "What we need is in my bottom dresser drawer." Still holding his hand tightly, she led the way into her darkened bedroom. Dropping to her knees, she rummaged through a drawer. "Ah, here's the box." She paused, apparently uncertain, for a brief moment.

Logan's eyes had adjusted, and with light from the street and neighboring apartments, he noted her slight hesitation. But he didn't really expect what came next.

"This is your last chance to back out, Logan. I've gotta warn you. All that bragging I did to Dane about not being virginal—well, I'm not…very experienced."

He knelt beside her and touched her face reverently. "Why me? We don't have a history. And this may be the one and only—" Logan's voice broke when he saw her lips trembling. "I'm trying to be honest, Daph."

She bit down hard to control the weakness in her voice. "I know. I know all that, okay? But, you're the first guy who didn't laugh when you heard about my other screwups, Logan. I don't want to go through life constantly wearing that label, no matter what I do. The last time I tried this—okay, okay, the only time, but the guy I was with made two attempts. It was—he said…that I, that I couldn't—"

"Shh! Of course you can." Logan kissed her silent, and kissed her again as he brought both of them to their feet. The packets fluttered from her hands, but Logan saw they'd fallen close enough to the bed for him to scoop one up when necessary. Her eager kisses had begun to affect him again.

He was barely able to strip back the spread and tumble them across the sheets.

Wanting, needing, to feel more of her, Logan tore the top of his borrowed sweat suit over his head without stopping to unzip the front.

There was nothing wrong with Daphne's technique. Nothing at all. She wasn't at all shy about ridding herself of her own shirt. She struggled a bit when it came to the zipper on her jeans. Logan stilled her hands, and said in a gravelly voice that sent shivers along her bare arms, "I want to—let me."

Because his sole aim had turned into making this a good experience for her, Logan found renewed stamina. Rather than rush, he spent time touching her. And he urged her to explore every part of him, which she did as he guided her hands. She moved carefully at first, then as the heat built between them, experimented with greater abandon. The light that filtered into the room allowed him to revel in the natural pout of her full lips, and in the shining eyes that glowed just for him. As well, her hair caressing his face, teasing his chest, was everything he'd dreamed about and more. Much, much more. Logan felt himself slipping. Just…slipping.

That was one of his last coherent thoughts as he moved her overtop of him, coaxing her to take the lead. Although she might have gone into this inexperienced, she was a fast learner. And so beautiful she robbed him of breath. As her knees gripped his hips and they spun out of this universe into another world together, Logan grabbed at a passing thought: that he was in deep, deep trouble here.

Daphne collapsed on top of him, every bone and muscle in her body floating free. Only the soft whir of the overhead fan, combined with the thrumming of Logan's heart under her right ear, let her know she was still alive.

The ride had been glorious, magnificent, stupendous. Now she knew why so many of her friends raved about making love. Except...Logan hadn't used that term earlier. What she considered wonderful lovemaking was, to Logan, simply sex.

Raising her head, Daphne saw Logan had his right arm thrown across his eyes. "Oh, no. Did I do something wrong?" she blurted. She rolled off him and tried to wrap herself in the tangled sheet.

He slid his arm up enough to expose one eye. "Wrong? Nothing's wrong. Babe, if they gave awards for this sport, you'd take home the trophy. I just need some time to recover." Finding her with his left hand, he pulled her down and snuggled her into the curve of his side.

As Daphne lay still as a mouse, slowly digesting what he'd said, she felt his breathing even out, and it dawned on her that Logan had fallen asleep.

He didn't think she'd messed up at all. Smiling, she burrowed into his warmth, and found a corner of pillow on which to lay her head. She'd never slept through a whole night with anyone before. When the same lethargy that had left Logan relaxed in sleep began to claim her, Daphne thought she could easily get used to sleeping with a partner. And even though in her waking state she knew her partner wouldn't be Logan Grant, when the sandman came and sprinkled dreams behind her eyes, her dream man looked a lot like him.

DAPHNE WOKE UP to a bedroom flooded with daylight. She sat up, kicked her way out from under a tangled top sheet and scraped back her hair. That was when she discovered she was stark naked. And like a bucket of cold water dumped on her head, last night's activities came flooding back. In all, she and

Logan Grant had made love three times. The second time at his instigation, and the third at hers.

Her gritty eyes finally found the bedside clock. It had fallen on the floor. She reached down to grab it. But that revealed all kinds of aching muscles. "Ooh," she moaned.

Her bedroom door flew open. She shrieked and snatched up the wrinkled sheet, covering herself as best she could. Her intruder turned out to be Logan. He'd showered, obviously. He had on the second set of sweats her brother had lent him, and his face wore what Daphne immediately judged to be a morning-after expression of guilt.

"Are you all right?" he inquired. "Your phone rang about half an hour ago and woke me up. You were sleeping like the dead."

"Who was on the phone?"

"I don't know. I didn't want to answer in case it turned out to be your mom. I figured that wouldn't be too cool."

"No. I'll, uh, give her a ring after I shower."

"You, ah, might want to soak in the tub this morning. I'm told a warm bath helps ease the— You never said if you're okay this morning. We went at it pretty hard for a first-timer."

She waved a hand negligently. "I'm fine, Logan. It's just— what time is it? My clock got disconnected from the wall."

He let his gaze run lightly over the dishevelment of both the woman and her bedroom. "It's almost noon. Like I said, you were dead to the world."

"What?" She leaped off the bed. "Logan, we're supposed to be at Lori Jones's party at one-thirty. It's across town and we can't leave here unless we're both in full costume."

"Crap. I forgot about that." He raked a hand through his neatly combed hair, messing up the dark gold layers.

"A bath might be what I need. A quick shower is what I'll

get. While I shower, would you go put on the costume I made for you?" Wrapping the sheet around her, she glided toward her bathroom with as much elegance as she could muster.

Logan wanted to say to hell with the Jones party. Parts of his anatomy were demanding he take Daphne back to bed. But, of course, that was impossible.

He gave himself a mental shake as she disappeared. Then she stuck her head back out. "Good, you're still here. I need you to throw all that stuff on the table into the same beach bag we used the other day. And when you finish packing, set out the white, red and black paint pots. If you get everything ready, we can make this commitment and save my professional reputation."

Logan didn't know why her words jabbed him so hard. Probably because he'd spent the whole night ruining her personal reputation. At least that was how her hulking brothers would look at the night's events.

That and other things had run through Logan's mind this morning as he'd awakened feeling like a million bucks and then gazed down on her naked, sun-kissed back. He'd been assailed by longings a man in his position had no right to feel. The first thing he'd done after showering was phone Simon Parrish. He'd applied pressure on his boss to get him out of here today.

That would be best for everyone, he mused, haphazardly slinging items into the beach bag.

Simon refused to promise anything. Logan had come as close to begging for a favor as he ever had since joining the agency. Simon still hadn't been moved.

After seeing Daphne just now, Logan knew that if his boss didn't arrange to break him out by the time he and Daphne returned from today's gig, he'd take matters into his own hands and leave anyway.

Having decided that, Logan costumed up and sat still while the woman he longed to kiss turned him into a pointy-headed, laughable creature no lady in her right mind would want to kiss back.

"There," she said, leaning to the side to view her handiwork. "I like this disguise, Logan. In those pants you look thirty pounds heavier. I doubt the guy who saw you last time will even know you're the same clown."

"You're clever, all right."

"Maybe those jokers in the car won't follow us this time."

"Did you phone your mom?" he asked as they locked the apartment.

"She wasn't the one who phoned. It was Perry. He'll probably be here by the time we return from the party. Don't you wish we had another night alone before he barges in?" she said, turning a wistful eye on her companion.

Logan said nothing. How could he explain the surge of hope that washed over him? With one of Daphne's brothers here, maybe he could survive another night. A different hope soared as they reached Daphne's small car, and Logan didn't detect any interest directed their way from the car parked across the street. The white one with the dark windows had replaced the blue one again. Then another thought struck. "Daph," he mumbled, half out of one side of his mouth. "Until I have time to sweep your car for bugging devices, don't talk about anything except the party. Above all, don't say my name."

She gave a nod of understanding.

He sank into the passenger seat, thinking maybe everything would work out, after all.

"Dang," Daphne muttered. She gave a quick jerk of her head to indicate they'd attracted a tail.

Closing his eyes, Logan crossed his arms over his chest.

She wanted to hit him. If she hadn't fallen for him so hard, she might have. And it wasn't good news that her Mr. Right had dropped from the sky, either. Not good news at all, Daphne noted, suddenly glum.

CHAPTER EIGHT

DOING HER BEST to forget the car that rode her bumper, and the possibility of a bugging device, Daphne took a different route to the Jones party. She was pressed for time, and it would undoubtedly be faster to take the off-ramp closest to April Ross's home. Lori's and April's houses were probably a few blocks apart. However, by driving a mile farther and doubling back, she hoped the men, who might not be as familiar with the city, wouldn't connect the dots between the two residences. This way, they were also farther from where the organization had lost Logan.

Logan had nodded off, she saw with some envy. How could he sleep when her sweaty palms slid around the steering wheel? She reminded herself that was why he was the special agent and she was a party clown.

"Wake up," she said loudly. "We're here."

Logan came so instantly alert, Daphne wondered if he'd been playing possum all along so he wouldn't have to listen to her nervous chatter.

"It's a good thing we did come dressed for the job. This address isn't actually Lori's home. She mentioned she'd be holding her event at the neighborhood park."

Logan's uneasy gaze swept the open expanse. He swore

succinctly, and Daphne understood why. The partygoers were set up at picnic tables under a small stand of trees. Kids ran around playing tag over a huge area of grass. Or else they hung upside down from monkey bars connecting two huge jungle gyms. At a glance it was easy to see that anyone could wander up and watch the proceedings.

What was of greater worry to Daphne was that any sharp-shooter who wanted to pick Logan off would have ample opportunity. She waited to voice her concern until they'd un-loaded the gym bag and were well away from the car. So if any bugs had been placed, she was out of range.

"I hear what you're saying, Daph. But our best defense is to act as natural as possible. Guys like that can smell your fear a block away." He squeezed her arm. "I know this is a bad setup. What I want you to do is keep the kids away from me as much as possible in case anything goes down."

"Goes down?" Her eyes were dark pools of horror. "Oh, Logan, you don't even have a weapon to defend yourself."

"I do. But I'd never bring it out in a situation like this. I considered giving Simon this address and letting him cover us. I'm glad now I didn't. There's no place to stash agents. A presence here would only worsen our chances."

"I can do this, Logan," she said. "We can do this." March-ing straight up to the group of adults sitting at the table, she said, "My partner and I are providing entertainment for a birthday party. I think we're at the right place. Is one of you Lori Jones?"

A tall, willowy blonde separated herself from the others. "I'm so glad you found us. The later it got, the more I wor-ried that I'd forgotten to mention Ellie decided she wanted her party at the park. Ellie," she called, cupping her hands around her mouth.

That brought all the children galloping across the field. When Daphne looked up to see which girl led the pack, she noticed the two men from the white car. They were sauntering nonchalantly around the perimeter of the playground. Her heart dropped when she saw that one of the men carried a sack from a fast-food chain and his friend had two soft drinks. He held both in one hand, which left his shooting hand free.

It was clear they intended to eat lunch at one of the tables. So before they got within hearing range, Daphne quickly explained to the children that Buzzy had awakened with a bad sore throat. "He didn't want to miss Ellie's party, but it's probably better if you let him do his tricks without getting too close." She smiled at the assembly of mothers, only a couple of whom she'd met at April Ross's house. "I doubt any of your moms want you missing the first week of school because you caught a virus. Clown colds are harder to get rid of than normal sniffles," she added with a wink at Lori Jones. "I mean, look at Buzzy's red nose. None of you kids want to end up with noses like his."

Children were so delightfully frank. All of them drew back a respectful distance, issuing a variety of icks and yucks and eeuwes. One big-eyed waif sporting long pigtails tied in large loops eyed Buzzy dolefully, but said to Daphne, "He might not be able to talk, but he can hear us, I'll bet. We should be careful not to hurt Buzzy's feelings."

"You're absolutely right. What's your name?" Daphne asked.

"Gracie," the child said, which set off a round of introductions. Connecting each name with a face, Daphne soon settled down. She got involved with the party and stopped thinking about the two buffoons having lunch at the far end table. She'd half expected Lori or one of the other moms to charge over there and demand to know why two men in suits were hanging around a neighborhood park. Daphne was sure her mom would've done that, as would Dane's wife. Either these mothers felt there was safety in numbers, or they were used to seeing men in three-piece suits stuffing their faces at picnic tables in their park.

For an icebreaker, Daphne took out a package of balloons. Lori hadn't provided any. Too bad she hadn't brought a canister of helium. Halfway through blowing them up, she discovered Logan making balloon animals out of the elongated ones that were most malleable. "Will you look at that talent, kids," she called. "I wonder where on earth Buzzy learned that trick."

Ellie, the birthday girl, raised her hand. "Didn't they teach you at clown school?"

"Not me," Daphne exclaimed. She handed off a balloon to the last child in the circle. "I learned how to juggle baseballs, though. Wanna see how I do that?"

All the children chorused immediate consent. Logan, however, made a show of rolling his eyes and nixing her choice with wild antics, which soon had the kids roaring with laughter.

Daphne really expected baseballs to be easier to juggle than the plastic bowling pins she'd kept dropping at the last party. She was more surprised than anyone when three of the four balls she got in the air fell, bonking her on the head.

As the children at Nat's party had, these kids found the routine exceedingly funny. Even sympathetic little Gracie giggled herself silly. And wouldn't you know, Logan kept the baseballs in the air without missing a beat.

Lori Jones approached Daphne, who stood to one side still rubbing her forehead.

"You guys are terrific. The friend who gave me your name said what really sets your act apart from other party clowns is the way you painted the kids' faces. She suggested I bring something for the children who aren't in the makeup chair. So I filled plastic bags with trinkets, squeeze rockets, plastic slide puzzles and other time-wasters."

Daphne turned one of the packages over in her hand. "These are great gimmicks to occupy little hands, Lori. I paint faces at the end of our act, and then that's it, unless you want us to help serve cake and ice cream."

"No, as a matter of fact, Ellie's aunt is going to bring sno-cones for everyone. I just have to call her about the time you start working on the next-to-last face."

"Then Buzzy and I won't stick around after I finish the faces. Oh, wait. I'll give you some pipe-cleaner critters I made as a special treat for each child."

At the table, Daphne handed over the sack of snails, worms, butterflies and centipedes she'd twisted out of chenille pipe cleaners the week she babysat Dane's kids. She'd known they'd come in handy one day.

Lori leaned across the table, her smile turning to a faintly worried expression. "I noticed two men seated at the far picnic table who've been watching us. Do you or your partner know them?"

Daphne wasn't sure what to say, and Logan was tied up with his juggling demonstration. Then an idea popped into her head. One Logan might not like. "I assumed the men lived in the neighborhood, Lori. Otherwise, it's odd that they'd choose to eat here where it's hot and noisy. Hmm. If I were a parent, I wouldn't want strange men hanging out near my children's playground."

"It is suspicious. Our area used to be so safe. Nothing's

safe anymore. But wouldn't you think they're too obvious for child molesters?" She bit her lip. "What if they're trying to snatch a child for a parent involved in a custody fight? Stacy Martin's parents just had a nasty divorce."

Shrugging, Daphne continued unloading her paint supplies.

Lori fidgeted a moment, then picked up her cell phone. "Those men aren't actually doing anything wrong, and I hate to disrupt Ellie's party. My sister, the one bringing the sno-cones, is dating a cop. Maybe he'd swing past here and ask them some questions."

"Oh, that's good, Lori. What if he arrived with the sno-cones? The kids would be huddled right here, and their interest would be focused on the treats."

Before putting her plan into action, Lori removed a check from her pocket. "I'll give you this now. There's no reason to detain you over what might be nothing."

Daphne readily accepted and stored the check the woman gave her. It dawned on her that she hadn't yet banked April's check. Logan Grant had certainly muddled up her life.

Or maybe she couldn't truthfully say he'd done anything but spice up a normally dull existence. Just being with him made her happy. Recalling how he'd thrilled her last night, she flashed him a veiled smile.

Logan read the smile, in spite of the clown paint, and came to a conclusion any man would reach. She wanted him. Wanted more of the pleasure they'd indulged in last night. Only a fool who saw that smile could interpret it any other way. But maybe Logan was a fool. A fool for letting her get under his skin. He'd already fallen for one unsuitable woman.

He considered all the reasons Daphne was unsuitable. Not for the same reasons Liz had been. Liz was a hard, clever woman with whom he'd shared the intensity of a tough job. Daphne personified house-in-the-suburbs, two-point-four kids and a dog in a pristine backyard, if ever Logan saw a woman who fit that description. Last night she'd shown him how loving and giving a person she could be. And that scared the hell out of him.

When the kids lost interest in his juggling, Logan withdrew from the main gathering. He sat on the ground under one of the trees, content to watch Daphne begin her paint magic. Once more he was impressed with the way she turned everyday boys and girls into passable likenesses of angels, witches, princesses and kings. She used only a few pots of coloring and some rudimentary props—and her skill.

Yesterday, before they'd digressed, she'd said something about using makeup to change a person's appearance more easily than plastic surgery. He'd let the comment pass. Maybe because it sounded preposterous, or because she'd rattled him. What exactly had she meant? When they got back to her apartment, he'd ask her to show him examples.

She finished the last child, capped her paint and tossed all the loose items lying on the table back into the beach bag, then blew kisses to the kids.

Out of the corner of her eye, she saw the woman delivering sno-cones pull up, and right behind her, a black and white. Daphne hurriedly motioned for Logan to get up. If she acted in a rush to leave, it was because her plan seemed to be falling into place. "Princess Ellie, Bozo and Buzzy wish you the best birthday ever, but now it's time for us to go home."

"What's up?" Logan lengthened his stride to match Daphne's, and bent to murmur in her ear.

She smiled and waved merrily at a blonde carrying a tray

of colorful icy cones, and did the same to the police officer walking three paces behind the woman.

"Shh. Let's make tracks. Lori Jones is worried that our shadows might want to snatch a child. The cop is her sister's boyfriend. While he questions them, I thought we could skate."

"Brilliant." Logan all but sprinted to the VW. His glee was short-lived. Even as he rubbed his hands together and directed Daphne toward the quickest route, the big blue car that traded surveillance with the white one shot out of a side road and swung in behind them.

"Ouch." Logan fumbled in the glove box and came out with a pad and crayon. He wrote and held it where Daphne could see. "Remember there might be a bug. I think our friends at the park saw the cop and they phoned their pals."

Daphne took one hand off the wheel and scribbled fast. "How could they know the cop came to see them? Couldn't he have been a parent coming to pick up a child?"

I blew that, Logan wrote. I should've had us walk normally, not rush like we did. It was a dead giveaway.

"If they were going to shoot us, wouldn't they have done it already?" Daphne had to flip the page to finish her statement.

Logan slumped in his seat and fell silent.

Daphne scratched on the pad again. "I could've discouraged Lori. Instead, I egged her on. Now the cop will find out they're carrying guns. He'll arrest them and the organization boss will be twice as steamed, right?"

Logan cracked open one eye, sighed and took his time writing. "Depends on how it plays out. Those men aren't dummies. The way they were dressed, they may convince the cop they're FBI. Or if the cop's not clean, he could let them go.

How they react depends on whether they think Lori acted on her own—or if there's some suggestion that you were the instigator."

Daphne spent the remainder of the drive wishing she'd let well enough alone.

Both were grateful to reach Daphne's street without being blown off the map.

"Perry's here," she announced, pointing to the tractor portion of a big red rig that took up two parking places. Daphne pulled in close behind it.

Logan had been writing on the pad. He turned it toward her. "I'm getting out first. You pretend you dropped your keys inside the car. If you hear bullets, I want you to take off fast. Drive to this address. Tell Simon I said he needs to give you protection."

Her throat felt parched, and her knees shook. Daphne doubted she'd be able to carry out Logan's instructions. She let a second pass after he got out. Staring at her floor mats, she was afraid she might barf all over them. Two seconds passed, and Logan tapped on her window. She let out a screech and bolted upright. Grabbing her keys from the ignition, she flew out the door.

"Where's the blue car?"

"Down the block, turning around. Don't look. I have the beach bag. Remember how we did this last time. You unlock the door, and I'll bring up the rear."

They entered the building without a hitch. Only this time Logan didn't lag behind. He led the charge up the stairs.

As they rushed into Daphne's apartment and slammed the door, a man with sleepy eyes and rumpled red-gold hair reared up off the couch.

"Oops, sorry to wake you, Perry. This is my friend Logan Grant. Logan, the only one of my brothers you haven't met."

The men shook hands, with Perry trying to stifle a big yawn. "Sorry, it's got nothing to do with the company."

Logan saw that the man's grin and the shape of his face was more like Daphne's than like Dane's or Kieran's.

"Did you bring food?" she asked, pulling off her clown hat and hair.

"I picked up everything on the list Dane gave me. Plus, I threw in extra beer. Can I interest you in one now?" he said, directing his query to Logan.

"You sure can. Just let me get human first." Crossing the room, Logan spied a suitcase propped open against the wall. "In case Dane didn't tell you, I've latched on to a couple pairs of your sweats. I don't suppose you happen to have any spare jeans, T-shirts or underwear? I arrived on a wing and a prayer," he joked.

"There's a care package on your bed. Dane gave me sizes. He said he'd add the cost to your tab."

Logan underwent rapid-fire mood changes. He felt humbled by the kindness these men had offered him, and their willingness to take him at face value. Guilt for the way he'd paid them back already—by romping across the bed with their sister. "I owe all of you," he said. "With luck I won't be in your hair much longer."

Daphne padded toward him in stocking feet, having pulled off her clown slippers as he'd done on entering the building. "What makes you say that? Do you know something you're not sharing?"

"I know a lot I'm not at liberty to tell you, Daphne. Unless the main man gets jittery and waves off the shipment coming in by boat, on Saturday, at the latest, this operation will end. One way or another."

"Oh."

Logan avoided commenting on the disappointment lurking in Daphne's eyes, saying instead, "I'll go scoop out a handful of that face cream to take off this greasepaint. I'll set the jar outside my door and you can pick it up whenever you're ready."

"I'll just follow you. Perry, give us ten minutes or so, then open three beers. And don't fall back asleep."

"When did you get to be old enough to drink, kid?"

"Very funny." She threw her clown slippers at his head and scored a direct hit with one.

Unfazed, her brother guffawed lustily as he gathered them up and hurled them back. Daphne nimbly dodged both.

Logan stood back, thoroughly enjoying their banter. As a kid, he'd always wanted a brother. April had been such a girlie girl, and his time to pal around with other boys ended the year he entered junior high school. That was when his father, a rural sheriff, dropped dead of an embolism, and his mother went to work as a dispatcher to support what was left of their family. Money was tight, so as soon as they could, Logan and his sister asked around town for odd jobs.

Unlike the Malones, the Grant family had gone their separate ways. The Malone brothers shared traits easily seen by a casual observer like Logan. As he made his way to the bedroom he'd come to think of as his, he mulled over the good times Daphne's family must have at weekend barbecues and holiday get-togethers. After Logan's dad died, his mom hadn't made much of an effort to carry on with family traditions. It wasn't that Connie Grant didn't love her kids. She did. But after Garrison Grant's death, she pulled back, not allowing anyone to get too close to her. Including April and Logan. Oh, they all stayed loosely in touch, but there wasn't the same kind of intense, all-out family involvement shared by the Malones. Until now, that fact had never really struck Logan. Losing his dad at such a crucial time in his boyhood, and the subsequent altered state of their family, had definitely affected him. It probably had to do with why he'd been tagged with the lone-wolf label.

"Are you okay?" Daphne caught up with Logan outside his room. "Perry's not always a cutup. He's really smart. He reads more widely than any of us. Because of that, and because he refuses to settle down and apply himself, he takes a lot of heat from Mom and Dad. Especially Dad, who had high hopes that one of his kids would follow in his footsteps and be a doctor."

"Your dad's a doctor?"

"Psychiatrist. So you can see why Perry and I are such trials to the folks."

"If your dad's any good at his job, he ought to know why you're not falling in with the establishment."

"That's rich, Logan. I can't wait to tell Perry. He can point that out to Dad when Mom throws our next family gathering."

"Maybe you'd better not. You wouldn't want them to find out that the jab came from me. You're hiding me from your folks, remember." Logan went into his room, found the jar of face cream and scooped out an amount he thought would do the job.

Daphne had followed him in, and he didn't know why, but having her standing next to the bed where he slept and dreamed pretty racy dreams about her bothered Logan. Especially as one of her brothers, one who'd been imported specifically to stop any hanky-panky between them, was only a room away.

Shoving the jar into Daphne's hands, Logan gestured her toward the door.

"You're suddenly acting weird," she said, frowning at him over her shoulder as she stumbled across the threshold.

"How am I supposed to act? This isn't some garden party for me, Daphne."

Hurt eyes belied her painted-on smile. "You're mad because I planted the idea in Lori Jones's head to call a cop today, aren't you?"

"I'm not mad," he said, sounding weary. "You need to listen to what your brothers are trying to tell you, Daphne. I'm trouble. The sooner you can be rid of me the better it'll be for you."

"I get it. This sudden chill isn't about today. It's about last night. Well, don't worry that I'll foist myself on you once you leave here. I'm not as clueless as you and my brothers seem to think. I know all we had was a one-night fling." Reaching blindly for the doorknob, Daphne started to slam it in Logan's face. Having second thoughts, she closed it softly instead.

Inside the room, Logan stood with a handful of rapidly melting cream. He ducked into the bathroom and slapped it all over his face, hoping it'd be enough to do the job. He didn't trust himself to go ask Daphne for more. She'd been absolutely correct; the problem making him a sorehead was last night. But Logan wasn't comfortable brushing it off as a one-night fling.

It had been special. Daphne was special. Now, with Perry taking over the living room, Logan couldn't tell her what last night really meant to him.

As he stared at his almost clean face in the mirror, a sense of reason returned, reminding him that a woman like Daphne would be better off not knowing the truth. She deserved more than a one- two- or three-night stand. She deserved way more. But she obviously knew he couldn't give it. His guilt somewhat mollified, Logan dressed in the new clothes Perry Malone had brought him, and went next door to thank the man.

"Hey, whaddayaknow, everything fits." Perry glanced up from the TV to run a critical eye over Logan's jeans, boots, T-shirt and belt.

"I can't tell you how good it feels. If you ever need a favor, I hope my name's at the top of your list."

Perry laughed, and his eyes crinkled at the edges. "Dane and Kieran said you're in our fantasy-football group. Pull up a chair, and look at my laptop screen. Daph," he called. "Bring Logan a pad and pencil so he can list his players. You do have a computer, I hope. You'll need one to follow all this when league play starts next week. Any of the three of us can give you a disk with the forms we use. Oh, and we don't use our names, so you need to pick a handle."

"Like what? What's yours?"

"Trucker." Perry hiked up one shoulder.

Daphne dropped a spiral notebook and pencil in Logan's lap. "How about Rogue or Renegade? Do either of those feel right?"

Logan and Perry both eyed her sharply. She might as well have said bastard, for the way she spat the words.

"Kieran goes by Blue Man, and Dane uses Smokey," Perry went on as if his sister's little outburst hadn't occurred.

"Okay, I've got one. Big Heat. Fed or Feeb might scare people off. Street language lumps all cops under the term heat."

"Works for me." Perry called up his instant-messaging

feature and logged himself and Logan onto the site. Other players popped up to welcome the newcomer. A dozen guys in all were signed up for the new season.

Daphne knew they'd be engrossed for a while. Feeling decidedly left out again, she sorted through a stack of paperbacks Perry had dumped out of his suitcase. She selected one that interested her and curled up in a corner of the couch. She listened to Perry explain the game to Logan as they chose their players. Actually, she drifted in and out, finding Perry's familiar voice soothing and Logan's deeper tones affecting her in quite the opposite manner. Barely two chapters into the novel, she closed it and stood to announce, "I'm going into my bedroom to work on a mask."

Perry shooed her off with an offhand twitch of his hand. He continued pulling in screens and chatting to Logan, who processed her words and stored them for later. He, at least, offered a quick though vacant smile.

"Sheesh! You guys are so not a bundle of fun," she muttered.

Several hours later, there was a light rap on her bedroom door. Daphne straightened, rotating her shoulders to ward off a stiffness she'd just noticed. "Come in. The door's unlocked." She grabbed a towel to scrub bits of dried foam latex off her gloved fingers. Sinking down on the stool she used when she built a mask, she raised the goggles she wore and tested the gel on the Asian female face she'd just cast.

"I was just coming out to stick this in the oven to bake," she informed Logan, whose head popped through her door.

"Perry wanted to know if we should stick something in the oven for dinner. He noticed it preheating when we went into the kitchen to grab beer."

"Oh, goodness. I lost track of time. I'm afraid we'll have

to make do with something cold, or something I can cook on top of the stove. This head needs to bake for three to four hours uninterrupted." Standing, she reached for the lid to the mold.

She hadn't fit the two pieces together when Logan walked over with his hands jammed in his back pockets.

"That looks like a face."

"It is a face. A gel mask. They're the most realistic kind. She'll be a geisha when I'm finished painting her. Kieran's wife, Diana, asked me to make this for her to wear at a fashion designer's Halloween costume party. All the models try to outdo one another. Two weeks ago, I made a life cast of Diana's face. This will fit her perfectly. She's not going to tell anyone in advance what she'll be wearing. I know they'll never guess who she is."

Carefully picking up the mold with both hands, Daphne turned. "Step aside, please. Can you get the door? Mask making from latex foam is a lot like cooking a soufflé. So don't sneeze."

Perry stopped pawing in her cupboards and watched as Logan sped around Daphne and opened the oven door. Both men gave her plenty of room to place the mold inside on the middle rack.

"Why do I get the feeling we aren't going to eat that for supper?" Perry remarked.

"You're right. And don't be clomping around in here, either." Snapping off her gloves, Daphne tossed them in the trash, then washed her hands thoroughly. "Go back and watch TV for a while. After I put away everything in the bedroom, I'll fix tuna sandwiches."

"Ugh." Perry shook his head. "I've been counting on home-cooked meals."

"Then you'd better go to Mom's."

"And let her set me up with a date this weekend with some-body like Darla Landers? Remember her—the last piranha Mom found at her health club? I'll go down the street and bring us all barbecued chicken from Sam's Grill."

"Suits me. Just don't slam the door on your way out. While you're gone, I'll show Logan my other masks. If you're still interested," she said, sounding shy all of a sudden.

"I am. After seeing the one you just put in the oven, I'm even more curious."

Perry left immediately, and Daphne led Logan back to her room. "I intended to have you view them in the daylight. The effect is more dramatic. But you guys pooped away the afternoon on football stats."

Logan said nothing. He was a little nervous skirting the bed where they'd made love last night. Nevertheless, he followed her to the far wall, where she opened doors to a cabinet he hadn't noticed before.

When Daphne tilted the lampshade and let the light play across the dozens of realistic-looking masks stored on rows of shelves, Logan gave an involuntary gasp. "Holy cow!"

"What?" Daphne crowded in closer to see if something was wrong.

"These are incredible," he breathed, reaching out to touch the cheek of an old man with longish gray hair. "If I wore this teamed with a shabby suit and, say, I carried a cane, I'll bet I could walk right past Billy Holt's snitches sitting out front." Logan was so entranced, he let Billy's name slip.

"I don't know." Daphne thought Logan was getting carried away in his eagerness. "It'd take hours to make you up that well. I'd have to age your hands with wax, too. Anyway, you don't have a suit or suitable shoes. Old men don't usually wear boots."

"No, no. But this is the answer, Daphne. The answer to springing me. Perry can go out tomorrow and buy what I need, while you do your thing with my hands. You know, work your magic."

Daphne hurriedly closed the doors on her masks. She was still protesting when her brother arrived back with the food.

"Why are you so against that idea, sis?" Perry passed out the boxed dinners and dropped a pile of napkins in the center of the table. Steam curled out the minute they sat and opened the boxes. "You'd be helping Logan—if this works."

"That's the crucial if, isn't it? If my makeup works. In the theater, no one's life is at stake if someone in the audience happens to see through a disguise."

"That's the beauty of this plan, Daphne." Logan wiped barbecue sauce from his lips and fingers, using two napkins. "The men in that car won't look twice at an old geezer leaving this apartment building."

She stabbed unhappily at a chicken leg sticking out of her box. "If anything went wrong, how do you think I'd feel? I won't do it. It's too risky."

Logan reached across the table and took hold of her chin, forcing Daphne to meet his eyes. "I work in a risky business, Daph. Where's the woman who was willing to take a few risks herself to help me at Nat's party? And at today's party, you marched us right past men you knew were probably armed."

"That's not fair, Logan. We took those risks together. You're talking about walking out of here on your own."

"I am. And I'm also absolving you of any and all guilt."

Perry's head swung from one speaker to the other. He

studied Logan's earnest face and then his sister's. "Sis, you
hold the key to helping this man get back to doing a job that
may—probably will—benefit thousands. If I understood Dane
right, the organization he escaped is very likely responsible
for dumping a lot of drugs on L.A.'s streets."

Logan hated to add to Daphne's anxiety. But he could feel
her weakening. "Not only are they involved in drugs, but I
have reason to believe the mastermind of this organization is
bringing illegal arms in the next shipment. If I read the mani-
fests right, we're talking about enough automatic weapons to
arm all the hoodlums on the West Coast and then some. Worse
than arming hoodlums, I can't swear to the fact that he's not
planning to supply domestic terrorists."

Daphne pushed back from the table. "You guys are ganging
up on me. And you both know I can't refuse when you tell
me all this stuff. Which doesn't mean I have to like doing it."
Looking miserable, she stood. "I'm not hungry. I'm going to
my room until Diana's mask is done. Don't either of you say
another word to me tonight."

Logan muttered, "I'm really sorr—"

"Not a word," she said in a shaky voice. She rushed from
the room after delivering one last, brokenhearted glance at
Logan.

He pursed his lips, and wadded the entire stack of
napkins.

"I'm not going to ask what was behind the look in my
sister's eyes, Logan. I can guess, though. You have my word
I'll do whatever it takes to help you leave. After that, it'd be
best if you faded completely out of her life."

Logan sat there, ripping the paper napkins to shreds. He
wanted to throw the chair, strike the wall, or belt Perry Malone
in his unsmiling mouth. Instead, he finally rose, saying curtly,

"I'd like to argue with your logic. But I can't. If Daphne asks where I am when she comes out of her room, tell her I've gone to get a full night's sleep before an important mission."

168   JANICE KAISER

"Fill the syringe with your body," that Lukan ID, replaced its to weight. "I am almost true to reduced exercise or all her. I've done in me a full night's sleep before i go back in circulation.

CHAPTER NINE

THE SMELL OF FRESH COFFEE permeated Daphne's apartment when Logan rolled out of bed the next morning. He'd slept well. Far better than he'd expected. Due, undoubtedly, to the fact that he had a plan to get back into circulation.

In the kitchen he found brother and sister deep in earnest conversation. "You two look gloomy this morning. Problems?" Logan took down a cup and poured it full before he turned to see why they'd fallen silent.

"I'm complaining about her damn lumpy couch," Perry growled. "My back's killing me. Daphne's rehashing the subject she had her teeth into last night. She's afraid she'll make you up and then you'll walk out of here and get killed. She claims she didn't sleep a wink all night."

Logan downed a swig of coffee. "I slept like a baby." He dusted his knuckles across Daphne's chin. "Have faith, babe. I wish you'd shown me those masks earlier. I'd already be out of your hair." Logan offered Perry a smile. "I predict I'll be vacating the guest bedroom by noon, buddy. That mattress is great. Tonight you can catch your Zs in a real bed."

"He knows it's a firm mattress," Daphne said, slapping bread in the toaster. "It's his bed from home. Everything in this apartment used to be his and Kieran's."

"Well then, there's really no sense in holding this wake. Daphne, you said something about the time it'll take to make up my hands and to shape the mask to my face. How long, would you guess?"

"Depends on how well the mask conforms to your nose and cheeks. If it slips, you can't breathe well or see."

"You can fix it so it does fit, right?"

She nodded without enthusiasm. "It'll take a while, but yes, that's what I learned in school."

Logan turned to Perry. "I don't want to look too senior GQ. Maybe a little shopworn. There's a Salvation Army thrift shop over on Slauson. It'd be great if you could find a suit and dress shoes there in my size." Logan stated his jacket size. Perry had already bought him underwear, socks, pants and boots.

"How do you propose Perry smuggle something like a suit into the apartment?" Daphne buttered the toast and shoved one piece at each man. "I don't like this at all, Logan. We said from day one that our watchdogs will be monitoring anyone bringing in sacks of clothing. It'll look extremely fishy if half an hour after Perry waltzes in with a suit, you waltz out."

"Shuffle, darlin'," Logan said with a grin. "We talked about an old man. He'd move slowly and carefully."

"The thrift shop might not stock everything."

"They've got stuff in there you wouldn't believe," Logan said. "I hung out in that area, blending in with the homeless, picking up leads from two-bit gangbangers. Anything you buy in the thrift shop you could carry out rolled up under your arm, or stuck in a grocery bag."

"That's supposed to ease my mind?"

"Don't worry," Logan said softly. "I feel in my bones this is going to work like a charm."

"I'm glad one of us thinks so."

Perry drained his cup, rinsed it and turned it upside down on a paper towel. "I say we ought to trust Logan's judgment, Daph. He's been in this cloak-and-dagger business longer than we have."

Daphne shuddered. "It's even worse when you put it that way."

"If it works, you can add it to your résumé," Logan teased. "Think how that'll impress people—I was a makeup artist for the FBI. Has a certain panache, don't you think?"

Daphne slugged him hard. "I don't know why I'm worried about saving your sorry hide, when all you do is crack bad jokes. Sit. I need good light to do the first fitting. You'll need time to walk around the apartment getting used to the feel of it." She sighed. "If you weren't so anxious to leave, I'd make a lifecast of your face and neck. That kind of mask fits like a second skin." She swept her hand toward the kitchen table, where the mold she'd cooked last night sat on a Styrofoam head. It looked alive except for the empty eye sockets. The cheekbones were delicate, the chin gently rounded, and the eyes slightly almond shaped.

Both men gaped at the lifelike face. Logan was first to comment on the workmanship. "It's so real it's almost creepy. I can see why you keep all those masks behind closed doors, Daphne. You wouldn't be able to sleep in there otherwise."

"Stop. I can't stand all these backhanded compliments. Now sit, and I'll get started. Perry, I think the thrift shop opens at seven-thirty. I went there with Mom a few times to drop off bags of clothing collected by her church women's group."

Her brother tore off a corner of a magazine and jotted down a list. "I have shirt, tie, suit or sports coat, slacks and shoes."

"Keep in mind that you're after stuff somebody's grand-father would wear. I recall reading in my textbook that when you're aging someone, it works better to buy his or her cloth-ing a size larger. People shrink as they get older. Oh, and make it a bow tie, Perry. Old men often like ties that clip on because their hands are too shaky to tie knots. And when I get through working over Logan's hands, they'll look wrinkled and arthritic."

"You can really do that?" His eyes brightened in amazement.

"If I can't, I'll never be hired by a studio." She picked up the head and asked Logan to clear everything else off the table while she prepared the items she'd need.

"Sis, give me the keys to your car. I'd rather not fire up my tractor just to run a few blocks. Not only that," Perry added when his sister appeared to hesitate, "did it ever occur to you two that this elaborate ruse might not be necessary, after all? I'm about Logan's height. A little skinnier, to be sure. But if the guys out front only saw you dressed as a clown, they might think that's who I am—one and the same person. Especially if I drive away in the Volkswagen."

Daphne and Logan exchanged looks of dismay. "I don't know," Logan said slowly. "If they're really charting the com-ings and goings here, they'll have noted that you arrived in the big tractor rig two days after they followed Daphne and me here."

Perry tossed the car keys from hand to hand. "That's why you're the fed, and I'm a trucker. I wouldn't have thought they'd keep such close tabs."

"If they're that clever, Logan," Daphne murmured, concern darkening her eyes again, "what makes you think they won't see right through any disguise you attempt?"

"Because I'm gonna give the performance of my life, sweetheart," Logan said, winking Bogart style.

That ought to have eased her churning stomach, but it didn't. Daphne felt she'd laid out all the objections she had any right to voice. If they meant something to each other, she could ask Logan not to go, for her sake. Since they were little more than two people who'd shared a few days and one incredible night, she didn't have that right.

She returned ten minutes later, her arms full of props, including a trifold, lighted makeup mirror, which she plugged into the wall socket. "If you were willing to wait another day," she said lightly, "we could do this properly. I can borrow a wheelchair from Mrs. Bellows who lives on the second floor, and it'd be simple to make you look infirm. I have a uniform I wore to cosmetics class. As long as we're pretending, I'd wear a wig and wheel you right past those creeps."

Logan grasped her fluttering hands. He gazed full into eyes that were heavy with anxiety. "I let you shill for me once, Daphne, when I shouldn't have put you in such danger. The next time, I let you talk me into going out in public with you, and that was just plain stupid. My gut was twisted in knots during the entire party. From here on out, I'm risking my neck and no one else's."

He could tell she didn't like the finality of his words. But, like a trouper, she spread out her tools and set to work.

Logan watched his transformation in the mirror. First she tucked his longish hair under something she called a bald cap. Then she fit the latex mask over his face and he instantly looked old.

"Not a bad fit," she said, fussing to comb the bushy gray eyebrows. After heating a waxy substance in a small pan, she used a brush to paint around Logan's mouth, nose and, more delicately, around his eyes.

She asked him to talk and he did, at first without moving his lips.

"No, Logan. Talk normally. Say, the guys from the car take it in their heads to ask you something, even something simple, like the time. They'd spot you for a phony in a minute."

He practiced until the pull against his skin felt natural.

Daphne had just shaken out the gray wig and fit it carefully over his head and the exposed edges of the mask, when the front door opened and Perry strolled in.

"Whoa, brother!" He whistled through his teeth. "If you gave him a mustache, sis, he'd pass for Mark Twain."

She stopped fluffing out the hair at the back of Logan's wig and gazed at her brother in astonishment. "That's who this is. I mean, Mark Twain was my assignment. I do have the mustache in the other room, but I think that'd be a little much, don't you?"

"I do," Logan agreed. "So, Perry, did you get everything?"

"Wait till you see. And by the way, the dudes in the blue pimpmobile out there all but took my picture when I opened up the VW and crawled inside. They were only slightly less curious when I returned. I'm glad I asked the woman at the thrift counter to stuff all those things in a grocery sack from a local store. Anything else and they might have shaken me down."

"See, Logan," Daphne exclaimed. "They're on extra alert since I stupidly had Lori sic her sister's cop boyfriend on them."

"Hey, hey! Let me go put on the new duds. We'll leave it

up to Perry, okay? If he says I can fool them, then I want you to promise to settle down."

She nodded. Just barely. Her heart remained in her throat as Logan gathered up the sack and sauntered toward his bedroom. "You have to remember you can't walk like you own the damn world," she yelled after him.

Immediately he slumped his back and shoulders. Not even that helped allay Daphne's fears. How could she live with herself if she got him killed?

When Logan came into sight again, both Daphne and Perry were stunned. His metamorphosis was complete. Not only did Logan look smaller in the too-large clothes, as her textbook indicated, but with his bobbing head, he seemed to have a palsied step. He even spoke in a gruff, thin voice that sounded asthmatic.

"Fix my hands, little lady," he said, pausing in front of Daphne. "Oh, and close your mouth before you catch a fly." He cackled gleefully, and for the first time, Daphne thought he might actually pull off this charade.

"Logan, I take back most of what I said. You walk the walk and talk the talk. If you can manage to walk hunched over like this for however many blocks, I believe you'll succeed."

"Thanks, babe." He gripped her hands again. The emotion that overcame him was visible in the jerky way he rubbed his thumbs back and forth over her knuckles. She stopped him when he would've brought her hands to his lips.

"Don't—don't spoil my hard work," she chided in a husky voice. And she yanked her fingers back, discreetly trying to dash away tears skimming the lower lids of her eyes. "Sit, you goofball. If I'm going to take credit for this masterpiece, I want you walking out of here in full regalia. I, ah, let me warm the wax. I'll only be a minute."

Perry's eyes bored into her as she snatched up the small pan and hurried over to the stove. He pulled out the chair beside the one Logan had chosen and straddled it, much as Logan had done the first night he'd spent in this apartment.

That memory and others punched Logan in the gut. Punched him hard. He'd been anxious to go, to get on with his assignment. Until this very minute, he hadn't stopped to evaluate how he'd be affected by leaving. In his business, a man couldn't afford to let feelings enter into any of his undercover assignments. Logan had thought he'd be able to forget these last few days, to consider them simply part of this mission. Apparently not.

"I put the directions for getting into the fantasy-football Web site in your suit pocket," Perry said. "I listed all the e-mail addresses you'll need to get set up. Instant-message me when you find a computer. You don't reckon they'll send you on duty straight away, do you?"

Perry's question forced Logan to swallow the lump in his throat. "If I have anything to say about it, I'm taking part in the upcoming bust."

Daphne came back and started aging his hands. There was so much she wanted to say, but she couldn't admit the things running through her mind, not with Perry sitting right there. Anyway, they wouldn't be appropriate. And she couldn't allow herself to cry, sending Logan off in a puddle of tears. So she clamped her lower lip between her teeth, and let the men's words wash over her as she added bulging veins, age spots and a couple of arthritic knuckles to hands that brought her exquisite pleasure.

"There," she said, fifteen tough minutes later. "My work is finished, Logan. The rest is up to you." She almost lost her grip on the handle of the pan holding the warm, malleable wax. They both grabbed for it, but she slapped at his wrist. "Don't. You'll spoil everything. The wax needs a minute to set." Quickly, she turned away. "To say good luck might imply you'll need it. Just go, Logan. Godspeed."

He hesitated, rising clumsily. His eyes behind the mask clashed with those of Perry Malone. Logan hoped Daphne's craftsmanship hid the raw ache tormenting him. "Perry, how much do I owe you for all the clothes and stuff?"

"You owe Dane for the jeans, boots and T-shirt. What I spent today isn't worth repaying. Call it my donation to the homeless shelter. That's where all the proceeds from that shop go."

"Fine. I owe Dane's wife for sending my niece a birthday gift, too. Tell him I'll look him up in the phone book when this is all over and I'll drop a check in the mail."

"You won't stop to see us?" Daphne stood at the sink, running water into the pan, her back to the men. They both heard the quaver in her voice.

"I'll be pretty busy," Logan said, his own voice none too steady. He shared another veiled glance with Perry, when Daphne simply nodded several times.

"Sending a check would probably be best," Perry said pointedly, beginning to edge him toward the door. "I'd shake hands with you, but Daph would kill me, since I'd wreck all her hard work."

The door was open and Logan had one foot over the threshold when Daphne rushed out of the kitchen. "Oh, wait a second. Your phone. The one Simon sent with the pizza. I saw it on the coffee table. Here, I'll tuck it in your pocket. But you can't stick your hands in your pockets, okay? You don't want to ruin the wax."

"You keep the phone. When I get to the office, I'll call you on it. Just to let you know I made it. Okay?"

"I'd like that." Daphne rubbed her palms nervously up and down her thighs. She stopped abruptly and wrapped her arms around her waist. "Well, goodbye again."

Logan took two steps. He turned back and blocked the closing door with his foot. "I forgot to ask how I'm supposed to return the mask and wig to you."

"Keep them," she said quickly. Now she wanted nothing more than for Logan Grant to be on his way. Her mind had skipped ahead to the promised phone call. Daphne didn't think she'd breathe again until it came.

Perry nudged Logan's shoe aside and continued shutting the door. "Yeah, man. In your line of work, you might be able to put that disguise to good use sometime."

Logan tipped his head briefly in acknowledgment, but before he even reached the landing below, he knew he'd never be able to look at the mask or the wig again without remembering Daphne Malone. Without remembering every nuance of her easy smile. Every velvety touch of her soft skin.

It didn't pay for a man in his position to indulge feelings like that. With a shake of his head, Logan hurried to the front door of the building. He took a deep breath before he shoved open the front door. Showtime. Then he blanked his mind to everything except ambling safely down the street, around the corner and away from the blue car.

The closer he got to his office without having anything happen, the easier Logan breathed. Once he'd let himself into the agency building using his palm print, he felt cocky enough to whistle. It was a darned good thing Daphne hadn't covered the underside of his hands with wax. At the time, his brain had been too addled to consider how he'd get into the building.

Now that he was past the first checkpoint, he decided it would be fun to burst straight into Simon's office. Of course, he'd run the risk of being shot by one of the agents. But not if he convinced Lupe, their go-to girl on the front desk, that he had a private appointment with Simon.

Logan punched into the office, using his private key code. He was almost disappointed to find Lupe's desk vacant, as were the desks of agents who sat in nearby cubicles. A glance at the wall clock showed him why. Feeding time at the zoo. In other words, most had gone out for lunch.

Logan slipped past cubicles where two agents were talking on their phones. Neither paid him any attention. Afraid to grin in case he screwed up Daphne's mask, he opened Simon's door and limped inside.

The older, balding man looked up from papers spread out over a messy desk. "Who the hell are you?" he demanded, half rising from his chair. "And how did you get past security?" Simon's hand shot to a shoulder holster he'd probably worn so many years, it fit him as well as Logan's mask fit the contours of his face.

"Relax, boss. It's only me. Logan." He did chuckle then. Simon's slack jaw said it all. Logan had to laugh when his boss stumbled backward and actually fell into his chair.

"Logan?" Simon's breath came in short spurts.

"Yep. You aren't going to expire on me, are you, old man?"

"Look who you're calling old." Simon got up and made a slow circuit of Logan. His sharp eyes missed no part of the disguise. "I thought you were holed up in an apartment with that girl, the one I did a security check on. I talked to her a couple of times on the phone."

"I was." Logan sat gingerly on the edge of a straight-backed chair across from Simon. "Let me catch my breath. This mask is hotter than hell. Plus, walking eight blocks like an old duffer used more energy than a mile sprint."

"Get your breath. Then tell me why you took it upon yourself to disobey my direct order to stay under wraps until we put the Holt project to bed."

"If it hadn't been for my months of work, Simon, you wouldn't be anywhere near putting this one to bed. I want in on the capture. I deserve it."

Parrish leaned back, stuck both feet on his desk and dug a stick of gum out of a pack tucked in his shirt pocket.

Rocking back in his chair, Simon presented the picture of a relaxed man. But Logan knew better. The longer they went without Simon speaking, the tighter grew the knot forming in Logan's stomach.

"I've never known your ego to get in the way of a project, Logan. What's this about? You angling for brownie points—or a big bust to throw back at Liz?"

Logan tried to turn away from Simon's gaze, but his latex neck refused to budge. "I just like to finish what I start, Simon."

"Bullshit! You're a detriment to all of us. Billy's put out the word to smoke you on sight."

"But if I don't crop up somewhere, won't he and his cronies be nervous enough to pull the plug on the whole shebang?"

"They can't." Simon cracked his gum. "I told you I had a second man in the organization. The ship left Thailand weeks ago as scheduled. Our spotters say it refueled in Honolulu and steamed out the day it had to in order to make the marina at Del Rey this weekend, which is the date you gave me. I have almost everything in place to give Ratsami the surprise of his life. And you're not going to throw a monkey wrench in the works, you understand?"

"Yes, sir." Logan seethed inside.

"So, tell me. What magician pulled off this costume?"

"Daphne," Logan said without thinking. "She helped in my original escape."

"I thought you said she was some kind of party clown."

"Temporarily. Until a movie studio hires her to do makeup. She does great work, huh?" Logan sat up straighter and gestured at his face.

"More than great," Simon mused, narrowing his eyes to study Logan. "What else does she do? What other disguises?"

"I don't know. Well, I saw a cupboard full of masks she's made. Last night, she cooked up one for her sister-in-law to wear at some costume ball. A geisha. Just looking at it, I'm convinced she'll fool everyone."

Simon turned the package of gum over and over, all the while studying Logan with pure concentration. "Get her on the phone."

"Excuse me?" Logan threw his shoulders back.

"This Daphne—get her on the phone."

"Why?" Logan tried to frown, but realized it was impossible.

"Because I intend to hire her," Simon bellowed.

"Hire her? For what?"

"Has that mask fried your brain? I think you've provided me with the last piece in my puzzle. I've been trying to figure out how I'd openly place agents at the marina. A group large enough to do the job without calling on local cops, since we're pretty sure Holt has a man or two inside. We have to assume he's been tipped off about our agents here, who they are and what they look like. Your little lady friend is going to change the appearance of four or five team members so they don't have agent written all over them. I didn't think of this earlier or I could've flown in a makeup artist from headquarters. Luckily this woman's already here. I'll plant a squad under Billy's nose. On a yacht in the marina. We'll have them look like party-goers. The idle rich." Simon chortled at his own cleverness.

"Good idea, but it won't work," Logan said severely. "It takes Daphne hours to make somebody up to look as legit as I do now—even if she didn't use masks, but altered faces using makeup and props. Somebody with her talent would have to live with the team. I mean, you couldn't move a yacht into a berth at the last minute. That would send Holt an automatic warning. A red flag."

"That's why I plan to hire her, Logan. She'll go out on the boat with Ron Thorpe, Randy Tabor, Mellie Banks and a few others I'll decide on later."

"Thorpe? No way in hell! Throwing a sweet woman like Daphne at Thorpe is like tossing her to the sharks." Leaping up, Logan slammed his palms on Simon's desk so hard some of the wax Daphne had used on his hands splintered.

Simon raised an eyebrow. His hands remained rock steady, as did his voice when he responded. "Ron should be too busy with agency work to move in on your woman, and I'll threaten him with a reprimand if he does. Ron's our senior man, Logan."

"Daphne's not my woman. I don't have a woman. But reprimands haven't fazed Thorpe in the past, now, have they?"

"I don't need your permission to hire her, Logan. Nor do I really need you to phone her, since you obviously have strong objections. I have her number right here." Parrish brushed aside a stack of papers and pulled out a scrap with a couple of phone numbers written on it.

"I left my safe cell with her," Logan growled, stomping over to stare out the window. Their floor was up high enough that he could see the ocean shimmering in the distance. "I planned to call and tell Daphne I'd made it here safely. I guess she'll know that, though, if you phone her."

"Any reason she can't come down and sign a contract today?"

"Only that she's a babe in the woods, Simon. She's a civilian, not an operative."

"She'll be a makeup artist, plain and simple. Anyway, correct me if I'm wrong, but didn't this lady save your ass, my friend?"

Logan had no comeback. Still, he felt edgy and prayed Daphne would have enough sense to turn down Simon's offer. Or, if not, that Perry would make her see reason.

Wrong on all counts, apparently. Daphne agreed to come and discuss Simon's offer. Simon used his speaker phone, so Logan could hear both sides of the conversation. There was no mistaking the excited lilt in Daphne's response.

"She'll be here in half an hour. I guess you heard me say she could bring her brother. What's he like? Is he liable to punch me out?"

"I wish," Logan muttered. "Either of her other two brothers might. Perry's the most mild-mannered of the three."

"No wonder you say she's not your girl. With a last name like Malone and three brothers. I grew up in the Irish quarter of Boston," he said with sudden seriousness. "Those guys protect their women. If I had any other choice, I might rethink this, Logan."

Logan cracked his knuckles and the last remnants of

Daphne's work on his left hand crumbled. Bending, he scooped up the wax and dumped it in Simon's wastebasket. "You don't need me hanging around during the interview. I have extra clothes in my office. Think I'll go into the men's room and change back into me."

"No. Don't do that, Logan."

"Why not? I'm not planning on looking like my own grandpa for the rest of the day."

"You'll need the disguise to return to her apartment because I don't want Billy's watchdogs getting suspicious of an old guy who left the building and didn't return. That might start them thinking about disguises."

"I'm not going back. I'm checking my in-basket and e-mail. Then I'm going home."

"No can do. Your complex is crawling with Holt's sharp-shooters. Which is why I know he's got some inside info on our agents."

"Okay. I'll wear this disguise until I get there. No big deal."

"As good an agent as you are, Logan, today your brains are mush. You think those bastards don't know by now which apartment is yours? A light pops on and bam. Our guy said they have their best shooter whiling away his hours in an apartment directly across the alley from yours. Billy means business, son. He can't afford not to. Part of my deal with your girl will include giving you safe haven until this task ends."

"She's not my anything! So no, I'm not going to her place. I can't."

"Why?"

Logan latched on to the first reasonable excuse to pop into his head. "Her brother's a long-haul trucker, home on a break. Last night he slept on the couch because I was in her one guest room. This morning he said the couch killed his back and he's not crashing there another night."

"Then you take the couch. Or the floor. And don't claim you have a bad back. I just got copies of everyone's physicals. You're in top shape, Logan."

What Logan said to that didn't bear repeating. And Simon distracted him, anyway, by shoving a sheaf of papers into his hands. "These are the facts we've built on the organization so far. While we cool our heels waiting for Ms. Malone, give them the once-over. See if you have anything to add, or tell me if you see flaws. I'm going out to let Lupe know I'm expecting visitors."

"Lupe wasn't at her desk when I came in."

"Ah, so that's how you managed to barge right into my office. Her sister's in town. They were meeting for lunch, but I'm sure she's back by now. Unlike others who shall remain nameless, Lupe would never break a standing order of no longer than one hour for lunch."

Logan toyed with the idea of throwing Simon's stapler at his fat head as he marched out of the office. Deciding to curb the childish inclination that would surely get him fired, he flung himself back in the chair, but ended up so engrossed in what he was reading, he lost track of time. It seemed impossible that a half hour had slipped by but it must have, as Simon strode through the door with Perry and Daphne in tow. Logan knew that, because he caught a glimpse of Perry, and a shapely pair of legs besides. Otherwise, Simon's wide girth blocked the guests from seeing into the room.

Logan was unprepared for Simon's angry statement. "The least you could've done, Logan, was tell me the lady's pregnant."

Logan shot to his feet. "What? Who's pregnant?"

Simon moved, and sure enough, there stood Daphne, cling-ing to Perry's arm. She wore a flaming-red wig and a sleeve-less maternity dress that bulged in front as if she were seven or eight months pregnant. Logan's sagging mouth refused to close, mostly because he'd begun to laugh.

Daphne let go of Perry. She ignored Logan's laughter, and spoke to Simon. "My brother thought my dressing this way was silly. I pointed out that if you're hiring me to help with an important case, maybe it'd be to everyone's advantage if I didn't come here looking like me. I don't have red hair, Mr. Parrish. And I'm not expecting a baby."

Simon's gray eyes took on a twinkle. "Ms. Malone. Not only are you a genius at creating illusions, but you have a sharp mind, as well. I like that, young woman. I like that a lot."

Perry muscled his way to the foreground, alleviating any need for Logan to protest Simon's decision to hire Daphne. The Malone brother Logan knew as quite friendly, puffed up like an adder. "I'm here to tell you in person that you're not hiring my sister to work for the FBI."

Simon dealt the interloper one of his evil glares. He shut the door and addressed Daphne. "Am I wrong in assuming you're of legal age to make job decisions for yourself?"

"Ye-es," she said, darting Perry a worried glance. "Er, no. I am over twenty-one."

"Well, my request is fairly straightforward. I need to disguise an entire team, and I think you have the expertise to help me do that. If your first efforts produce the effect I need—well, I foresee making use of your services on a regular basis."

"So you're offering me a permanent job with the FBI?" Daphne's eyes, which Logan noticed were no longer tawny gold but dark brown, almost popped out of her head. Logan thought she'd also been clever to wear contact lenses.

Perry stepped forward again. "Sir, Daphne has a…checkered past when it comes to jobs. Things happen to her. I hate to call my sister a klutz, but…she's a klutz."

Simon took a seat behind the massive desk. He motioned for everyone to find a chair. He contemplated a moment, then turned to Logan. "Agent Grant, give me your unvarnished assessment of Ms. Malone's professional abilities."

Logan teetered on the edge of blurting out all the negative job experiences Daphne had shared the first day they'd met. Damn, he didn't want her in harm's way. He especially didn't want her falling under the spell of a Romeo like Ron Thorpe. But he had another objection, perhaps the hardest one to ignore—the fact that another woman he'd cared for had ended up stabbing him in the back because of a job.

Everyone in the room waited in silence. Simon expected the truth. Logan knew Perry wanted him to lie so Simon would refuse to hire Daphne. And she gazed at him with love and hope in her eyes, begging for a chance she knew full well he could dash. "I, uh, am living proof Daphne has the talent and the guts to do anything asked of her."

Averting his eyes, not wanting to see the anger stirring in Perry Malone, Logan also needed to escape the joy that leaped at him from Daphne's smile.

Simon advised them all to stay seated. Hitting the intercom, he growled, "Lupe, is that contract I dictated ready to sign?"

"Simon, I found nothing amiss in this report." Rising, Logan motioned to Perry. "Let's go to my cubicle while Simon and Daphne go over her contract." Seeing Perry about to object, he added in a low tone, "Please. I have a proposition for you."

"This had better be good, Judas," Perry muttered for Logan's ears alone.

"I think it's worth your time to hear me out." Logan led the way to his cubicle, ignoring the curiosity aimed at them by agents who hadn't seen him come in, and who had no idea why their boss had allowed some old guy to use a coworker's office.

Perry refused the offer of a chair. "What's this about? I'll hear you out before I tell my brothers what a fool thing you did. After that, they'll tear you limb from limb."

"I agree. Unless the four of us work in tandem to watch out for Daphne."

Crossing his muscular arms, Perry nodded at Logan to continue.

"I've been ordered to lie low and it sticks in my craw for any number of reasons. This operation's going down near Marina del Rey. Kieran said that's where you guys berth your fishing boat." He barely waited for Perry's nod. "I'm proposing we trawl for bottom-feeders on our own, if you get my drift."

Perry obviously did. He grinned and pumped a fist in the air.

Because Logan had already ruined the wax job on his hands, he clasped Perry's large mitt between both of his, and delivered a handshake Perry wouldn't soon forget. It bothered him a bit that he hadn't spelled out exactly what Daphne's mission entailed. But then, maybe the less her brothers knew, the better for all concerned.

CHAPTER TEN

DAPHNE, STILL DRESSED as a pregnant woman, exited Simon Parrish's office just as Perry and Logan stepped out of Logan's cubicle. She saw them and waved her contract aloft, ending in a little soft-shoe victory shimmy that had several other agents stopping their work to stare. In fact, the threesome garnered a great deal of attention, and Logan felt a little smug on Daphne's behalf.

As none of his coworkers knew him disguised as he was, Logan realized their trio did present quite a bizarre picture.

For that reason and others, he rushed Perry and Daphne out the door without attempting to introduce them around. He said nothing until they were alone on the elevator. "According to Simon, my apartment's staked out more rigorously than yours, Daphne. Much as I hate to ask, I need to go back with you and change out of these clothes. At least, I now have some cash to work with—and I know there's a point Holt will pull his men off stakeout." He displayed an envelope tucked in the inside pocket of his suit jacket. "Agents always keep cash in their desks to use in case they need to lie low. Writing checks or using a credit card can get a guy killed faster than anything."

Daphne hugged herself. "Pinch me, somebody. I can't

believe your world's soon going to be my world, Logan. Look at this." She proudly displayed a check with enough zeros to cause her brother to do a double take. "Mr. Parrish gave me an advance to use for clothes he wants me to wear on this project, and for makeup supplies. Plus, I have my own safe phone." She pulled it out of a small purse slung over her shoulder.

As they left the elevator, Logan did his best to scowl under the tight mask. It frustrated him to think he'd been the one responsible for getting Daphne into this fix. "That's not information you want to spread around in public." He thought he managed to convey his displeasure in his tone. And was sure he had when Daphne turned, the sparkle suddenly snuffed from her expression.

Perry, leading the pack toward the main door, obviously missed the undercurrent between Logan and his sister. He waited for them at the door, pulling car keys out of his pocket and kicking impatiently at a plant stand holding a huge potted palm. "What kind of duds did that guy upstairs tell you to buy, Daph?" he burst out when they caught up to him. "Seems to me that's a lot of dough for those smock thingies haircutters wear." Discussing beauticians' attire obviously made Perry uncomfortable.

"Silly, you'd know what Mr. Parrish expects of me if you and Logan hadn't dashed off like spoilsports. I'm supposed to hide a team of his agents in plain sight on a big expensive yacht someone's parked or is going to park at the marina. That is so cool. Everyone on board has to pretend to be part of the elite yachting crowd. This money—" and she waved the check in Perry's astonished face "—is to buy me slinky cocktail dresses, designer swimwear and shorts, as well as wigs and makeup."

Logan thought Perry was going to explode right there in

the lobby. Logan knew exactly when it dawned on the other man that Logan had been aware of the entire scope of the operation.

Perry grabbed Logan's shirt front and twisted the collar tight around his fake neck. "You SOB."

Daphne dropped her purse, her contract and the check, and dived between the struggling men. "Perry Malone, what on earth has gotten into you? Stop! Turn Logan loose this instant. You're hurting him, and you're going to ruin my mask."

"I'm not doing half of what Dane and Kieran will do when they hear about this."

Logan fell back against the wall, grateful for the air now flowing into his lungs. If he wanted, he could wipe the floor with the younger man. Instead, he counted it fortunate indeed that the building lobby remained empty. Saying nothing, he knelt and gathered Daphne's belongings. Handing them over to her, he said, "This is an argument we need to hammer out back at your place. You two drive, and I'll walk. I just need you to unlock the entry when I get there."

Daphne opened her purse and handed him a set of keys. "Perry has his own set, and we're in his truck."

"Pretending to be pregnant, I'm surprised you were able to climb into that thing."

Logan slanted her an oblique glance. It still rattled him to see her rounded belly. He found himself wondering if that was how she'd look if she was really expecting a baby. April had complained about more than weight gain before she had Natalie and during her current pregnancy, but Logan had to admit he hadn't paid much heed. And he didn't know why such trivia plagued him now, when he had more important stuff to think about. Getting and keeping Daphne's volatile brothers on his side, for one thing.

"Why don't you ride home with us, Logan?" Daphne glared unhappily at her brother's stony face.

"It's a bad idea for us all to arrive together. And Perry needs time to cool off."

"He has no business acting like this. It's just another example of him—of all my family—treating me like a child. A lamebrained one at that."

Perry thrust open the door. "It's because you pull such idiotic stunts, Daphne. This latest being a case in point."

"I think you're missing the real issue, Perry. Which is— it's my life. Have you forgotten how everyone in the family was against you buying a truck and being constantly on the road? I remember precisely what you told them they could do. And here you are years later. All I'm asking for is the same consideration you wanted."

Logan noticed their voices were rising and people out on the sidewalk had begun to take an interest. "Perry, my friend, if you don't want an angry mob coming to the rescue of your poor pregnant sister, you'd better bite your tongue and move on down the street."

The others saw what Logan meant. They fell silent. Logan slipped his hands in his pockets, watching Perry boost Daphne into the tractor cab. She looked so fragile perched high on the seat of the rig, and a pang of fear crept into his heart.

After Perry drove off, he stood there through several changes of traffic lights wrestling with what he'd done. He could go upstairs and try to argue Simon out of sending her on this job. But chances were better than good that Simon would tune him out.

Head down, Logan strode back toward her apartment, kicking aside any stray bit of litter that fell across his path. It wasn't until he'd turned the corner onto her street that he realized how close he'd come to blowing his cover. And this time the white car sat squarely in front of the steps leading into Daphne's building.

Logan gave himself a good hard shake and assumed the half-limping gait of an old man. He'd forgotten the joy attached to simple freedoms like going out on daily strolls. One thing he was positive about, though—tonight, one way or another, he planned to leave Daphne's apartment. Billy's men were getting restless. How long before they got it into their heads to pull a door-to-door search? He'd seen them do that via two methods. One, pretending to be cops or feds. The other by intimidation and brute force. The carnage they were capable of leaving behind sent chills up his spine. Logan could feel himself getting too involved. With Daphne. With her family. But especially with her.

Sweating under his mask, he sensed the men in the car monitoring his progress up the steps. He didn't have to fake the nervous twitch of his hands as he rammed the key into the lock. If luck remained in his corner a while longer, their eyesight wouldn't be good enough to see that his hands looked younger than his other features. It took every ounce of control to enter the building slowly and not race up the stairs. Logan retained his measured gait until he was well out of view. Riding the wave of that small success, he didn't expect to unlock the door to Daphne's apartment and find her sitting on the couch, crying her eyes out.

"What's wrong?" Logan locked the door and quickly crossed to her. Perry stomped around in circles.

She wadded a partially shredded tissue and wiped her eyes. "Those men downstairs stopped us on our way in. They asked us what we knew about a couple living here who occasionally dress up as clowns."

Stripping off his gray wig, Logan didn't feel the expected rush of air. He'd forgotten Daphne had stuffed his hair under that skullcap.

"Why don't you ask her what kind of agent she'll make?" Perry snapped. "She froze out there. Froze, I'm telling you."

"I did not. I shook like a sapling in a hurricane," Daphne admitted reluctantly.

"Same difference," Perry muttered.

"Will somebody tell me what they asked and what you told them? They're still out there and you two are both alive, so one of you must have appeased them."

"Perry did. He said we only moved in a few weeks ago. I think he said he'd been on the road but was home now until after the baby came."

"That's about all I said. I let them think we'd just been to the doctor and I needed to get her upstairs so she could put her feet up. Of course, if they'd been really observant, they'd have caught me in that lie. Do her ankles look puffy to you?"

Logan let a hot gaze run the length of Daphne's long, slender legs. He knew their slenderness belied their strength, given the way she'd clamped them around his hips in the throes of their tussle across the bed the other night.

Shrugging away the swift reaction he felt in remembering, Logan dropped down on an adjacent chair. "You passed their test, and everything's okay. So, why are you crying?"

"Because Perry's insisting I call Simon and quit. He's phoned Dane and Kieran. You don't want to know what they had to say. Between them, they listed every minor and major infraction I've ever made in twenty-six years." Her shoulders slumped and tears trickled down her cheeks again. "I know they're right, Logan. There's hardly anything I can point to that's ever not ended in disaster. I can't fight facts. I was just waiting for you to get here. Will you phone Simon? Thank him for the opportunity, but say I can't chance bungling this assignment for everyone else."

Logan noticed that she'd removed the contact lenses. The impact of seeing her beautiful eyes wet with tears drove a nail through his chest. "Tell me how I go about shedding this mask so I don't wreck it," he said brusquely, brushing aside her plea.

Dutifully, Daphne rose. "Let me get my kit." She left the room and came back a minute later with a case similar to a doctor's bag. "I didn't use much spirit gum to affix the mask. There's some on the back of your neck, and I'll loosen it carefully. At the hairline I had to blend the mask with your skin." She took out a bottle, which she uncapped, and little by little removed the adhesive. She apologized when it became apparent that she was pulling his hair.

Reaching up, he grasped her wrist. "It's okay, Daphne. The disguise did the trick. Do whatever needs to be done to get it off in one piece."

She worked swiftly and quietly, but Logan could hear her breath catch every so often. She was obviously trying not to cry. Logan got angrier and angrier at the man who hovered like a hulk in the background, and at his absent brothers as well. He wondered why they were too blind to see how capable their delightful, fun-loving sister was. He wasn't happy about Simon's hiring her, but didn't her brothers care that they were tearing her down? Dammit, he cared.

"There," she breathed at last, sliding the mask off and onto the Styrofoam head, where she pinned it after cleansing the inside. "Now you need to go shower in case you're allergic to any of the mastic remover I used."

"In a minute." Logan pulled off the cap and scrubbed at

his hair with one hand, while with the other he snatched up the safe phone he'd left lying on the coffee table. "I'm going to start with Dane. Someone tell me how to reach him."

Though frankly curious, Perry supplied the number.

Logan lashed out as soon as Dane came on the line. "You fathead! Who's calling? Logan Grant, that's who. No, no. You listen to me. You have a kind and decent sister here who's sobbing her heart out. She's unbelievably talented. You and the rest of your family ought to hang your heads in shame for undermining her like you do. I'm not overjoyed that my boss offered her a job. I'm less thrilled that she said yes. But I'll stand behind her because, dammit, she has the right to say for herself what she does or doesn't want to do." Still fuming, he pressed the disconnect button.

"I'll take on Kieran next."

His disdain clearly turning to respect, Perry volunteered his brother's number without missing a beat.

Daphne hung over Logan, alternately wringing her hands and fluttering them. "Logan, I appreciate what you're trying to do, but you've never seen Dane or Kieran when they're well and truly furious."

Logan moved her hands aside. "Kieran? Ah, good. You're on another line with Dane? Hang up. You can talk to him when I've finished." Then he pretty much repeated word for word what he'd said to the older brother, adding for good measure, "You want to come over here and knock my block off, feel free. I'm not going anywhere until it gets dark. My advice is to give some thought as to how it'll look in the morning papers. A local cop, fireman and federal officer busted for tearing up an historic apartment. And for what? Because two heavy-handed, pea-brained men who ought to know better refuse to see their sister's no longer a child, but a grown woman." Click went the off switch.

"Hey, you left out the meatheaded trucker," Perry said amid gleeful laughter.

Logan glanced up from where he sat rubbing his face, which still felt tight after getting rid of the mask. Not joining Perry's laughter, he got to his feet. "I'm going to take a shower. That way I'll be clean and dressed when the morgue comes to collect my broken body."

Perry called down the hall at Logan's disappearing back. "Hey, Grant. I wonder if my brothers picked up on the message you sent loud and clear. You must really love Daphne not to see what a screwup she is. I mean, I love her, too, but…"

His words slammed into Logan with the power of a freight train. An out-and-out denial sprang to the tip of his tongue, but in his shock and dismay, he couldn't force it past his lips. Refusing to consider that there could be even a hint of truth in Perry's hurled allegation, Logan finally stammered out, "You're talking crazy, man." He floundered in the hall, his heart beating hard and fast. He looked right, then left, and didn't know which way to turn to avoid facing Perry's charge. "And you know what," he yelled back the moment he was able to assemble a coherent sentence. "I've decided not to wait around for the death squad. After I shower, I'm packing and I'm out of here."

Perry almost fell from his chair in his rush to scramble up and confront Logan. "Oh, that's brilliant. Like you have more sense than we do. Something you need to learn is that the Malone brothers talk big. We're not looking to meet our Maker, though. You, on the other hand, are gonna do something really dumb just to avoid our razzing."

Logan stared at him in the dim light of the hall.

"I'll go pack my gear while you clean up, Logan. Since you're determined to get yourself killed, the least I can do is hang with you. We have a deal, after all, and I need to get you down to the marina. Daphne has all sorts of theater props lying around. I swear I'll find something that'll work well enough to sneak you out of here to where I parked my rig."

Not trusting his voice, Logan blinked his concession.

Fifteen minutes later, he emerged much refreshed and feeling satisfied with the plan he and Perry had forged. Having swept all spare items that belonged to him into the grocery bag in which Perry had delivered the Salvation Army suit, Logan carried it into the living room, only to experience another shock. Simon Parrish loomed over Daphne, who sat in the recliner shredding another tissue.

She wasn't crying, but her eyes were red and swollen, indicating that she certainly had been. Right now she was blabbering a mile a minute.

"Simon, what are you doing here?" Logan burst out. "Are you trying to get us all shot? How did you get past our watchdogs? I know for a fact that a good share of Billy's goons can spot an agent a mile off."

"Not the ones out front. Anyway, I've been doing this work since before you were born, kid. I think I'm proficient enough at skirting jerks like them."

"Obviously," Logan drawled. And his boss did look very different. He'd traded his usual white shirt and tie for a short-sleeved plaid sport shirt. He wore baggy khaki pants, tennis shoes and a baseball cap. A pair of mirrored shades were hooked at the throat of a T-shirt worn underneath the sport shirt.

"Suppose you tell me, Logan, why I got an irate phone call from a man who said he's my makeup artist's oldest brother.

He threatened to kick agency butt all the way to D.C. and back to L.A. if I don't tear up her contract."

Daphne hunched farther over her knees.

Perry, already lounging near the only escape route, waited to see what Logan intended to say to the older man.

Dismissing Simon with a shrug, Logan looked straight to Daphne.

"Don't look at her," Simon commanded. "She fed me some poppycock about how you recommended her without really knowing her history."

"Hogslop! I'm willing to lay money on the fact that any negative history she's accumulated can be dumped squarely on the doorstep of her overbearing brothers."

"Mr. Tightwad of the Agency stands ready to place a bet?" Simon's pewter eyes glittered with interest. "Hmm." Spreading his feet, Parrish folded his arms and brushed a thumb back and forth across a protruding lower lip. "Well, she did say she might reconsider if I stuck you on the yacht with her instead of the agent I've been considering."

Logan's hope surged. But it fizzled and died the minute he saw the sudden outpouring of foolish love in Daphne's watery eyes. Love as clearly evident to Simon and Perry...

Rolling down the top of the sack, Logan hardened his resolve and let his gaze move past his boss. "Like you said earlier, bringing down Ratsami's dirty organization is our only goal. It's time to let go of individual egos. Perry, did you locate a camouflage you think will work for me?"

Simon shifted his stance. "I thought I told you to stay put, Logan. Where in hell are you going?"

"Underground. Perry has a safer hideout." Logan made it clear that he was ready to head off.

Daphne's brother unzipped the side pocket of the duffel

bag that sat at his feet. He dragged out a man's brown wig, spiked in the new style so prevalent on TV. A phony, slightly oversize nose and jug ears completed the ensemble.

Logan stuck the nose over his, but it promptly fell off. The ears stayed, but looked totally fake.

"Mercy, you two," Daphne said, hopping up. "If you're determined to leave here, Logan, at least give me a minute to fix it so your disguise isn't so obvious." She picked up her leather kit, which still sat where she'd put it when she removed Logan's mask. A few wads of spirit gum, followed by a couple of whisks of her makeup brush, and the others in the room were nodding their approval. She also worked on Logan's chin, and when he glanced in the wall mirror, he saw she'd done away with the cleft he'd been born with.

"If you wait a sec, I'll get a pair of contacts that will make your eyes the color of Perry's."

"What if he can't get the contacts out again?" That came from Perry.

She sighed. "I'll show you how to tug on your lids and pop them out." She dashed out of the room, and came back as quickly. "This is the case, and this is wetting solution to keep your eyes moist." Daphne pressed the bottle of solution into Logan's hand. Opening the case, she extracted one lens, then rose on tiptoe and leaned full against his chest.

Reacting to the brush of her soft breasts, Logan sucked in his breath and stepped backward—straight into Perry.

Daphne sighed. "You have to hold still, Logan. I'm good at this, but not if you keep moving."

He did his best to stop breathing. To stop being moved by her touch. To stop melting in his shoes from the merest hint of her sweet, light scent.

"Blink," she ordered. "I'm done."

Logan did, all the while wishing she'd remove her hands from the front of his shirt. Please let her remove her hands. But he blinked as he'd been told, and gnashed his back teeth in order to remain upright.

Smiling, Daphne trailed her fingers past his shirt pockets and over his taut belly—lingering, it seemed—before she stepped back. "You'll be fine, Logan, if you can keep the lenses from popping out between the apartment and Perry's truck. Oh, here. Don't forget your phone," she said, grabbing it up and pressing it into Logan's free hand. His other hand still had a death grip on the contact-lens case.

"Perry, you make sure you watch your rearview mirror. If I'm going to be part of the team, I don't see why you guys can't tell me where you're going."

Logan loved her small pout. It managed, like nothing else had, to engage his brain and eject it from where it had lodged, much below his head. "Are you saying you've changed your mind and decided to accept the job?"

"I want to," she murmured. "I really do. It's right up my alley. And who knows how soon one of the studios will have an opening."

Simon, who'd remained silent for a time, played a trump card he must have held, just waiting for the perfect opportunity. "Need I remind you that most citizens finding themselves in similar circumstances would consider it their civic duty to help their federal government?"

Daphne sawed her lip with her bottom teeth. But Logan knew even as Perry opened the door and they let themselves out that Simon had scored the points he needed to assure her compliance, to say nothing of her undying loyalty.

"Just one thing, Simon," Logan said in afterthought. "Give me your word you won't team her with Ron Thorpe."

The agency head unwrapped a stick of gum and stuck it in his mouth. Carefully refolding the wrapper, he tucked it in his shirt pocket. "Go on, get! Worrywart. How about Lee Harriman? Better? I'll promise you Lee instead, if it'll make you happy."

Logan pictured the big, jovial man who'd raised five daughters of his own. "Fine. Lee suits me fine." Logan and Perry left as Simon led Daphne to the kitchen table, about to go over every step of the part she'd play on the yacht.

"Guys, wait a sec," she called, slipping away from Simon's light grip on her elbow. "Perry, don't breathe a word of this to the folks. Cross your heart? And Logan, promise me you'll stay safe."

Dainty as a butterfly, she bestowed a kiss on each man before she blushed and withdrew, slamming the door hard and shooting the dead bolt home.

"Well," Perry exclaimed as the two clattered down the stairs. "Suppose you tell me again that you have no feelings for my sister."

"Drop it," Logan warned.

"Why? It's easy to see Daphne's wearing her heart on her sleeve."

"If you get the chance, you'll have to throw cold water on any hopes or dreams she has connected to me."

Perry said little for the next few, tense minutes as they left the building and strolled seemingly without concern to his truck. He took care to unlock the passenger door first, so Logan could vault inside and be out of the men's sight.

"You know something I don't get?" Perry remarked. "Wouldn't you think that after having those same nuts parked in front of the building this long, someone would have reported them to the cops?"

"Maybe they have," Logan returned, glad to move on to a subject other than his feelings or lack thereof for Daphne.

"Then why hasn't someone hauled them off?"

"That's the biggest snag in this entire operation, Perry. We're almost certain the organization has a stoolie or two working for the local police. Kieran agrees."

"I don't know why I'm surprised," Perry mused aloud, adjusting the side mirrors once the engine roared to life. "I'm not naive, but on the other hand, I go through life expecting the folks I deal with to be honest."

With one eye on the passenger-side mirror, Logan grunted an expletive.

"Oh hell, are we being followed?"

"Nope. Not by those guys, at least. I was merely wondering how my life would be if I viewed everyone I met as a potential good guy."

"Come on. It can't be that bad. You hafta trust your fellow agents."

"Not all of them," Logan said, thinking about his ex-wife and a few others he could name.

"Jeez, are you going to burst my bubble and tell me some of you squeaky-clean feds aren't so squeaky clean?"

"By and large I think we all start out with high ideals. Guys like Simon, they hit their heads against brick walls year after year, fixing what they can. A percentage of us burn out early."

"Where do you fit in the scheme of things?"

Logan relaxed against the seat and laced his fingers. "I plug away. But if Simon hadn't tapped me to come West, I probably would've turned in my badge. I have two buddies who offered me a job in private security. That's an up-and-coming field."

"Why would you have quit?"

Logan was worried that their conversation might circle back to his reasons for not wanting to get involved with Daphne. So instead, he made some inane comment about the thickening traffic.

"Yeah, this time of the afternoon on nice sunny days, all roads lead to the beach. You know, when Dane, Kieran and I were kids, we rode bicycles from our house to Redondo. Nobody worried if we showed up an hour late for dinner. But these days..." He shook his head. "That's another sign the criminals of the world are blowing our sense of security all to hell."

"Cross your fingers that after this operation ends, the good guys' score will be up by one."

"Will do. Are we really going to do some fishing, Logan, or is our staying on the boat all a sham?"

"We have to fish to make our cover look real."

"We're two against how many?" Perry asked. "Maybe we really ought to fish and let your teammates handle the collar."

"Look, Perry, if you're getting cold feet, I can rent a fishing vessel and go this alone."

"No way." Perry turned his probing gaze on Logan. "Especially not since you involved my baby sister in this deal."

Logan heaved a huge sigh. He sat up and massaged his temples. "Daphne's your sister, but she's a long way from being a baby."

"You'd know that how?" Perry lashed out.

"Come on. If we're going to carve pieces out of each other from now until we part ways, we won't be any good to her should she need us."

"You think she may?"

"No plan is foolproof." Logan found something of interest out his right-hand window.

"You do care what happens to her, right, Grant? Maybe I'd stop picking at you if you'd level with me about that."

"I care for her." He sounded gruff. "She's fun, warm and hell, she's pretty much perfect."

"Then why are you trying so hard to deny how important she's become to you?"

Logan rubbed his lips for a long time before he surrendered and gave Perry an answer. "If you know her and understand her as well as you think, you've got to realize she has her sights set on what Dane has. And what Kieran has. And for that matter, I guess what your younger sister has. A husband. A home near her family. And babies."

"She says not. Daphne claims that all she wants is independence and a career."

"If you bought that, Perry, I have a bridge called the Golden Gate I'm ready to sell you."

Perry rolled down his window, stuck out his elbow and breathed deeply of the salty air. "We're getting near the marina. I know this little hole in the wall where the beer is cold and the fish and chips are fried to perfection."

"I'll have to go aboard your boat and ask you to bring me back a doggie bag. No beer, though. From now on I need a clear head."

"Anybody ever call you a wet blanket, Logan?"

That wrenched a grin out of Logan. "My ex-wife. Almost daily after we got married."

"She was a party girl?"

"You could say that. I was out on assignment so much, I somehow missed hearing until too late that Liz kept a head count as she slept her way through the office."

"Ouch."

"Water under the bridge."

"But not the Golden Gate, right?"

"She's still in D.C. if that's what you're asking. In case you're worried about her showing up on this assignment, don't be."

"I guess I was wondering if—as Kieran believes—you left your heart back in D.C. With her."

"Why would anyone think something that stupid? Haven't the cops on the West Coast heard those she-done-me-wrong songs?"

Perry threw back his head and laughed. "Point made. All right. My portion of the grilling of Logan Grant is over for the night."

"Only yours?" Logan tossed off the query lightly, but he didn't like the way Perry avoided answering him for a long moment.

"You see that leaky old tub floating at the end of pier seventy-nine?"

Logan, who'd also lowered his window, squinted into the deepening shadows on the docks and saw the boat Perry pointed out.

"Well then, the other thing I should say is that I'm parking between Kieran's pickup and Dane's minivan. I'll do my best to keep them from roasting your buns until after supper. But then, I'm afraid you've gotta take their heat."

"You knew they'd be here waiting for us?"

"Yup." The younger Malone brother grinned. "As someone who's been on the butt end of their pounding my whole life, I'll give you one more piece of free advice, pal. Don't ever let either of them find so much as a pinhole in your armor. Otherwise you'll be dead meat and you won't have a second's peace from now until hell freezes over. Shovel it back and they'll welcome you into the Malone family with open arms."

It wasn't until after the four men had claimed berths on the boat, and the boisterous Malone trio had gone down the dock to scare up some food that Logan stopped to ponder Perry's sage advice. What Perry had said hit him squarely between the eyes.

Lord help him, but while they were gone, Logan indulged in a little fantasy about joining the Malone family and what that would mean. To his own shock and surprise, he didn't find the notion appalling. Not at all.

CHAPTER ELEVEN

BEFORE DAWN the next morning, Kieran Malone shook Logan awake. He landed instantly on his feet, and began yanking on his jeans. Rapid alertness sometimes saved an agent's neck. "Rise and shine, buddy. Perry's topside hauling anchor. Coffee's on in the galley," Kieran said.

"We're going fishing?" Logan asked, even though the rumble of the big inboard drowned out his words.

"Why else are we here?"

"Honestly? I thought you two showed up last night to give me the third degree."

Dane slapped Logan's shoulder and laughed. "I work seven twelve-hour days and get seven off. Kieran needed to use up some of his overtime. The city doesn't like to pay for overtime, and they're fussy about employees clearing it off the books before the next fiscal year. So for five whole days, we're doing nothing but sailing the ocean blue. Well, as blue as the ocean in Santa Monica Bay gets."

A look of envy crossed Logan's face. "I figure I'd better stay out of sight. This bay is probably crawling with Holt's point men. I wonder how wise it was of you to come, Kieran. Simon also thinks dirty cops spoiled our last raid, which would've put a few of Billy's strong-arms in jail."

Kieran nodded. "The chief said Internal Affairs relieved two suspects of duty. They know they're being investigated in-house. That's two down, Logan."

"Right after you called and lowered the boom on both of us yesterday," Dane said, "Kieran shared a little bit of this background with his chief. He's aware something may be afoot this weekend."

"He'll give us backup if we need it, you mean?"

"Yep." Dane rummaged in a footlocker and tossed some things on Logan's bunk. "Here are some extra cutoffs, hats and deck shoes. In your jeans and black T-shirt, my man, you'll stand out like a sore thumb."

"Hey, thanks." Surprisingly, now that he had the proper clothes for a fishing expedition, Logan's enthusiasm picked up.

"What are we fishing for?" he asked some forty minutes later as Perry dropped anchor and the others broke out nets and some heavy-duty rods.

"Mostly bonito, mackerel and rockfish. With luck and the right bait, we occasionally land good-size yellowtail and striped marlin."

"That sounds like serious fishing, not just goofing around."

Dane set up the swivel seats and holders for the rods. "It's all legal, Mr. Fed Man. We have a commercial license. That's how we originally paid for the boat. I figured if we show up at the dock with a good catch tonight, that establishes our reason for hanging around the bay."

"Smart." Logan was developing a firm liking for Daphne's brothers, who seemed more easygoing in this atmosphere.

Dane's white teeth gleamed through his day-old beard.

"That's what I keep telling these yahoos. I'm more than just another pretty face."

His joking set the tone. In spite of the real reason Logan needed to be here, close to the agency's action, he was able to relax and enjoy the day. With the temperature in the low eighties, a salt breeze cooling his bare back and a cooler full of soft drinks—Logan thought he could get used to this life real quick. Although he tensed each time a yacht steamed into the bay... "I wish we'd asked Simon the name of the damn boat he's renting to use as the agency's cover."

Perry unhooked a flopping baby yellowfin and tossed him back in the water. "You think they'll bring in the yacht this early? Rent on a baby like that won't be cheap."

"It'll be a fraction of the cost to the taxpayer in increased police services if Ratsami's cargo makes it to the streets."

"Drugs, huh?" Kieran hauled in a keeper. "I figured it must be the uncut stuff."

Logan, who'd long since decided these three men were trustworthy, rebaited his hook and threw out the line before he fully confided in them. "Reports from overseas operatives give us reason to believe that as well as bringing tons of high-grade opium, Billy Holt's looking to raise the crime quotient by expanding his trade to include automatic weapons and rocket-propelled grenades. China's best."

"I thought these dudes were local yokels," Perry murmured.

"Not the ringleaders," Logan confirmed. "I have it on good authority that the main man is traveling with this shipment. This is to be a gathering of the clan, so to speak. While pretending to work with Holt, I was privy to some of the plans."

Kieran whistled through his teeth. "No wonder they put a price on your head."

That statement, or maybe Logan's earlier remark, sobered them all for a time. Perry broke the thoughtful silence, saying, "Even wearing that god-awful hat of Dane's, you're fairly recognizable, Logan. You'd better plan on staying below and out of sight anytime we're in port. Like a good mole, you can come out at night."

Logan's answer was to flop his next fish, a good-size salmon, across Perry's chest—after he'd carefully rubbed on suntan lotion. Now he had to wash up.

They were still laughing at Logan's antics when a fifty-foot yacht called The Good Time Girl came around Point Vicente on a course aimed at Santa Monica.

Logan had a feeling about the boat. He knew Simon had a good friend, a former U.S. senator whose life he'd once saved, who lived on some prime real estate near Rancho Palos Verdes. Logan had attended a black-tie party there right after Simon set up the West Coast office. It was dark when they'd arrived, but he remembered stepping out on the wraparound deck and seeing a full moon glinting off a yacht tied up in a cove. It could be the one that just passed.

"I wish I'd brought a pair of binoculars," he grumbled, never taking his eyes off the fast-moving boat.

"Ask and you shall receive." Kieran snapped down his reel, slid off the fishing seat and crossed the deck. He returned with both a spyglass and high-powered field glasses. He handed them to Logan.

First, he tried the spyglass. "Damn, she's inbound but traveling too fast for me to recognize anyone on deck from this angle."

"Pretty showy. Surely you don't believe that's the cruiser

Daphne gets to hang out on?" Perry had finally managed to wash off the smell of fish. He gazed after the yacht, pausing every now and then to sip from a beer. "Man, if so, you guys do travel in exalted circles."

"It's rare," Logan mused aloud, still trying to focus on the yacht. "With most of my assignments, I'm lucky to get a bed in a flophouse. More often than not, you'll find me hunkered down for the night under an overpass or in an alley."

"You do get the luxury posts," teased one of the brothers. "Maybe if your boss had offered Daph one of those assignments, she wouldn't have been so ready and willing to raise her hand."

Logan gave up on the field glasses and set them aside to use later. "I know you guys don't want her doing this. But Simon's not going to stick her on the front lines. Everyone on the team will know she's had no training. They'll do everything they can to protect her."

"I'm afraid you don't know our sister if that's what you think," Dane lamented.

Perry gestured with his beer can. "And if you really thought she'd be so safe, why did you argue at first when your boss insisted on putting her on the boat?"

The line of Logan's fishing rod pulled tight. He dashed over to reel in the biggest catch of the day so far. A hefty striped marlin. He was glad talk switched to fishing again and they got off the subject of Daphne. Logan didn't like it when the men made disparaging remarks about her. It irritated him a lot. Too much for someone who had no right to feel possessive. Yet he couldn't seem to control the emotions her very name evoked. Soft, tender emotions. He frowned. If there was anything he didn't consider himself, it was tender.

He much preferred words like rugged. Tough. Gutsy. Yeah, gutsy was good.

Daphne had been pretty gutsy, too, that afternoon he'd popped in on her, looking like a total derelict.

Whenever Daphne Malone wiggled her way into his mind, Logan quickly began to recall other things about her. Like how soft and smooth her skin felt plastered to his in the throes of love—uh...sex.

"Hey, Logan," Kieran said, nudging him in the ribs. "Why are you scowling?"

"I'm not," Logan snapped.

Dane yelled from the other side of the boat. "I need somebody with some muscle. These nets are full. We must've had the good luck to anchor in the path of a school of bonito."

Pulling nets, Logan soon discovered, was darned hard work. Even with the winch that spanned the deck of the Boston trawler.

"Jeez, considering all the engineers who fish, you'd think one would've invented an electric crank for this job."

"Ha," Kieran shouted. "That's the trouble with feds. All their muscle is between their ears."

Logan waited until they'd hauled in and dumped both nets. Then he walked up behind Kieran, grabbed him up, keeping both of his arms pinned at his sides. Deliberately and efficiently Logan flung him overboard.

Stunned at first, the other brothers soon roared with mirth. Once they'd thrown a line to Kieran and watched him climb back on deck, they took turns going for a swim.

"This is the life, isn't it," Logan remarked as they lounged on the deck buck-naked, drying off. Their cutoffs hung over the side rails.

"You might at least apologize," Kieran growled.

Logan smiled lazily. "I will. As soon as you write a letter to all special agents everywhere saying you're sorry for besmirching their physical prowess."

Kieran's crude response made them all laugh again.

It felt good to joke and trade insults with a group of men. Logan recognized that this was a part of his life he'd let go by the wayside. He guessed he could blame that on his divorce, too. The occasional get-togethers in bars had lost their appeal.

As if reading his mind, Dane shifted so he could see Logan, and asked, "What do feebs do for fun in their spare time? Most fire stations have softball teams. I play center field. Kieran's on his precinct's bowling squad."

"An agent doesn't keep regular enough hours for stuff like that."

"Nor do long-haul truckers," Perry put in from the other side of the deck.

Wearing a grin, Dane sat up and threw Perry's shorts at him. "The only thing truckers do in their spare time is drink. You're all a bunch of lushes. That's why Mom works so hard at finding you some nice little homebody. She wants to nail your feet down."

Dane's statement might have led to another tussle, except that a speedboat full of women in bikinis roared past. Evidently someone spotted the drying clothes, because they cut their engines and circled back around, giving wolf whistles and catcalls.

Perry, the only one of the men who was decent since he'd pulled on the half-dry shorts Dane had thrown at him, hung over the rail and flirted. He got back at the others by threatening to bring some of the women on board. All that saved the men's modesty was the simple fact that the speedboat sat much lower in the water than their trawler.

Logan was really the only one who feared Perry might make good on his threat to invite the beauties aboard. When he did no such thing and eventually sent the women off, promising to make an appearance later at one of the beachside nightclubs, Logan understood what good guys the Malone men really were. Perry made it clear his brothers were married, and that they didn't play around.

That point stuck with Logan long after they'd dressed and lifted anchor. If the Malones, who worked in fields where males frequently strayed, remained loyal to their spouses, Logan supposed fidelity characterized the Malone women, too.

Remaining faithful in marriage held a high priority with Logan. It ranked right up there with honesty, integrity and service to his country. He couldn't say where or how he'd come to have such strong feelings. After his dad died, he hadn't had a male role model. Logan just knew he wasn't open to compromise in any of those areas, and his experience with Liz had only confirmed it.

As agreed, he went belowdecks well before they pulled into port. It was stuffy down there and he wished darkness would fall so he could go back on deck again. Restless, he found a stack of paperbacks and chose a spy thriller that had hit the bestseller lists a couple of years back.

The boat rocked, and gruff voices shouted and swore. Things hit the hold above his head, and Logan knew they were off-loading their catch.

Some time later, Perry bounded down the ladder. "Hey, we didn't do half-bad. Your marlin brought in the single best price." He named a figure.

"Great. But a lot of good money does me stuck down here."
Not answering, Perry stripped unselfconsciously and from his
duffel, pulled out a pair of black chinos and a white pullover
that showed off his tan.

"Going out on the town, are you?" Logan said a bit
enviously.

"Thought I'd hit a bar or two, dance with a few of those
pretty women, and maybe find out what other strangers might
be mingling with the locals." Checking his wallet, Perry but-
toned it into his hip pocket.

"That's a good plan. Except Holt's men won't be in bars.
Billy has a strict rule against even social drinking this close
to a shipment. Punishment for disobeying isn't pretty."

"Really? So where are those goons likely to hang out?"

"Watch for muscle-bound types in groups of two or three.
Check the balconies of posh hotels. Especially the ones overlooking the marina. And ritzy boats. I expect Holt leased one
with enough speed to double as a getaway vehicle in case
anything goes wrong. Damn, I should be the one out trying
to spot them. I know these guys."

"Yeah. But the downside is they also know you, Logan.
Don't do anything stupid while we're gone. Our deal was we'd
be here in case of an emergency—and only an emergency.
Now, what kind of food would you like Dane and Kieran to
bring you? Burgers okay?" At Logan's nod, he said, "They'll
be back long before me. I heard Dane talking about buying a
new poker deck. My final advice—don't play either of those
crooks for money."

He left and Logan lay back, letting the book rest open on
his chest. He played a mean game of poker himself. It was a
tough challenge to pass up. But maybe Perry was counting
on that.

The gentle rocking of the boat lulled him to sleep.

It was dark in the cabin when he jerked awake, bothered by the loud voices of his companions arriving back on the boat.

Kieran dropped a bag from a burger joint in the middle of Logan's stomach, causing him to jackknife upright.

"Logan, you were dead-on right about that yacht, The Good Time Girl, being the feds' decoy. We saw Daphne. She didn't see us."

"How far are we from them?" Logan asked, unwrapping his burger.

"Big as that boat is, she's sprawled clear across the end of pier seventy. We're on the bay side of seventy-nine."

Logan chewed slowly. The truth was, he wanted to go top-side and have a gander. While he ate, the other two men broke open fresh decks of cards. In the dim, wavering gaslight, they each set up to play solitaire.

"How about a game of poker?" Kieran said casually, glancing up when Logan rose to dispose of his leftovers.

"Maybe later. I want to go above, get some air, maybe try the binoculars on the inhabited boats we can see from here."

Dane scooped up his cards and tucked them in their box. "Sounds good. I need a stretch. Come on, Kieran. If Logan recognizes one of Holt's men, we'll all want to see where they're docked."

One at a time they clomped up the ladder. Logan's gaze was drawn to the gaily lit yacht. Laughter, men's and women's, drifted across the softly lapping water.

Logan retrieved the binoculars from where he'd stashed them earlier. Claiming a spot at the railing of the trawler, between his two friends, he fitted the glasses to his eyes and waited for the partyers on the yacht to come into focus. Like radar, it seemed, he immediately found Daphne. Her dark hair was clipped atop her head in some intricate weave with bits of what—crystal?—sparkling like diamonds among the dark strands. She wore a black, strapless dress that left her shoulders bare. Shoulders that looked sun-kissed under the deck lights, as if she, too, had spent some hours in the sun. Unable to help himself, Logan played the field glasses slowly along her slender body. She held a half-filled flute of champagne in one hand. The other gripped the yacht rail. A dreamy smile parted her lips, causing Logan to linger there a while. It wasn't until she moved, pressing her right side into the rail, and a foreign object, a man's navy jacket sleeve, rested on her shoulder, that Logan turned his attention to the other person who shared the deck with her.

Reluctantly, he swung his binoculars. All at once, his breath hissed from his lungs. "That rat-fink bastard, son of a sea cook lied to me!" Logan roared.

"Who? What do you see?" Kieran demanded, edging closer.

"Simon!" Logan kept the binoculars trained on a man he'd like to yank off the yacht and drown.

"You're calling your boss a rat-fink bastard…." Dane snatched the glasses out of Logan's hands without finishing his sentence. "Nothing looks out of whack to me. In fact, everybody appears to be having a better time than we are. Which guy is your boss?"

"Simon's not there." Seething, Logan prowled the deck, slamming one fist into the other. "He gave me his word that he wouldn't team Daphne with Ron Thorpe." Obviously part of Daphne's job was to turn Ron into a dashing and debonair middle-aged yacht owner. The Thorpe he knew had blond hair; this Ron sported black hair with a touch of gray at the temples. He wore an ascot, of all things, which suited the pompous windbag.

"This Thorpe guy," Kieran muttered. "He's not a good agent?"

"Oh, he's an okay agent."

"So, what's your beef?" Both men turned puzzled gazes on Logan.

"He thinks he's hot stuff. Can't keep his hands off women. You pull duty with him and all he can talk about is how many women he's laid."

"Is he married?" This from Dane, who took another look at the yacht through the glasses.

"Three times divorced. Claims he learned his lesson the last trip through divorce court. Now he's going to love 'em and leave 'em before he has to pay alimony."

"Nice guy." Dane handed the glasses to Kieran. "Take a look-see and then let's go deal up a round of poker."

"Aren't you concerned about your sister?"

"There's a lot of activity on that deck. All feds, I assume. Anyway, what can we do?" Kieran asked, then shrugged.

Logan didn't know. But he stewed over it all the same. So much so, he couldn't keep his mind on the cards. Dane and Kieran fleeced him without half trying.

FOR HER PART, Daphne continually edged down the yacht rail in an attempt to avoid the agent who, for the past three hours, had been bending her ear with tales of his single-handed saves for the agency. He also insisted on more personal assistance from her than any of the other nine agents she'd disguised.

Daphne had always found braggarts boring. She'd immediately noticed how different Ron Thorpe was from Logan

Grant. Unassuming Logan, who in several days hadn't even mentioned his successes and good deeds. Daphne had learned about them yesterday through gently pumping Simon Parrish after Logan and Perry left.

She wondered where they'd gone. "Do you happen to know where Logan Grant is now?" she blurted to her companion.

"Grant?" Ron let his arm slide off Daphne's shoulder. "Nobody's seen or heard from him lately. Frankly I think he's dead. Or else he's too ashamed of blowing a deal last week to show his ugly face around the office."

Daphne itched to slap Ron's smug face. That she didn't took every bit of her eroding willpower.

"Since you only recently hired on with the agency, you probably aren't aware of what a loser Grant is." Ron launched into a lengthy description of how Logan's former wife had made him the laughingstock of the D.C. office.

"Poor Logan," she murmured, understanding completely now why he was so gun-shy when it came to marriage or commitment.

"Poor, my foot. Any man who works in our field and can't see through a shallow piece of work like Liz deserves what he got. Makes you wonder, though, how much he misses on assignments."

Daphne took another small sip of her champagne so that she wouldn't throw what was left in her glass at the man who was fast giving her a headache. Thankfully, his cell phone rang, and after glancing at the readout, he withdrew, saying their boss was calling him.

Taking the opportunity to dump the remainder of her drink overboard, Daphne tried to figure out where she might go to escape Thorpe. There was only the three-man crew and new agents aboard, plus her. All except Ron seemed to be busy all the time.

Mellie Banks, one of the few other women on board approached. This morning she'd been a svelte blonde, but in less than two hours, Daphne had turned her into an auburn-haired beauty.

"You poor thang," Mellie cooed in a soft, southern drawl that belied her proficiency in the art of judo, which Daphne had seen her exhibit. "Tomorrow we'll find a quiet corner and I'll teach you some simple moves. You may need 'em to discourage our friend Ron."

"Oh dear, I was afraid he's not the type to understand the meaning of no."

"The only thang bigger than that man's ego is his gall." Mellie batted her enhanced lashes.

"Hmm. I held my own in a household with three older brothers. They were bigger and stronger, but I fought dirty."

"That's the spirit. Uh-oh. Don't look now, but he's off the phone. Come on down to my stateroom. You can show me again how to remove and apply these weeds you call eyelashes."

Daphne laughed. It felt good. Maybe she could pump Mellie for tips on being a good agent. Simon had assured Daphne time and again that all he expected of her was to alter the appearance of the agents he'd handpicked for his mission. She didn't plan on involving herself in the capture or anything. But since Logan had vouched for her on more than one occasion, and had even taken on her brothers, she felt it was crucial not to do one single thing to embarrass him.

"How long have you been an agent?" Daphne asked Mellie. They sat curled up in matching stateroom chairs, munching on beer peanuts Mellie had produced after the eye makeup lesson.

"Almost six years. I'd planned to make it a career, but a year ago I met a man. Currently he's a White House journalist. I saw him frequently when I was stationed in D.C. Neither of us wanted anything serious—until Simon asked me to join this new team. Now my boyfriend's phone bills and mine are atrocious. A week ago he asked if I'd consider coming back after this job. I think I'm going to do it and resign."

"Can't you transfer back to the other office?"

"I checked. There aren't any openings. And with budget cuts…"

"What if two agents are married? Do they get split up, or when one's transferred, do they automatically transfer the other?" Daphne asked the question, knowing she had absolutely no right to make even a casual query.

"I've only met one agent couple. The marriage didn't last, which I think is why agents tend not to marry among the team." She fell silent a minute. "One half of that couple is here with our group. Well, not here on the boat. In California, though. Logan Grant. A nice man. So hot to look at a girl can get singed." Mellie grinned mischievously. "If he ever comes out of hiding, you can ask him if he and Liz would ever have been transferred together. Although, maybe not. Logan's pretty bitter. Can't blame the guy. He got a raw deal. Some women are too stupid to live. Liz Danby Grant is one of them, in my estimation."

Daphne would've liked to get more information about Logan from Mellie, but she noticed the other woman trying to hide a yawn. "Hey, it's late. I need to make the rounds of the agents to be sure everyone has jars of cream to remove all the makeup. Bright and early in the morning, I get to make everyone up again."

"You sure do have a knack for it, Daphne." Mellie took a look at herself in the mirror. "I really love this shade of red. When I phoned my boyfriend, he said he'd like to see me as a redhead. I may have you show me how to mix the colors you used. By the way, don't let Ron corner you in his room. I've noticed him pretending to be helpless. He might be team leader, but insist on removing his makeup in the lounge where there're other people around."

"I'll do that, thanks." Daphne left the stateroom, partly apprehensive about Ron, but encouraged by Mellie's complimentary words. If she got nothing else out of this experience, and if Simon never asked her to work on another mission, she'd leave knowing she had what it took to be a makeup artist for the FBI.

LOGAN STAYED UP half the night fretting over what was happening on the yacht. He tried several times to reach Simon, but his number was blocked. Logan knew that meant only one or two appointed agents working this takedown were cleared to have calls sent through. There was, however, a general number for messages. "This is Logan. Quit hiding behind a number block, you slimy worm. You gave me your word you wouldn't pair Daphne Malone with that octopus, Thorpe. Call me, Simon. If not today, then tomorrow."

About four in the morning, Simon called him back. "Where are you that you know who's working surveillance?"

"Maybe I'm telepathic. Any way you cut it, I don't like the visions I'm channeling."

"Channeling, my big toe. Stay out of this, Logan. And lie low. I won't have you ruining this gig because you're thinking with a part of your anatomy other than your brain." He sighed loudly. "Look, I had no choice but to put Thorpe in charge. Lee Harriman came down with the flu, and Ron's the next senior agent. As for you—Holt's put too hefty a price on your head."

Thoroughly annoyed, Logan clicked off. He fell asleep on the hard wooden bench from sheer exhaustion. Perry woke him up when the sun was barely peeking over the horizon.

"Dane said you should come below, or risk being fingered."

"The hell with Dane." Logan launched himself off the bench.

"Not a morning person, huh?" Perry noticed the binoculars still hung around Logan's neck. "Ah, this bad mood of yours is about Daphne and what's-his-name, Thorpe."

Logan stomped along the deck and practically threw himself down into the sleeping quarters. "After you guys got embroiled in your fantasy football, I came up on deck and endured watching your sister removing Ron's disguise. He kept touching her and rubbing up against her."

The three men involved in pouring their morning coffee shared a knowing look. "Sounds as if you're staking a claim on Daphne, hotshot." That was Kieran's take.

"I'm not. But if you coddle her the way she claims, you'll put a stop to this."

The brothers all shrugged. "Can't. We're not supposed to meddle in her life anymore. She told us that, and I believe you said something to that effect, too." Dane headed for the ladder. "And we can't exactly interfere with an FBI mission, can we?"

Logan jammed a hand through his hair. "So what are you going to do?"

"Go fishing," the three said in unison.

Logan hated every minute they fished out in the bay. He did little to help. Perry complained he was a hindrance, and more than once told Logan to go soak his head. Still, the men walked a wide circle around him. He was even more furious when he found out they'd brought cold cuts to eat for supper and weren't really in any rush to head back into port.

"Ah, there's nothing like getting away from harbor lights." Dane popped the top on a ginger ale.

"If you don't lift anchor and sail this tub back to the dock so we can see whether Daphne's still managing to fend off Ron, I'll take the lifeboat and row there on my own."

The Malones took a vote. "Jeez, Logan. None of us want to be responsible for you splitting a blood vessel or anything. Kieran's gone to hoist anchor," Dane said.

It was quite late, almost midnight, by the time they motored into the berth and tied up. From the moment they got within range of the yacht, Logan stationed himself in the bow and kept his field glasses glued to the deck of the pleasure craft. Half a dozen people milled about—all of them agents. Logan recognized their alertness and readiness, even though they were in disguise, thanks to Daphne's artistry. They all gave the appearance of enjoying themselves. Two people who were nowhere to be seen were Daphne and Logan's nemesis. Where the hell was Ron? As team leader, he should be on deck, keeping tabs on everything.

"Everything looks quiet along the dock tonight," Perry observed, peering over Logan's shoulder. "Think I'll turn in early. Kieran said he feels in his bones something's going to break soon."

"It would if he'd go across the bay and bust Thorpe in the nose."

"Logan, I've gotta tell you. For a guy who isn't romantically interested in the girl, you've turned into a man possessed. I've heard sleep deprivation can do that." Perry gave him a manly little punch on the shoulder. "Well, good night, sport."

Fuming, he imagined all manner of atrocities—for instance, Daphne in her bed, trying to fight off Ron's unwanted advances. And who would hear? Not the revelers milling about the upper deck.

For another ten minutes, Logan weighed what he was about to do against common sense and all the warnings he'd been given. The ship they awaited probably wouldn't come into range tonight, he reasoned. Cloud cover left the night perfect for a small craft to skim the distance between the yacht and the trawler unnoticed. Not the lifeboat, but a small rubber dinghy he'd discovered. He could get over there, check on things himself, and be back in half an hour or less.

As silently and stealthily as a cat burglar, Logan slid the dinghy into the murky water. Climbing over the rail, he dropped into it with a loud plop. And froze. But no one seemed to take notice.

Taking extreme care to stay in the shadows, Logan rowed across the open bay and around to the dark side of the yacht. His arm and back muscles strained.

Climbing up the slick side of the luxury boat wasn't easy, either. Logan was winded, but satisfied with his accomplishment when he finally crawled over the top and landed on the canvas cover of a life raft.

He knew where the crew slept. He didn't know which stateroom was Daphne's. Maybe Simon and the others had been right; he wasn't using his brain. Although, since he'd come this far, he wasn't about to go back until he made sure she was safe.

Tiptoeing down the hand-polished wooden steps, he paused with an ear to the door of the first cabin. Easing the door open, Logan saw at a glance that the room was empty. Deciding this was the only way to find her, he worked his way down the long hall. In the second to last room, he met success. Daphne's bunk was so narrow, he stood there feeling foolish about imagining two people thrashing on its surface. A bead of light from the deck above bounced off an open porthole a foot or so over her head. The urge to sneak a closer peek physically tugged at him.

What could it hurt?

Promising himself no more than a few seconds, Logan slipped inside and glided silently across the room. Silently—until he stubbed his big toe against something hard that hurt like hell.

The thud caused Daphne to rise six inches off her bunk. She screamed without knowing who her intruder was. A man, from his size. Possibly that obnoxious Ron Thorpe. Except she'd kneed him earlier and he'd slunk off to his room in a sulk.

Her intruder dived toward her, attempting to clap a hand over her mouth. She screamed and kept on screaming until light flooded her room and four agents, all in full disguise, crowded into the small space, weapons drawn.

"Logan, what the hell?" Mellie Banks sheathed her weapon first and motioned to the others in the room to do the same. "Special Agent Grant, you look like crap."

"Mellie?" Logan could tell from her voice who had spoken.

"Logan?" Daphne slithered down the wall she'd been trying to melt into in her panic. "Where did you come from and what are you doing here?"

"Your brothers and I are, uh, doing a little recreational fishing nearby."

"My brothers? Perry, you mean?"

"All of them. And me."

"You didn't come to fish, you came to spy on me! None of you think I can handle this job. I can. I will," she said with conviction. "I want you to get out of here, Logan. Now. Get off the boat." Daphne pointed.

"My visit has nothing to do with the job."

"Really?" Her eyebrows dived toward the bridge of her nose.

"Uh...I've seen Ron Thorpe manhandling you."

"That's none of your business."

"It is. I...care. I care a lot, Daphne."

"Ha! If you did, you'd trust me to handle him. I want you to leave, Logan."

"Daphne...ee." He took a step nearer, but she staved him off.

"She's not the only one who wants you gone, Grant." Thorpe looking like himself hobbled toward them. "Simon does, too. He's on the phone and he's livid."

Logan uttered the f word. "What's he got, sonar?"

"I phoned him. I'm the team leader." Ron thumped his chest.

Wresting the phone out of Ron's hand, Logan said, "Hi, Simon. I know I'm not supposed to be here. But since I am, I might as well stay." He listened, winced a few times and eased the phone farther from his ear. "That's plain enough. I'm to leave the yacht even if I have to swim."

Expression thoughtful, Logan trailed an almost reverent finger along Daphne's tense jaw. "Be mad if you want, but

I'm not abandoning you to that shark. I'll be watching, and I'm only a good yell away."

Logan stepped back, turned and elbowed Ron into the hall. Reaching behind him, he flipped the lock on Daphne's door and slammed it tight. A line of people parted as Logan shoved the phone hard into Thorpe's midsection. "You lay another hand on her, Ronnie-boy, and you'll be picking up your teeth off the yacht deck one by one. Oh, and by the way, tell Simon there's no need to fire me. I quit!"

CHAPTER TWELVE

BEHIND HER TIGHTLY CLOSED DOOR, Daphne's shaking legs gave out. She felt the mattress sink beneath her weight. Murmurs from the hall filtered under her door. Then one voice stood out, Logan saying, "I quit!"

Quit? Being a special agent? Even the most feeble-minded person could tell he loved his job. Daphne thought the world needed more, not fewer good men like Logan Grant.

Spurred to act, she swung off the bed, grabbed her shorts and a T-shirt and threw them on. But she forgot Logan had locked her cabin door and she wasted precious minutes because her fumbling fingers turned the lock in the wrong direction. In her present state of mind, her fingers just slid off the metal. Frustrated, she forced in a few deep breaths before calming down enough to break out of her room.

The hall, which moments ago had teemed with agents, now stood empty.

Spinning right, then left, Daphne didn't know which stairs she should choose. One set led fore, the other aft. Which way had Logan gone?

They were facing heaven only knew what kind of mission. Daphne didn't want him leaving with nothing but cross words between them. She thought back to their conversation before he'd stormed out and told the others he quit. When he'd suddenly appeared in her room, she'd flown off the handle. But Logan had told her, "I care. Care a lot." Lord have mercy. For a man like Logan to say that and to say it in front of his colleagues—some who knew his history with his former wife—that "I care a lot" was tantamount to a declaration of love.

She had to find him. Had to make him spit out exactly how much he cared. She'd go first. Tell him that every hour they were apart felt like a lifetime. Other people, including her family, might think her silly. After all, she'd spent very few days with Logan Grant. That didn't matter. Daphne's heart knew. She knew.

Closing her eyes and choosing the corridor on the right, she ran as fast as her feet would carry her.

On deck, she spotted a group gathered next to the railing on the bay side of the craft. Daphne forgot if it was port or starboard. And didn't care. Agents milled aimlessly about, some wearing fancy party clothes, some in robes and slippers.

She charged behind the throng and began to elbow her way between them. "Excuse me. Please let me pass. Thank you." She reached a point where only two people blocked her from seeing the water—from seeing why everyone's eyes were focused below. Those people were Mellie Banks and Ron Thorpe.

"Mellie, I have to locate Logan. It's important. I must." Daphne's voice cracked as Ron turned, still blocking her path.

Agent Banks glanced up, surprised. "Can't, hon. He's gone. In that dinghy, rowing across the bay."

"He can't go yet," Daphne declared, kicking at Ron to move him aside.

"Don't you dare call out to him," warned Ron in a low, threatening voice. "Simon put me in charge. One idiot trick like the one Grant just pulled is enough to blow our cover." He hooked her around the waist, and she rammed an elbow in his groin.

She knew it hurt him, but Ron clapped a hand over her mouth. And Daphne understood. She did. She wouldn't be the one to cause problems. But that didn't stop the tears from streaming down her face and dripping over Ron's fingers.

Mellie saw. Brushing the agent away from Daphne, the other woman flung a comforting arm around her.

Near the stern of the boat, someone shouted. Curse words rolled along the line of agents who had yet to disperse, swelling like an ocean wave. All eyes turned toward where the agents were pointing.

Daphne, along with Mellie, leaned over the rail to see what had caused the sudden fracas. At the mouth of Santa Monica Bay, bearing down on the marina fast was a hulking shadow. A ghost ship, running silent and black.

"Holy hell!" Ron began barking orders.

"What is it? What's happening?" Daphne gripped Mellie's arm hard, even though her eyes remained trained on Logan in his bobbing rubber boat. He didn't seem to be making headway now because of the waves being stirred up by the larger vessel.

"This is it. Showtime," Mellie murmured, her voice throbbing with excitement. "That can't be anything but the shipment we've been waiting for."

"But...but...but," Daphne stuttered. "I thought it wasn't due until this weekend."

"It's early, and that's why we're here. Look, I've gotta go toss on some work clothes and get to my post. Hear our engines firing? We'll be moving out to intercept. Simon can't afford to let that ship reach the dock. Too many chances of bystanders getting hurt. You'd better go below and sit this one out. It could get ugly, Daph."

"But…Logan. Does he see that ship? Can he get out of its way?"

"Honey, around the office in D.C., Logan was known as the man with nine lives." Mellie rushed off. Everyone seemed to be rushing. All lights on deck were extinguished. Daphne felt a hard lurch. She heard the whish of prop wash as the engines reversed them out of the slip, sending them into the channel. Running along the railing, she searched the churning water for a glimpse of Logan. Panic seized her when she couldn't find him.

At last she saw his boat, and her heart slammed erratically. Had he seen the ship, or was he just intent on getting back to her brothers' fishing boat? Maybe he was so upset with her, he was blind to everything.

Suddenly pandemonium blew up around her. Nobody here seemed to give a damn about Logan. Nobody but Daphne. An agent she'd met only once almost ran her down in his haste to reach his post. "Wait!" She grabbed his arm. "Do you need your cell phone? If not, can I use it a minute?"

"What for?"

"To call my brothers. Their fishing boat's moored across the bay."

"Tough luck for them. It may be raining bullets all over them shortly."

"That's just it! One's a cop. A good cop," she said. "The other is a veteran firefighter. They could hold back curiosity-seekers if nothing else. But if I don't call, they'll probably snore through the whole thing."

He handed her the phone and shook himself free. Praying that either Kieran or Dane had his phone on the boat, Daphne punched in the first number from memory. It rang five times. She almost skipped to the next number, but a gruff, sleepy voice mumbled, "'Lo."

"Dane. Dane! It's me, Daphne. Wake up! Wake Kieran up and listen to me." She spewed out the whole story, her sentences choppy, her words tumbling one after another.

"Whoa, whoa! Slow down. Logan's done what? He's where?"

"Go on deck, Dane. Look toward the yacht. Please! I love Logan, Dane. I love him like you love Holly. And...and... he's smack-dab in the line of danger. Oh, why am I talking to you? I'll—I'll help him myself." Clicking off, she sought out the agent who'd lent her the phone and thrust it back in his hand.

Things were beginning to happen. A lookout on the approaching ship apparently spotted the yacht as it attempted to swing around to block their passage. Or maybe someone on the ship was in contact with their partners on shore. All agents on the yacht noticed when a smaller pleasure craft in the marina revved its engines.

Daphne ignored the hubbub around her. She followed the yacht's railing until she found a place where she could gaze straight out at Logan's bobbing boat. With the practiced eye of an artist, she calculated the angle between the big ship, the yacht and the craft now pulling away from the marina. The dot in the center that was Logan Grant bounced up and down at the very point they all threatened to intersect.

ACROSS THE BAY, Dane Malone had made little sense of his sister's garbled call. Three things stood out, however. The words go on deck, her I love Logan, followed by a word that always meant something to him—danger. As he yawned and yanked on his pants, he rousted Kieran and Perry. "Hit the deck, guys. That was Daphne calling. Our friend Logan's gone and done it. He's got himself in a mess from the sound of it."

"He's a federal agent, for pity's sake. Can't he get himself out?" Perry mumbled, head still buried under his pillow.

"Listen up! Our little sis said she loves the poor sap."

That ejected Perry and Kieran from their beds as nothing else had. "She loves Logan?" Kieran stuck one leg in a pair of crumpled shorts and then the other. "Well, I guess we know the feeling's mutual. If ever I've seen a lovesick dog, it's Logan Grant."

"I don't know that I want to help rescue the idiot." Perry nevertheless found a flashlight and followed his brothers in throwing on a minimum of clothes. "Because if Daph bites the dust, I guess you guys know what that means. Mom'll have nobody left to pester about settling down except yours truly."

"Quit whining." Kieran shoved his younger brother up the ladder.

The old fishing boat rocked as the three big men converged on the side facing the bay. The same curse word exploded from all of them at once. "It's the shipment," Kieran whispered tightly, scrabbling to find the binoculars he'd tripped over on his mad rush to reach the rail. He found them, but before he could lift them to his eyes, Dane tore them out of his hand. His older brother trained the glasses on the deck of the yacht. Not finding Daphne, he slowly panned in an arc.

"Hell's bells and little fishes! I think Logan's figured out what's going on. He's paddling with everything he's got. He's just not making any headway. And if he doesn't soon, the spray from the yacht is going to swamp him—if that ship doesn't flat run over him first."

"That'll never happen," announced Perry sagely. He'd unearthed the spyglass and had it trained on the advancing freighter. "I don't know what charts that captain used. Don't you remember, Dane? The year after we bought the trawler, big shots from the Santa Monica Bay Association voted to ban entry of everything but pleasure craft up to forty-five feet, and small fishing boats like ours."

"I've got news for the association. No ban is going to stop that ship from docking wherever she damn well wants."

"The ban won't stop her," Perry said almost gleefully, "but the gravel reef they spent millions erecting about fifty yards in front of her will."

"Hot damn! I remember," Kieran shouted. "What are we waiting for? Let's fire up this baby. We'll run out there and save Logan's butt."

Dane was already starting their engine. They didn't have as much power as newer boats, but more power would create more wave action and be twice as detrimental to Logan's precarious position.

Not two seconds later, everyone in the bay heard a rending screech. Perry's prediction came true as tons of metal hit tons of gravel. The front of the freighter rode the reef right out of the water.

"Hot dog!" Kieran yelled. "Unless I miss my guess, that captain tore a fair portion off the bottom of his ship."

Perry hopped up and down with glee. "Same effect as crashing into a concrete wall."

The Malones watched lights pop on in high-rise hotel

rooms flanking the bay, throwing theater-like spotlights on a
host of people who preferred not to be in the spotlight at all.

STILL FIGHTING a strong current in the center of the bay,
Logan half rose out of his seat. A fist of fear slammed into
his gut. He didn't have a clue where his mind had been, but
certainly not on the show suddenly erupting around him. The
yacht he thought was solidly anchored moved toward him with
purpose. A darkened freight vessel he'd glimpsed a moment
earlier had begun to take on water. Badly crippled, it was
listing sideways. Too close to him for comfort.

Whipping his head from side to side, Logan saw a fast-
approaching speedboat on his left, running without lights. Off
to his right he identified the shape and outline of the Malones'
Boston trawler.

Connecting the dots in rapid-fire succession, Logan tumbled to the fact that this was the mission going down. The
mission Simon had cut him out of. And of all the players in
the bay, he judged he had the best chance—maybe the only
chance—of getting the drop on the smugglers. Except that
he had no weapon.

With luck maybe he could steal one. The freighter's crew
hung above him, racing around shouting like demented fools.
Billy Holt and company had to be in the speedboat, which
had suddenly cut its engines.

Logan assumed there was commotion and indecision in
that sector, too. As stealthily as possible, he let the waves take
his rubber raft alongside the crippled ship. Sliding the oars
out of their locks, Logan dropped them into the bottom of
his dinghy. By standing up and jumping, he was just able to
grasp a knotted rope that dangled over the side of the listing
freighter.

Several agents aboard the yacht, Daphne included, saw and noted what Logan intended to do. But no one would ever know if his plan would've succeeded. Too many things happened simultaneously.

The crew began to abandon the crippled ship. Their frightened chatter told the story. Most of them didn't speak English, but the language of fear was universal. Clearly they thought their boat was going to sink.

DAPHNE LISTENED TO Ron Thorpe's screaming voice on the bullhorn. "Get them! Don't let the bastards swim to shore. We can't have them disappearing. Simon will have our heads. My head!"

Around her, agents—some still wearing makeup—began to jump overboard, their weapons held aloft in an attempt to keep them dry. She paid scant attention. Her eyes were glued to the progress of one man. When it seemed Logan would meet his goal and board the smugglers' craft, the ship's captain—and Daphne guessed it was the captain from the amount of gold braid on his hat—decided at that very moment to escape via the dangling rope. If bulk counted for anything, his weight alone threatened to crush Logan.

Daphne felt it and winced when the two men collided. She may have been the only one who saw the accident. Her breath caught when the two fell and struck the water with a loud splash. The captain bobbed to the surface, but she didn't see Logan.

In the next instant, she climbed onto the yacht's railing and stood poised, ready to leap in and save the man she loved.

Kieran Malone spotted her. He cupped his hands and screamed. "Daphne, don't! Don't jump. We'll get Logan."

Teetering to and fro, she tried to wave off their slow-moving trawler. "I'll find him. You capture the men in the speedboat. They're the people who want Logan dead. Uh-oh, they're turning. They're going back to shore."

Anything his sister might have screamed after that was broken off. The yacht took a dip in a trough, and Daphne was pitched from her perch. Kieran hesitated only long enough to see her surface. Of the few things Daphne did exceedingly well, swimming was among the best. Placing two fingers between his teeth, Kieran garnered Perry's and Dane's notice with one shrill whistle. It took a few hand motions to get across his message about changing course.

Once Dane understood, he spun the wheel. Perry kicked the engine up several notches. The trawler had it in her to go fast. Soon they were hot on the trail of the getaway craft. On a straightaway it had speed enough to outdistance them, not so in the tight confines of the shallow bay.

As they bore down on the fleeing criminals, the brothers also managed to scoop some of the floundering agents out of the water. As a result, they had plenty of authority backing them when they cut between the dock and Holt's contingent. They nabbed the lot without anyone firing a single shot.

Ron Thorpe continued to lumber up and down the deck of the yacht, all the while bellowing orders into his bullhorn.

Daphne heard Thorpe address Logan. "You, Logan Grant, single-handedly screwed up my assignment. If you live through this, I don't care if you've already quit, I intend to see that Simon censures you anyway. You'll never work for any law enforcement agency again."

Treading water below, Daphne fervently wished someone would shove that damn bullhorn down Ron's throat. She craned her neck to figure out where Logan was. Wet hair kept flopping into her eyes. Once she adjusted to being in the water rather than looking down from above, she did get her bearings. Even so, the water was horribly black and murky. The only plus—it wasn't cold.

She moved in a half circle, all the while muttering a prayer for Logan and the other agents, many of whom grappled with fleeing crooks and sailors.

The rubber dinghy bobbed up and bumped Daphne in the back of the head. Reaching behind her, she steadied the light-weight skiff. After three tries, she heaved herself over the edge and inside it.

In the eerie lights dancing across choppy waves, she saw two men struggling in the water. Fighting, she realized. It was Logan and the ship's captain. Each time she paddled closer, the men moved.

Suddenly, suddenly, they showed up a few feet in front of her. Her breath stalled. The captain had Logan in a choke hold.

Picking up one of the two oars she'd discovered in the bottom of the dinghy, Daphne swiped at the rippling currents and finally made some headway. The dinghy rose and fell as the water around the men churned. She was close enough now to stare at the back of a balding man's head. Her mind on saving Logan, she raised the oar and beaned the jerk who had both pudgy hands wrapped around Logan's neck. He stiffened and sank like a rock.

Choking and spitting, Logan felt his assailant's body slipping away. His first thought was to catch hold of the man's heavy jacket. Logan had been struggling so long that at first he couldn't comprehend what had happened to the guy who'd been determined to kill him. Heart attack? Could be; he was as big as a house.

It wasn't until Daphne leaned out of the rubber boat and

called, "Logan, tell me what else I should do," that he knew he wasn't alone out here, after all.

"Did you just bonk this guy?" Logan wiped water from his eyes, yet tried to maintain a firm grip on the limp captain.

"Yes," Daphne said anxiously. "With an oar. I didn't kill him, did I?"

"I think he's breathing. But I've gotta say, I owe you another humongous favor. Until you clobbered him, I was as close as I've ever been to meeting my Maker."

Her heart sang. "That's the nicest compliment I've ever had."

"Depending on how hard you hit him, it may only be a temporary fix." With the luxury of time in his favor at last, Logan scanned the bay. "The water's lousy with agents. Simon really did have all the bases covered."

"Do you want to try and roll that guy into the boat, Logan? I know he must weigh a ton. Maybe between us we can tow him to somebody with a pair of handcuffs."

"The yacht's closer than the dock."

"Not the yacht, Logan. Please."

"Why?"

"Ron's there. I guess you didn't hear him shouting at you. He'd like nothing better than to hand you over to Simon for punishment. Instead of helping clean up this mess, Ron's shouting through a bullhorn. He keeps blathering on about how you're to blame." Daphne slid out of the boat and immediately set to work helping Logan roll the ship's captain up and over the soft edge. It took a lot of effort.

"I hate to be obtuse," Logan said as they kicked their way toward shore, pushing their weighty cargo. "What does Ron blame me for?"

"Everything. First, for the fact that you came on board his

secure yacht undetected. Second, because he's afraid he won't get to hog the glory. I heard him tell another agent that this assignment's his ticket to a long-overdue promotion."

"That's rich. Instead of a promotion, Ron's gonna have to explain how he almost let that freighter sail down his throat." Logan broke off talking because he'd stumbled on a jetty. He helped Daphne get her feet under her. His aim was to land their catch on a catwalk flanking the main dock. Two already-dripping agents jumped into the water and waded out to lend them a hand.

"Hey, Logan, I thought I recognized you," one said. "Buddy, you oughta be pretty damn proud. This is a good night's work. Port authority's got a crew coming to unload the ship's cargo, and tugs to clear her from the channel. We've got paddy wagons lined up to haul off these dirtbags. God only knows how things would've ended if you hadn't decided to sneak aboard to see your girlfriend."

A harsh denial sprang to Logan's lips. Then, thinking better of it, he draped an arm around the soggy woman to whom he owed his life. He rubbed a wet cheek over her tangled hair, and admitted to himself how good it felt to pretend she was his girlfriend.

Daphne placed a possessive hand on the front of his ripped shirt and smiled into his eyes.

"Uh, thanks, Davidson," Logan said belatedly. "Truth of the matter is, I didn't have much to do with what took place tonight. The word probably hasn't reached everyone yet. But I'd already tendered my resignation before this battle got under way."

"Damn shame. You and the lady make a good team. Hey, it looks like this piece of pond scum is waking up. I'd better make the transfer before he starts swinging." The agent clasped

Logan's free hand. "Good luck. At least you can invite us all to your wedding."

Logan felt Daphne tense. "Sorry, babe. I should've set him straight. After things calm down, I promise I will."

"Must you?" Her voice was gritty and Daphne doubted Logan had heard her. Also, a burly security guard who wore the uniform of a local resort, showed up at that exact moment and yanked them onto the dock. When the guard saw that neither of them was really steady, he led them to an empty park bench.

"Nice capture out there, you two. Saw it all from the hotel patio. That's a mean right hook you've got, little lady." The guard winked. "You both seem a mite woozy. Can I have someone give you a lift home? Or if not home, wherever you need to go to file your reports?"

Logan released Daphne. "Go on home. As soon as I catch my breath, I need to hunt down your brothers. If they slept through the excitement, they're gonna hate themselves."

Daphne thanked the guard, but said she'd stay with Logan. The guard touched his forehead in salute and hurried over to break up a crowd of gawkers.

"My brothers didn't sleep through the excitement," Daphne said. "I thought you were going to get killed in that little boat. I phoned and woke Dane up. I saw them. They were in the thick of it. You know," she said, suddenly crestfallen, "Simon and Ron might try to hang this mess on you. It's like all my other screwups. The finger points straight to me."

Logan linked their hands. "How do you figure?" Reminiscent of another time, he pressed tiny kisses on her knuckles.

"It's easy, Logan. Look at the facts. If you hadn't met me at your sister's house, you wouldn't have ridden home with me. If I hadn't been so weak, you wouldn't have made love to me. Then I wouldn't have fallen so hard for you. Then I wouldn't have accepted a job with the FBI. Et cetera, et cetera, et cetera. All which ultimately led to my being on the yacht and you sneaking over the side to—"

She stopped abruptly and licked her bottom lip. Turning to Logan, she frowned. "You sneaked on the yacht to do what, Logan? Be brutally honest. My brothers sent you, didn't they? Oh, I know they did. And I've proved their point. Now they'll insist on looking out for me until I'm ninety and white-haired," she wailed.

She looked so forlorn as well as bedraggled, Logan knew he shouldn't laugh. But he did, which made Daphne try to disconnect their hands.

He, being stronger, didn't disconnect easily.

"Daphne, be still. Listen to me. Dane, Kieran and Perry have already cut you loose. For two days I've tried my darned-est to convince them they needed to save you from Ron Thorpe. I know Ron. He thinks he's God's gift to women. Your brothers ignored me, I swear."

She kept shaking her head.

"It's true. You should've been a mouse in the corner. I begged them. All three of 'em brushed me off. Dane pointed out that you and I both insisted they let you be independent, so they were going to butt out of your life."

Clasping her hands between his again, Logan studied the myriad onlookers milling around the dock. Facing her again, he said, "Daphne, sneaking onto the yacht was all my idea. I'd let myself make mountains out of molehills. Bottom line, I didn't—don't—want Ron Thorpe laying his hands on you like I saw him do repeatedly these last two days."

Daphne sighed and rested her head on Logan's shoulder. "I didn't want him touching me, either, Logan. Not too long before you showed up, I kneed him. Hard. I don't think he'll try touching me again."

"Really? You kneed Ron?" A smile found its way to Logan's lips. "Boy, I'd give a lot to have seen that."

"Why did you care if he touched me?"

"I told you why. On the yacht."

"Refresh my memory." Daphne felt his muscles bunch under her cheek. She indulged in a secret smile, loving the way her questions made him nervous and edgy.

"You told me to butt out of your life, too. You ordered me to leave your cabin."

"Before all that," she said. "I'm pretty groggy when I'm jolted awake. Didn't you, ah, say you cared? For me? A…lot? What exactly did you mean, Logan?"

He reared back fast. Admittedly, he was surprised to find Daphne wearing a soft, mischievous smile.

"There's nothing wrong with your memory, is there?"

"Nope." She skimmed a hand over his hollow cheek and down across his lips.

He nibbled at her fingers. "I've made one bad choice, Daphne. My first marriage. You and I—we've plunged awfully fast. Do you think it can be real?"

"Feels real to me. Does it to you?" she asked anxiously.

"Oh, yeah."

Daphne thought she'd melt on the spot. Now that she'd led him into these uncharted waters, she was incredibly nervous. Very, very nervous. "Then, ah, what do you think we should do about—about…our feelings?"

A loud, rough voice came out of the darkness, "Both of you quit pussyfooting around, and get to the point. This is where Logan says I love you. And Daph, this is where you say Same goes. Then you tell him to set a date. Otherwise, I may be forced to figure out how to load this double-barreled shotgun I took off one of those crooks."

Dane, Kieran and Perry Malone materialized out of thick shadow. Dane cradled a lethal-looking gun in his arms.

Hopping up, Daphne rose on tiptoe and bestowed a big kiss on each set of leathery cheeks. "Get lost," she commanded. "This is something Logan and I have to work out for ourselves." She paused. "By ourselves."

It was plain to see the men would rather stay. But after a long, studied perusal of Logan, who thanked the brothers profusely, the trio did an about-face and disappeared.

Logan wasted no time getting to the heart of what troubled him. "I quit the only job I've ever known, Daphne. I have nothing to offer you."

"Love?" she asked hopefully.

"That goes without saying."

"No, Logan, it doesn't. To me the words caring and love are miles apart. When a couple has love between them, I believe they can weather any storm."

"My world gets brighter when you walk into view. I take personal pride in everything you do. I want to keep you safe. When you pretended to be pregnant the day you came to Simon's office, I spent a long time wishing you were carrying my child. Is that love, Daphne? I'm not a good judge."

She leaned over, let her eyelids drift shut and kissed him long and hard. Drawing back, she murmured, "How about if we have this same conversation on our fiftieth anniversary? If you can say the same things then, that will be love."

"So you're willing to take a chance on a has-been special agent?"

"I am. Would you like to meet the rest of my family before

we do what Dane said and set a date? Before we fully commit ourselves?"

"I'd like to meet them. But I can't get any more committed."

Those words sang in Daphne's ears. Any doubt that might have lingered evaporated then. "I know I love you, Logan Grant. The only thing I want more than you at this moment is a shower. That bay water positively stinks."

Logan threw back his head and laughed. He clasped her hand, stood and flagged down a passing cab to take them to her apartment.

THREE WEEKS LATER, after all the fury surrounding the big drug and weapons bust had died away, and after Ratsami, Billy Holt and henchmen were arraigned in federal court, and after local and national media had stopped dogging their footsteps, Daphne and Logan sat in her parents' roomy kitchen, going over wedding plans. The ceremony would be held directly after Kieran's formal promotion to detective. Kieran and Logan between them had managed to identify three dirty cops who'd been supplying Billy Holt with inside information.

The phone rang. Callie Malone excused herself to answer it. Logan took the opportunity to refill everyone's coffee mugs.

"I like how you've made yourself at home here, Logan," Daphne said. "It's been such a zoo, what with having our pictures splashed all over the front page of every newspaper in the country. But things are quieting down. I must say, I thought by now Simon would admit he was wrong to let you go. I'm disappointed he hasn't come around. Are you…are you still okay about going forward with the wedding?"

"I'm looking forward to embarking on a life like your

parents have. Like your brothers and sister have. And my sister and Mike. The lack of a job worries me, though. I guess I can always hire out as a party clown," he said with a straight face.

She slugged his shoulder, then rubbed his arm and kissed him to make up for her impulsiveness. And Logan didn't object to her method of apology.

Callie came back into the room. "Okay, break it up, you lovebirds." She smiled indulgently as she handed the cordless phone to Logan.

"For me?" Taking it gingerly, he sat bolt upright and frowned at Daphne.

She shrugged. "Maybe it's someone who wants a party clown," she teased.

Glaring at her, Logan said a tentative "Hel…lo." He said very little after that, except for a few "yes, sirs." At one point, he said soberly that in two weeks he was getting married.

The conversation ran on for so long, and seemed so one-sided, Daphne began to feel alarmed.

At last, though, he took the phone from his ear.

Daphne leaned close. "Something's wrong. Tell me, Logan. Is this going to affect our wedding?"

"Wrong. Er, no. Uh, maybe. Not the wedding, but our honeymoon. It's Hollis Sidel on the phone. He's third man from the top in the FBI chain of command. It seems Simon's report landed on his desk, giving us a fair amount of credit. Sidel's intrigued by us. You and me," Logan said again when Daphne gaped at him. "He said that according to Simon you and I work extremely well together. The FBI upper echelon has an idea and Sidel wants to present it to us in person. He'll wire us tickets to D.C. for the day after our wedding. We're to discuss this, and I need to call him back saying yes or no."

"Oh. What do you think he wants? Does it matter?" She looked hopeful. "It means a free trip to D.C. and I've never been there." Daphne's worries fell away as Logan told the caller to book them a flight.

This time when he clicked off, he hauled her into his lap. "In a nutshell, Daphne, he and a couple of international agency directors think they could use us in Paris or Hamburg. They need disguised operatives. Are you interested? I can still call him and decline. But the salaries he mentioned for the both of us—well, if we stick it out for five years, I can see us being quite comfortable. Enough so we can come home and start our family without any financial worries."

Daphne fell back limp against him. "Me, in Paris." She sprang up and danced around the room. "If you're interested, Logan, then so am I. I mean—I'll be working in a new field of makeup artistry. Plus, this makes movie studios sound downright boring. But...I promise I'll never be like your ex-wife."

Logan propped his elbows on the table. His smile could only be called loving. "Daphne, from the moment we met, my life's been anything but boring. I intend to keep a journal of our adventures. Starting with Nat's party. Otherwise, in fifty years, our great-grandchildren will say we've made up all these tales."

Callie Malone appeared moderately distressed. "Your father's not going to believe this. You know how psychiatrists are, Daphne. They all have their favorite theories. Your dad's is birth order. When you kids were born, he made each of you a life chart. Which Dane, Kieran and Becky have followed to a T. And Daphne, he's so far off base with you—well, it's time to rip up the old chart and create a new one. Of course, there's still Perry. If I could just hook him up with a nice local girl, maybe he'd sell that truck and settle down in the neighborhood."

Logan and his soon-to-be-wife joined hands under the table. They shared a wry grin, sympathizing with the one remaining unattached Malone. "Poor Perry," Daphne whispered. "He already promised to come help us celebrate our wedding."

"Yeah. It'll be interesting to sit back and watch," Logan murmured in her ear. "I can attest to the fact that there's no stopping a Malone woman when she gets something in her head. Not that I'm complaining, mind you."

Rocking back in her chair, Daphne flashed him a thumbs-up. She spared a moment to reflect on how quickly her life had gone from potential disaster—to everything she'd ever wanted.

* * * * *

Fall in Love with...

MEN
in UNIFORM

MUBPA10

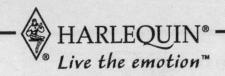

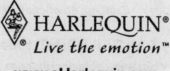

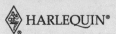

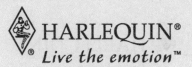

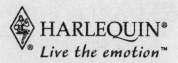

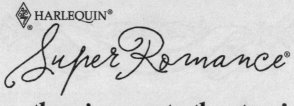
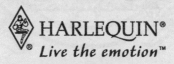

Harlequin® Historical
Historical Romantic Adventure!

Imagine a time of chivalrous
knights and unconventional ladies,
roguish rakes and impetuous
heiresses, rugged cowboys
and spirited frontierswomen—
these rich and vivid tales will
capture your imagination!

Harlequin Historical…
they're too good to miss!